CAST FOR MURDER

A VERONICA WALSH MYSTERY

JEANNE QUIGLEY

Edited by Bethany Blair
Cover design by Keri Knutson/Alchemy Book Covers and Design

Acknowledgements

Thank you to Bethany Blair for her expert editing, to Keri Knutson for her beautiful cover, and to Jill Marsal for her guidance.

Thank you to my mother, Oona, and my family for their constant support and enthusiasm.

Thank you to my cousin Eileen Habacker and my friends Charles Fortier, Barbara Silver, and Laura Devlin for reading and critiquing *Cast for Murder's* final draft. Thanks, Charles, for the terrific fact-checking!

Thank you to Tiffany Schofield, Nancy Moskowitz, Sandy Welsh, Sue Melnyk, Mary Etter, Carol Brennan, Dru Ann Love, Lori Caswell, Kathy Kaminski, Leslie Storey, Karen Owen, Shelley Giusti, Yvonne Hering, Christa Nardi, Jane Carraway, Angela Holland, Paula Mitchell, Carole Jarvis, and Katrina Wiese.

Thank you most of all to the cozy readers who have joined Veronica on her sleuthing adventures!

The Veronica Walsh Mystery Series

For my nephew Kevin; my nieces, Meaghan, Kelly, Shannon, and Colette; and in memory of my nephew Eric Robert.

The Barton Community Theater Presents
Noël Coward's *Blithe Spirit*

Cast, in order of appearance

Edith (a maid)	. . . .	Kelsey Devlin
Ruth Condomine	. . . .	Erica St. Martin
Charles Condomine	. . . .	Jerome Figueroa
Dr. Bradman	. . . .	Peter Jacobs
Mrs. Bradman	. . . .	Iris Silver
Madame Arcati	. . . .	Veronica Walsh
Elvira	. . . .	Lucy Kobayashi

Chapter One

My heart pounded. Butterflies ricocheted around my stomach, knocking each other out cold. My legs threatened to collapse like a cheap tent. A white light caused red dots to float across my vision. I fought an urge to burst into tears.

"Veronica, why don't you sit there?"

Gigi indicated the center seat at the long table. I took a steadying breath, collected my wits, and crossed the scuffed floorboards without slipping, tripping, or breaking a leg.

Which was exactly what I was there to do.

Claiming my seat alongside my new castmates, I inhaled, counted to three, and exhaled. My first acting gig in months had my adrenaline pumping; I had to get a grip on my excitement before we started our first table read.

Show director Gigi Swanson stood at the head of the table and addressed the nine of us. "Welcome to the Barton Community Theater's production of Noël Coward's *Blithe Spirit*. I'm happy to see some new faces along with the familiar ones. The next eight weeks will be very demanding, but also very rewarding and fulfilling. Now let's get started." Gigi sat down and opened a white binder lying on the table. "Act One, Scene One."

Sophie Morrissey, our stage manager, read the stage directions and then Erica St. Martin, playing Ruth Condomine, uttered the play's opening line.

" '*That's right, Edith.*' "

My attention slipped; my character, Madame Arcati, would not enter the scene for a few pages. I let my gaze drift around the table,

1

taking in each member of the ensemble. When I reached the table's head, Gigi looked up from her script, met my glance, and gave me a triumphant smile.

A Wednesday afternoon from the previous month flashed in my memory. The bustle of the Christmas season had fallen into a brief lull at my boutique, All Things, and my staff of four women and I were surveying the two floors, rearranging ornaments on the Christmas trees, refolding quilts, and wiping fingerprints from the display of blown glass. I was restocking the small candy counter at the back of the shop when Gigi swept in, her cheeks pink from the Adirondack winter.

"I'm pulling you out of retirement, Veronica Walsh," she declared.

"What?" My brain, stupefied from the swirl of my first December in the retail world, didn't immediately process Gigi's words. At that moment, retirement was an excellent idea.

"I want you to play Madame Arcati in our production of *Blithe Spirit*." Gigi's hooded, chestnut-brown eyes sparkled.

I gaped at the community theater's founder and president. Usually, her only request from me was for a donation. "Isn't the BCT an *amateur* theater?"

Gigi's grin turned impish. "Though all our past performers have been amateur actors, there's nothing in the theater's bylaws that forbids professionals from participating. The trustees, in fact, went bonkers with glee when I proposed inviting you to join our winter production."

I considered the role of Madame Arcati. Madame was an offbeat, juicy, fun role that had been played in past professional productions by the incomparable Angela Lansbury, Margaret Rutherford, and Geraldine Page. I wondered if my acting muscles had atrophied. I hadn't memorized a script in months since the cancellation of *Days and Nights*, the soap opera I had acted in for more than thirty years. Could I get back into the habit of learning lines, or had the math of payroll and twenty percent discounts assumed control over those brain cells? I made a quick decision: I could write my lines on my hand, if necessary.

"I'll do it."

A cheer went up across the sales floor. The boutique's manager, Claire Camden, bounced on the tips of her toes and pulled a tray of chocolate-covered vanilla creams from the display case. "This deserves a treat." The woman had an incorrigible habit of eating the inventory.

Gigi rounded the counter and embraced me. "FYI," she whispered in my ear, "you won't be paid."

Fine by me. I didn't need the paycheck. When the soap ended, I had returned to my hometown of Barton, bought All Things, and started the next chapter of my life. I no longer needed an acting job to pay the bills, but I sure did welcome the opportunity for a dose of the joy performing provided. I had missed it.

" *'I expect Madame Arcati will want something sweeter.'* "

Mention of my new alter ego brought me back to the present. A tingle shot up my spine and I was ninety-five percent certain only I could hear the choir of angels singing "Hallelujah."

When we finished the reading at nine o'clock, everyone's expression mirrored my excitement. "Let's talk nuts and bolts now," Gigi said.

She, Sophie, and production manager Nate Kelton went over the schedule. We would rehearse on Sunday afternoons and Monday through Thursday evenings. "This barn will be your second home," Gigi said.

No, we weren't sitting on hay bales set amid horse stalls, tractors, and various farm equipment. There were no offensive odors or neighs, clucks, and moos distracting us. The converted barn where the BCT staged its productions was located on the grounds of Townsend's Golf and Country Club. The cavernous structure, which seated two hundred theatergoers, also hosted wedding receptions, bar and bat mitzvahs, large parties of the retirement and anniversary sort, and off-site corporate events. It was a beautiful building of polished pine floorboards, thick overhead beams entwined with strands of tiny, clear light bulbs, and high windows on three walls that allowed in an abundance of natural light. A passage in the barn's right wall led into a separate building with kitchen facilities for catered events. Through a door to the left of the stage were a coatroom, the restrooms, a storage area for sets, tables and chairs, and a small room we would use for makeup and costume changes.

"And we'll become a second family. Without the squabbles and dysfunction," Nate added with a chuckle.

"What's Showcase Night?" Lucy Kobayashi asked about the event listed for the Friday evening the week before opening night.

"That's a promotional event," Sophie explained. "You'll perform a scene from *Blithe Spirit*—"

"The séance, I think," Gigi interjected. "You'll perform it in the main building for club members after dinner."

"It's a fun night," Nate said. "Coffee and cake will follow the performance, and a bit of fundraising, if we're lucky."

Left unsaid was the fact that Gigi's in-laws owned Townsend's and Zach, her husband, managed the club. Their generosity made everything possible: the BCT's use of the barn, Showcase Night, and the opening-night reception.

Gigi's countenance grew stern. "Last item. If you haven't gotten a flu shot, get it. Tomorrow! Don't tell me you're afraid of needles. We've got a tight rehearsal schedule. We can't afford to lose anyone. And if one of you gets sick, there is no place you can hide. I will find you."

"And she will be carrying a large vat of chicken noodle soup laced with Theraflu," Sophie cracked.

"I will not let you take the rest of us down." Gigi's formidable tone dissolved into a laugh.

The conversation became social and we introduced ourselves. I was proud of the diversity in our cast of five women and two men. Our ages ranged from twenty-three to the *early* mid-fifties (that would be me). Jerome Figueroa, our leading man, was of Cuban descent. Lucy's parents came to the United States from Japan and Vietnam, and Erica and her family emigrated from Haiti when she was eleven. We had varied occupations; among us were an electrical engineer, a yoga instructor, and a speech therapist. Peter Jacobs and Iris Silver, cast to play Dr. and Mrs. Bradman, were both math teachers.

After I introduced myself, Kelsey Devlin asked, "Will you share your tips on handling stage fright?" She was making her BCT debut in the role of Edith, and already wore a worried look.

"Deep breathing, prayer, and a good antacid," I replied. "And trust yourself and your castmates."

I left the barn an hour later exhausted, yet exhilarated, and unbothered by the twenty-degree temperature. I was back in my sweet spot: pretending I was someone else.

Chapter Two

Over the next few nights, I met the production's crew: the talented people who managed the lighting, sound, set construction, costumes, and props. The cast gelled during the week's rehearsals, creating a warm sense of family, and though we made occasional goofs, we handled them with humor and grace.

I met Donna Townsend on her way out of the barn when I arrived for Thursday's rehearsal. Gigi's mother-in-law, a frequent customer at All Things, gave me a warm greeting. A scent that evoked a pristine beach and crystal-clear, blue ocean reached my nose when she added a kiss on both my cheeks.

"We're grateful you didn't choose to hibernate this winter. The BCT will benefit tremendously with you in the cast, Veronica." The rustic lantern fixtures on each side of the door bestowed a glow on Donna's ash blonde hair, which was styled in a no-fuss bob.

I returned the compliment. "I'm glad I can finally take full advantage of your family's support for the theater. How lucky we all are you've provided a beautiful venue for productions."

"My hope for the new year is an even stronger bond between Townsend's and the theater. I hear you all are progressing nicely." Donna wished me a good rehearsal and dashed down the path to the parking lot.

I went into the barn and passed through the vestibule between the outer and inner doors. I welcomed the blast of heat from the floor vent.

Gigi sat at a round table set up in front of the stage, hunched over her laptop's keyboard. I heard a sniffle and what I thought was a quiet sob. She twitched when I greeted her.

"Sorry," I said. "Didn't mean to startle you."

"That's all right. I was absorbed in my thoughts." Gigi pulled a tissue from her pocket and dabbed her eyes.

I hung my coat on the rolling rack near the door and joined her at the table. I noticed her eyes were puffy. "Everything okay?"

Gigi nodded. "Just great." Her monotone suggested otherwise, but I wouldn't pry. She closed her laptop, a move that also erased the frown from her round face. "I'm glad you're here first, Veronica. I'd like to discuss something with you."

"Is this a performance review?"

"Not at all. Though I will say you're giving the fantastic performance I knew you would."

"I should ask for a review more often."

"Don't get a big head!" Gigi cracked before she turned serious. "I'm composing letters to our sponsors, thanking them for their support and offering advertising space in our program. Your signature on the letters will make a huge impression on them. You're by far the biggest name ever attached to our humble endeavors." She smirked. "I told you I'd milk your presence for everything it's worth."

I had an urge to "moo" and make a crack about being the new cow in the barn. Instead, I behaved like an adult, saying, "Of course I'll sign the letters. I'm a proud member of the production."

"Thanks. Maybe you can stop by the office Saturday morning? I'll have them ready."

I nodded my agreement. Gigi gazed at the stage for a moment, pushing a lock of her shoulder-length, golden-brown hair away from her face. "I'd value your help on another project." She faced me. "This one is much bigger than a mailing and will extend beyond our time on *Blithe Spirit*."

I nodded, waiting for the request for money or use of my fame. I was a two-time Emmy winner living in a small village; I was often asked to lend my name to one cause or another. Assuming Gigi's cause was the Barton Community Theater, I was all in with whatever she needed.

"The BCT hasn't had a capital campaign for funds in a few years. I'd like to build up our bank account. And if we can raise enough, we might be able to move into a home all our own. We'd even be able to have a fall production. We can't have one here because of all the weddings and other functions the club hosts between October and December."

I took a reflexive look around the barn. It was a gorgeous, ample space for the theater's needs and she probably had a sweetheart deal with her in-laws for its use. Why would Gigi consider leaving such an ideal situation? Did the answer lie in Donna's visit and Gigi's tears?

Since it wasn't mine to reason why, I asked, "So what role do you have for me?"

"Arm twister. Plain and simple. I'd give you a nicer title, though. How about Artist in Residence? Or Actress Emeritus?"

Gigi could raise a good chunk of the money she needed without my help with one turn around the club's dining room on a Saturday night, but she had her pride and the club a no-solicitation policy. I swallowed that snarky suggestion. "So you want the milkee to become the milker?"

"Yes. Are you with me?"

The impulse to make a bovine noise returned. Elegant Actress Emeritus that I was, I succumbed. "Moo."

Chapter Three

On Friday morning, I had breakfast at Rizzuto's Bakery with my mother, Nancy; my best friend, Carol Emerson; and my favorite person in the world, Mark Burke. I told them all about my first week as an out-of-retirement actress.

Mom shared my enthusiasm for the diverse cast. "Quite a difference from the days when you were working with professional actors. This group will bring varied views based on their life experiences. That should be exciting. I'm interested in how they interpret their roles."

"You said the same thing when I was in *Guys and Dolls* in the seventh grade, Mom."

"And it was true."

"Are tickets on sale yet?" Carol asked.

"Yes, but keep your wallet closed. Cast members receive free tickets for the opening-night performance. I will be proud to have my delightful mother, handsome fella, and best pal and her family in the audience."

"It's good to have connections," said Mom.

"Thanks, Veronica." Carol gave me a pseudo-hug by leaning her shoulder against mine. "All those times I've let you roam the shop, doing your *floral therapy* thing, have paid off."

"There's a reason for everything."

A movement at the window drew my attention. I saw Gigi standing outside, talking with a man. They appeared engaged in a tense conversation. The man, wearing a weathered navy blue down jacket and a gray watch cap, gestured with his hands, an irritated look on his unshaven face. Gigi wore a fixed expression of displeasure.

"Good morning, everyone!" The greeting, uttered with a strong Czech accent, came from my friend Dusanka Moravek. On a path from the front door to the register, when the young woman spotted us she changed course and made a beeline for our corner table. "I am so excited I will see you acting for real, Veronica!"

"I think you mean live, in person," I said.

"Yes." Dusanka nodded with vigor. I became fast friends with the newcomer to our country a few months earlier when we assisted each other; Dusanka gave me information for a murder case I was sleuthing around and I helped her secure a better job. "I am buying my ticket tomorrow. I have convinced all the ladies at Carlisle's to see your show, too."

"Thank you," I said, touched by Dusanka's enthusiasm. I stole a look out the window in time to see Gigi and the man parting. When the man entered the bakery, he was scowling and rude, allowing the door to close instead of holding it for the woman behind him.

"How do you like your seamstress work, Dusanka?" my mother asked, stressing the long "a's" of her name.

"I enjoy it very much. I like helping the nervous brides."

We chatted for another minute and then Dusanka headed for the counter and the four of us the exit. I bid Mom and Carol a good day and lingered outside the bakery window, giving Mark a more personal goodbye. Gigi stood by the building's corner, talking on her cell phone.

"What do you have today? American Public Policy?" I asked Mark, who was a history professor at nearby Arden College. I pulled the zipper of his parka higher, ran my fingers through his sandy hair, and looked into his kind, green eyes.

"Yep. And you? A record day in sales?"

"I hope not! I haven't recovered from Christmas yet. Give me another slow week and I'll be all ready for Valentine's Day."

Mark gave me a second kiss. "I better get going." After a third kiss, I watched him get into his car and waved at the departing vehicle.

"You know that man?" Gigi teased from behind me. She wore a purple thermal jacket and matching wool hat.

"I just met him five minutes ago."

"He looks like a good one. Hang on to him." Gigi's expression took a momentary, wistful turn. "Oh, hang on, I have something for you." She ducked her head and started rooting around in her purse.

My gaze took in the shops on both sides of Orchard Street. With the glittering, twinkling, colorful lights and decorations of the holidays packed away, the store windows had lost their allure and luster. Despite the antiques, books, paintings, and apparel on display, the dull storefronts offered shoppers little incentive to step inside and browse. Though I wasn't ready for Valentine's sales, Barton's main street certainly needed the hearts, Cupids, and splash of red a proper observance of the holiday required.

The man Gigi had been talking with left Rizzuto's with a large cup and a hard roll. He took a sizable bite from the roll and a gulp of his drink. Seeing Gigi and me, he glared at her for a moment before he noticed I was watching him. He turned on his heels and disappeared around the corner.

Gigi didn't notice the man. Before I could ask her who the guy was, she found the object of her search. "Here it is." She handed me a business card. "I forgot to give you this last night. If you're interested in doing research for Madame Arcati, give this woman a call. She's a medium." I caught the twinkle in her eye. "My Pilates instructor recommended her after I told her we were doing *Blithe Spirit*."

"I wasn't planning on doing any research for a dotty, middle-aged woman. And don't you dare say I'm playing myself."

"I talked with Agnes yesterday afternoon. She's a lovely woman. Maybe we should meet with her together, just for fun. Have a séance." Gigi checked the time on her watch. "Gotta run. I have a meeting this morning with a client about her master suite. We're talking toilets today."

"And you thought I had a glamourous career," I quipped about Gigi's interior design business.

"His-and-hers sinks. What do you think? Lisa is hesitant, but if I tell her the famous Veronica Walsh recommends them, she'll go for it."

"I hear they save a marriage every seventy-two seconds."

"A ringing endorsement. I'll see you tomorrow morning." With a wave of the hand, she charged into the bakery.

I glanced at the business card, expecting a crystal ball graphic and whimsical script font. Instead, I found the name *Agnes Steinert*, along with her phone number and email address, written in a no-nonsense type on cream-colored, sixteen-point cardstock.

I shoved the card into my purse and headed down Orchard Street for my shop on the corner. I had a business to run, a handsome guy to romance, and script lines to learn. I had no time for a lady who claimed to talk to dead people.

Chapter Four

Saturday was a bright, glistening day that charged my spirit, despite the twenty-five degree temperature and wind chill that made it feel even colder. It put the song "Oh What a Beautiful Morning" on my lips, a tune I carried off-key on the drive to the BCT office. I thanked my lucky stars *Blithe Spirit* was not a musical. I never would have landed the Madame Arcati role if Noël Coward had added lyrics.

At the curve where Grove Street became Club Lane, I slowed to the twenty-five mile speed limit and approached Townsend's. Behind the arched windows of the Tudor-style mansion, which was once the main building of a private estate, I imagined members dining on omelets, pancakes, and coffee while sealing business deals, seeking refreshment after a workout at the club's gym, or swapping holiday celebration stories.

I glanced at the hill on my left, an automatic move, though I knew no golfers were out on the course yelling "Fore" and exercising their right-of-way across Club Lane in their carts. I continued along the road, glancing at the outdoor tennis courts and the nearby squat building that housed the gym and indoor courts. When I reached the end of Club Lane, I made a right onto Old Bridge Road, and then another right into a parking lot that served the theater's office and the barn. Parked in the lot were Gigi's white SUV and a red Jeep, from which Sophie was climbing.

"I didn't know you'd be here this morning," she said. My explanation about signing sponsor letters made her grin. "Gigi wrings everything she can out of us."

We made the short walk to the theater's office, housed in a

cottage fifty yards from the barn. Constructed of the same stone used for the mansion, the one-story building was once the home of the estate's caretaker. Multi-paned windows on each side of the front door gave the place a cozy feel. An evergreen wreath hanging on the door, adorned with a red bow and small gold ornaments, added charm and brought a burst of color to the gray façade.

Sophie twisted the doorknob and stepped inside, leading me into a small front room warmed by radiator heaters. A desk and a printer stand were under the window on the left. On the white stucco walls hung posters from the theater's productions of *The Sisters Rosensweig* and *Noises Off*. A faded blue rug covered several feet of the hardwood floor. The fireplace on the right-side wall was long out of use.

A short hall led to a kitchenette, bathroom, and storage room, where a rolling clothes rack holding costumes from past productions blocked the back window, obscuring the view of the dense expanse of trees behind the cottage.

The only thing missing from the scene was Gigi. "She might have walked up to the barn for a minute," Sophie said when I inquired about our director.

We hung our coats on the stand beside the door and sat at the desk. Sophie opened the top drawer, clapping with glee when she found in it a check and a small wad of cash.

"Nice contribution," she murmured, eyeing the check. "Five hundred bucks from Carlisle Bridal."

"My friend dropped that off," I said. "Dusanka's a seamstress at the salon. She said she was going to buy a ticket this morning."

"You're definitely renewing enthusiasm in the BCT." Sophie gave me an appreciative look.

I let my glance slide over the desk. A laptop computer was open, its screen was black but its power button glowed silver. A vase of tulips sat on the far corner; the pink-and-white striped paper Carol used in her flower shop lay crumpled in a ball in the garbage can.

We sat and chatted for a few minutes. Sophie described the

backstage jobs she had done at the BCT before becoming stage manager and talked about her graphic design job in nearby Glens Falls. After she remarked on our similar fair-skinned Gaelic looks—she had jet-black hair and sky-blue eyes to my dark-brown hair and hazel eyes—we delighted in learning our families had both come from the same part of Ireland: County Mayo.

"We're almost Irish twins!" Sophie said, a laugh animating her oval face.

I considered my five-five height and Sophie's youthful age of twenty-nine and didn't come away amused. "Except you're three inches taller and I'm almost twice your age. *Almost.*"

Sophie checked the time on her iPhone. "Let's go see what Gigi's doing."

We put on our coats and traversed the paved path that connected the parking lot, cottage, barn, and kitchen facilities. Sophie tugged on the barn door, clicking her tongue when it proved locked.

"Maybe she went in the back door."

We trudged around the side of the barn. A wide, graveled area provided a border between the barn and a football field-size expanse of trees. Birdsong filled the air.

Sophie broke the serenity with an "Oh!" Lurching ahead, she let out a mighty scream that drove the cardinals, sparrows, and juncos from the trees. My glance followed her, and in seconds I saw the cause of her panic and it filled me with dread.

Gigi lay on her back a few feet from the barn wall, her arms straight out at her side. She gazed, unblinking at the sky. Her jacket was unzipped, revealing a gray turtleneck soaked with blood.

I rushed over and crouched beside her. "She isn't breathing. Does she have a pulse?" Sophie whimpered over my shoulder.

My heart breaking, I knew I wouldn't find a pulse. I also knew I shouldn't touch Gigi to check for signs of life. Her body was now a crime scene.

Chapter Five

I stood over Gigi for one more moment before grasping Sophie's trembling hand and leading her around the barn and onto the path.

"My God, what happened to her?" she asked.

"She was shot."

I hustled a wailing Sophie to the office and settled her in a chair. I grabbed my cell phone, plunked a box of tissue in front of her, and said, "I'm calling 911. I'll be right back."

I hurried outside and made the call away from Sophie's loud sobs. After giving the dispatcher the information she needed and ending the call, I stood on the path for a minute, absorbing the morning's shocking turn. Taking in my surroundings, I was stunned by the juxtaposition of the serene setting and the horrid scene behind the barn.

"Not again," I whispered to the sky that had cheered me less than an hour ago.

After gulping down a few breaths of air, I went inside. Sophie, wiping her mouth with a tissue, emerged from the bathroom. She pulled her hair away from her face, tucking it behind her ears.

"I puked," she explained. Her usually pale skin had taken on a sickly pallor; her eyes were puffy and moist.

"Are you okay? Can I get you something?"

"No, thanks. I'm fine."

"All right. The police and paramedics will be here soon."

"This is surreal." Sophie leaned against the desk. "I mean, Gigi was just here. She was sitting right here what, an hour ago?"

The faint sound of approaching sirens drew us back outside.

16

Through the sparse collection of trees between the office and parking lot, we saw two police cars turn off Old Bridge Road. An ambulance turned into the lot a few moments later.

Police officers Tracey Brody and Ron Nicholstone jumped from one cruiser and bounded up the path, followed by two officers from the second car. Three paramedics hustled behind them, carrying their life-saving equipment.

"You made the call, Veronica?" Tracey asked.

I fell in step beside her. "Yes. It's Gigi Swanson. We found her body behind the barn."

"All right. Stay here."

I stepped off the path, allowing the parade of EMTs passage. Two of the paramedics gave me grim-faced nods.

Sophie stood outside the office door, her arms crossed in a tight self-embrace. "I hope they take Gigi out of the cold soon," she said, her face shining with fresh tears.

While we waited in the office, Sophie called Nate and told him the grim news. During their conversation, I went outside and walked around to the back of the cottage, hoping I could observe the activity behind the barn. To my dismay, an ambulance blocked my view.

I lingered for a few minutes and then returned to the office. Sophie was off the phone and wiping her eyes. Before either of us could speak, Tracey walked in, a notepad and pen already in her hand.

"Are you all right?" Though the question was general, Tracey's lasting look at Sophie indicated it was more a check on the young stage manager than on me, who had the experience of finding a dead body the previous summer.

Sophie nodded. "Could you do anything for Gigi?" Her hope for her friend grieved me.

"We couldn't. I'm sorry." Tracey's wave indicated we should sit. Pulling a chair from the corner for herself, her gaze moved across the room. "Tell me what happened."

Tracey leveled her stare on me. "I was here to sign donor letters and Sophie came in to do some production work."

"What time did you each arrive at the office?"

"Veronica and I got here at the same time. Around eleven."

"Did either of you talk with Gigi this morning?" After we both replied no, Tracey asked, "Was this door unlocked when you arrived?"

Sophie again answered. "Yes."

Tracey asked several more questions, concluding with, "Where were each of you before you arrived here?"

A standard query, I knew, but Sophie bristled, flexing her jaw while I told Tracey about my bakery and All Things visits. Sophie, with a bit of asperity, said she was stuffing her face at Fortier's Doughnuts in Chestertown.

Tracey ignored the sass. "You need to leave. We'll be doing a full search of the office and barn for evidence."

"How long will that take? We have rehearsal tomorrow afternoon!"

"You'll need to make arrangements to hold it somewhere else." Tracey stood. "Now please leave."

Sophie's feisty flash of spirit evaporated and she gave a forlorn look around the office. "May I take Gigi's computer? She has a lot of notes for our production on it. And the check and cash in the drawer. And what if someone comes in for tickets for *Blithe Spirit*? We'll lose sales!"

"I'm sorry, but the computer is evidence. If anyone comes for tickets, we'll take their name and phone number and pass it along to you. And I'll bag the cash and check and make sure it gets to you." Tracey, a police officer of courage and compassion in equal measure, spoke with generous empathy.

Sophie was again sharp. "Make sure no one comes in here and steals anything."

"I will. I'll let you know when we're done." Tracey asked me, "Will you be at All Things this afternoon?"

"No. I'll be at home."

"All right."

The short exchange probably meant nothing to Sophie, but I knew Tracey would pay me a house call and warn me against snooping around the first murder case of the new year.

Tracey walked out with us and we parted ways on the path. "Are you okay to drive?" I asked Sophie when we reached the parking lot.

"Yeah. Is the Hearth's bar open? I need a stiff drink."

"How about some sugar and caffeine from Rizzuto's instead?"

"That'll work."

I followed Sophie's Jeep along Club Lane, alternating my attention between her bumper and the approaching police car that had exited Townsend's lot. In its passing, I saw Chief Bill Price behind the driver's wheel, with a passenger beside him and another in the back seat. The Townsends, I guessed.

"That was a close one," I muttered.

The chief wasn't a fan of civilians within a crime investigation perimeter, especially me, despite the fact I had solved two murders for his department. I knew Tracey would give me a calm but firm caution to keep my nose out of it; Chief Price would warn me with a glower, intimidating stare, and choice language.

Gigi had welcomed me into the BCT family and given me the opportunity to pursue my calling. I couldn't live with myself if I didn't help find her killer.

By the time I reached the curve where Club Lane became Grove Street, I had decided I was not only out of retirement as an actress, but as an amateur sleuth as well.

Chapter Six

Sophie griped about Tracey's question of our whereabouts when we regrouped at Rizzuto's. "Does she really think one of us pulled the trigger?" she asked while we waited at the counter for our orders. Sophie needed a double dose of chocolate: hot cocoa and a chocolate-glazed chocolate doughnut. I opted for a soothing cup of tea. "I'm surprised she didn't frisk us."

The two young women also waiting gave us curious looks. "We'll discuss it at the table," I mumbled.

We claimed a window table a few moments later. "I'll be mortified if they go to Fortier's and ask Terry and Christine if I was there. I've known them forever! They gave me my first job."

I blew across the rim of my cup and took a sip of the tea. "They'll understand. They know you and won't think you had anything to do with Gigi's death."

Sophie was quiet for a minute, taking several large bites of her doughnut and washing it down with gulps of the cocoa. Her ire diminished and her mood turned mournful. "Poor Gigi. She must have been so scared—" She broke off, grabbed a napkin from the table dispenser, and blotted her eyes. I reached across the table and patted her hand. Sophie nodded her gratitude and dabbed her nose with the napkin.

"I wonder if it was some kind of a freak accident. Deer roam the woods around the club. Maybe someone hunting illegally took aim at a buck and missed." I stretched for an improbable cause of Gigi's death in the hope that there wasn't another murderer in our village.

"Maybe. If only I had arrived ten minutes earlier. Or you had.

Maybe this wouldn't have happened." Sophie blew on her cocoa. "Or maybe we'd be dead, too."

Sophie's morbid swing prompted me to turn the conversation to possible suspects. "What do you know about Gigi's marriage? Were she and Zach happy?"

"I think so. Gigi and I didn't engage in much girl talk." Sophie gave the question more thought. "I guess the police spotlight will be on Zach. It's not good for him that Gigi was found on club property."

"Did Gigi have a problem with anyone at the theater?"

Sophie's eyes flashed displeasure. "No! We're one big happy family."

"Even happy families have troubles. Is there any resentment over me being in the cast? Any jealousy about that?"

One woman who might begrudge my presence was Iris, a veteran of BCT productions. She had starred in several shows and surely would have won the colorful Madame Arcati role, had it not been handed to me. She had welcomed me with warmth, though, and appeared happy about her stage return after the four-month break since the curtain fell on the last production.

"Nope. Everyone was thrilled when Gigi announced you'd be in *Blithe Spirit*. The actors were beside themselves that they'd be on the stage with you, and all of us were excited because we knew having you in the cast would draw a larger audience and more money."

"Even Iris?"

"Especially Iris. She called it an early Hanukkah present."

"What about people who auditioned and weren't chosen for roles?" I hadn't attended the auditions, per Gigi's concern I would distract the already nervous performers. "Was anyone upset they didn't win a part?"

"I didn't hear about anyone complaining. We announced who won roles last month. If someone was upset about not getting a part, we would have heard about it by now. And if anyone turned violent, it would be toward the person who got the part they wanted, don't you think?"

"A very angry person might have taken out his or her anger on the individual who assigned the roles."

"Gigi doesn't decide on the roles all by herself. Nate and I have input on who gets a part. I can tell you're already thinking about who killed Gigi. The killer must be found soon, Veronica, for the sake of *Blithe Spirit*. The production is supposed to be a joyful process."

"We need a director. Any idea who it will be?"

"The director's the only person at the BCT who has an understudy." Sophie gave a half-hearted wave. "That would be the stage manager. I guess my first duty is telling everyone about Gigi and figuring out where we'll hold rehearsal tomorrow. I suppose we can make it a table read, but I don't know where we can meet. I don't have a dining room and my kitchen table seats four. Nate said we should cancel rehearsal. I don't think we should. It will be good for us to be together. Like I said, we're a family."

"I agree. I'll host the reading."

Sophie visibly relaxed, lowering her hunched shoulders and sighing. "Thank you. That's one thing settled. I don't think it will be a problem to continue the weekday rehearsals at Townsend's. I'm sure we'll have their full support. But if we don't, we can probably work out something with the high school and elementary school." Sophie leaned her palms against her forehead and shook her head. "I've wanted to direct a show for a long time, but I didn't want to get the chance this way."

I patted her hand. "Don't dwell on the how."

She finished her cocoa and doughnut. I swallowed the dregs of my tea, hoping Sophie's sadness over her sudden promotion was genuine. If it wasn't, she was an adept actress who belonged on the stage, not behind it.

Chapter Seven

Twenty minutes later, Carol and I huddled at her flower shop's checkout counter, taking advantage of a lull in business.

"Wow," Carol said, stunned by the news of Gigi's murder.

"There was a vase of tulips on her desk. That striped wrapping paper you use was in the garbage can. Was the theater office on your list of morning deliveries?"

"Not that I know of, but I spent most of the morning at Saint Paul's and Saint Anthony's, setting up for two weddings. Amy watched the shop."

She waved me toward the back room where Amy Reynolds, Carol's floral designer, was finishing work on a basket filled with an eye-catching assortment of flowers.

"Amy, did we deliver tulips to the Barton Community Theater office this morning?"

"For Gigi Swanson?" I added.

"We didn't deliver. Gigi came here and picked out the flowers."

"Oh." My hopes sagged. "Did she say whom they were for?"

"They were for her. Gigi said she'd had a bad week and wanted a little pick-me-up."

Carol let out a sympathetic moan. "Poor soul."

"What time was Gigi here?"

"Around eight thirty. Is everything okay?"

Carol answered. "I'll tell you later."

"How sad she had to buy flowers for herself," Carol said when we were back at the checkout counter.

"She had very little time to stop and smell the tulips."

I placed Gigi's words to Amy in my mental filing cabinet alongside the woeful look Gigi had given Mark and me twenty-four hours earlier. I took in a deep whiff from a bucket of roses on the counter and realized everything wasn't coming up roses in the Swanson-Townsend marriage.

I entered Carlisle Bridal, the happiest place in Barton. Putting on a cheerful countenance, I congratulated the brides and their attendants and crossed the showroom, which provided a three-hundred-and-sixty degree view of white tulle, satin, chiffon, and lace. I descended the stairs to the workroom where Dusanka performed her seamstress magic.

I found her, alone in the room, at one of the four sewing machines a few feet from the bridal, bridesmaid, and mother-of-the-bride gowns that needed her loving attention. For a moment, I watched my friend delighting in her work. With her honey-blonde braid hanging over her shoulder and her lower lip caught between her teeth, Dusanka's gray eyes focused on the hem of a lace dress.

"Dusanka?"

She finished a neat row of stitching and greeted me. "I'm so glad to have you in my workshop!" Dusanka rose from her rolling chair and embraced me. "I bought my ticket to *Blithe Spirit* this morning and picked up tickets for the ladies here!"

"I know. I saw the check from the salon."

"The Carlisles are very happy to give to their new community."

"About what time were you at the office?"

"I was there at nine o'clock."

"Did you give the check to Gigi Swanson?" Dusanka nodded after I described Gigi. "Was anyone in the office with Gigi?"

Dusanka jerked her head. "No. But a woman was leaving when I arrived."

I paused for a few seconds before relaying the terrible news of Gigi's murder. "Dusanka, something happened and the police will want to talk with you."

"Did I do something wrong?" Dusanka's voice faltered and her eyes registered apprehension.

"No, of course not." I told her about the murder.

"How terrible! Did they catch the devil who killed her?"

"Not yet. How was Gigi when you talked with her?" I elaborated when Dusanka gave me a querulous look. "Was she upbeat? Distracted? Upset?"

"She was pleasant. I told her that I knew you, that you were my friend, and how excited I was to see you in the play."

"What about the woman you passed on the way into the office? Anything about her seem . . . unusual?"

"No. She was talking on her cell phone."

"Okay. She probably bought tickets. Did you see anyone else? Anyone arrive when you were leaving?"

"No. No one. It was very quiet. How awful that someone stole that peace."

I said goodbye and went upstairs. I looked around the showroom for a minute, soaking in the feel-good vibes from the gorgeous gowns. I felt as if I were in the center of a cream-filled cupcake. For a moment, I wished I were.

Chapter Eight

When I arrived home from the bridal salon, I made a turkey sandwich and ate it in front of my laptop. First I checked the website of the local newspaper, the *Chronicle*. Gigi's murder was the breaking news headline on the site's main page, but the linked article offered nothing I did not already know and deepened my sorrow with the reminder she was just thirty-five. A Google search of Gigi's name brought up the four-year-old announcement of her and Zach's wedding. The blurb included the information that Gigi had grown up in Ticonderoga and, at that point, had been a Barton resident for three years. There were several theater-related links. I clicked on a *Chronicle* article detailing Gigi's efforts in founding the BCT and a link for a review of its inaugural production, *Cat on a Hot Tin Roof.* I then checked out the website for Gigi's interior design and decorating business, Swanson and Roth Interiors. I wrote down her partner's name, Whitney Roth, and the office's phone number.

A search of Zach Townsend's name yielded dozens of links relating to the club, his father's position as the county executive, and his mother's philanthropic work. I read a couple of articles about Zach's club management duties and of his own community contributions.

Tracey rang the doorbell at three o'clock. "Can we talk?" she asked, crossing the threshold and removing her cap.

"Do you come with the good news that you caught Gigi's killer?"

"Sorry. No."

"Could this have been a freak accident?" I explained the deer hunter theory I had come up with at the bakery.

"No. Gigi was shot at close range in the heart. This was no accident. Can we sit for a minute?"

I let Tracey lead the way into the living room. She sat in a chair and I took a seat at the end of the couch. "Tell me about your castmates." Tracey sat poised with a notepad on her knee and a pen clenched between her fingers.

I reeled off the names of my fellow actors, their roles in *Blithe Spirit*, and the bits of biography they shared at our first table reading.

"What about people who auditioned and didn't get a role? Anyone upset over the rejection? Or angry over you participating?"

"I asked Sophie the same question. She told me no one seemed ticked off."

"All right." Tracey made a jot on her pad.

"Have you checked Sophie's alibi? She told me she's the backup director. I don't think for a moment she killed Gigi, but let's make sure we don't have a sort of *All About Eve* scenario here."

"We haven't checked it yet, but we will."

"Have you talked with Zach Townsend yet?"

Tracey's response was a terse, "The chief is dealing with the family."

I related my encounter with Gigi outside the bakery, specifically her remark about Mark and follow-up melancholic look, and of her flower purchase. "Sounds like there was trouble in paradise."

"There often is when a spouse is killed." Tracey paused a beat. "So you're the star of *Blithe Spirit*."

"Not the star. I'm Madame Arcati, one of the play's seven characters."

"But you'll be spending a lot of time with the group. You're in a position to help the department on this case, Veronica, and your questions indicate you've already started playing amateur sleuth again. Let's work together."

"How?"

"We'll be interviewing the whole cast and crew, but someone might say something to you that he or she wouldn't tell the police. Or something they didn't think was important to tell us. Can I count on you to share any observations you make or information you learn that could be helpful to the case?"

"In other words, be on guard for people letting down their guard?"

"Yes. People try to protect their friends when they're around a police badge, but openly talk amongst themselves. And you now have a reputation as an amateur sleuth. Some folks might be eager to talk with you about the murder. You might hear something useful to us."

"I do have a fine sense of hearing." I couldn't believe Tracey was asking my help on the case rather than warning me against having even a fleeting thought about who killed Gigi.

Tracey proved a skilled mind reader. "This is a request for information only. No leg work."

"Got it. I'm your informant. A backstage whistleblower. What does Chief Price think about this arrangement?"

"He doesn't know about it. Let's keep it between us."

"So we'll have secret meetings while wearing trench coats. I happen to have access to a deserted alley behind All Things. I'll be the one wearing the yellow rose behind my left ear."

"We're not turning this into a CIA operation, Veronica."

"Okay. I can keep it simple. Have you talked with Dusanka Moravek?"

"Yes. And she told me of your visit." Tracey gave me an amused look. "You move fast. I should arrest you for tampering with a witness."

"I didn't *tamper* with a witness. I'm very protective of Dusanka. What do you think of the woman she passed on the way in?"

"Nothing. She was there for tickets, just as Dusanka was. Hopefully, she'll step forward and let us know she was at the office.

28

She might have more information to offer than Dusanka has." Tracey stood. "Remember, I'm not deputizing you to question witnesses and suspects. Don't put yourself in danger."

"The only danger in Carlisle's is being caught in an avalanche of tulle and lace."

Mark and I refrained from discussing Gigi's murder until after we had eaten our dinner of hamburgers, fries, and brownies. After cleaning the dishes, we sat at my kitchen table with a legal pad and pen.

"Killing your wife on your family's business property isn't the brightest move. It's like putting up a flashing neon sign, *I killed my wife*," Mark said.

"It's a half-step up from committing the act in their home. So are you saying Zach didn't kill Gigi?"

"No. I'm pointing out that if he did, he didn't plan it well. Zach Townsend is a smart man. Unless he's too clever by half and killed Gigi behind the barn, assuming people would think it too obvious and wouldn't suspect him. A convoluted explanation, I know."

"I got it. Maybe it was someone else's plan to shoot Gigi at the barn to shift the suspicion to Zach."

Mark agreed. "Do you think this could have something to do with the theater?"

"Sophie was adamant there was nothing but love for Gigi at the BCT. I hope that's true. The possibility that there's a murderer in the group is unnerving."

"Maybe the show should be postponed until the police make an arrest. That shouldn't take long; you'd miss just one or two rehearsals." Mark's apprehension showed in his green eyes.

I stroked his arm. "I'll be fine. Safety in numbers."

Mark's jaw tightened. "It wasn't right, Tracey making you some sort of undercover agent. Is that some new police procedure? Are you the test case before they make it a community-wide policy?"

"I think her attitude is if you can't beat Veronica, ask her to join you. I'll be fine." I kissed his cheek and we lapsed into a short, comfortable silence. I broke it with, "If Gigi was planning on leaving Zach, it could have been because he was having an affair. The *other woman* will also be a suspect."

"*If* he had an affair. Gigi buying herself flowers could have had nothing to do with the state of her marriage. She and Zach could have been fine."

"I wonder if Gigi and the killer went to the barn together, or if the coward who shot her in the heart confronted her there." For what seemed like the one hundredth time, I had a horrible vision of Gigi lying on the ground.

Mark tapped my hand. "I think this is enough depressing conversation for a Saturday night. I'm going to light the fireplace. You'll join me?"

"Do you really have to ask?"

I scribbled a note regarding extra-marital dalliances before following Mark from the kitchen. Turning off the light, I prayed the Sunday morning headline would be that the police had apprehended Gigi's killer, making our conversation a waste of time.

Chapter Nine

My prayer was not answered, so I offered it again the next morning at Saint Augustine's ten thirty Mass. I was pleased that they remembered Gigi, a Lutheran, during the intercessory prayers.

Mark and I met Tracey in Father Bob's reception line. Tracey wore her uniform, with her brown hair pulled into a tight ponytail.

"Is this the end of a long night's work, or are you headed for a new day at the station?" Mark asked, looking with admiration at the woman who helped keep Barton safe.

"It was a late night, but I got a few hours of sleep before today's shift."

We greeted our pastor and walked outside into a crisp, sunshine-filled day. "I guess that means there hasn't been an arrest?" I asked.

"No. And you can rest easy. There's no *All About Eve* situation going on. Sophie paid her usual Saturday morning visit to Fortier's."

Terrific. I was glad I wasn't in sleuthing cahoots with the killer. "Good. What about Zach Townsend?" I whispered his name, not wanting passing parishioners to overhear me.

Tracey matched my low voice. "Zach doesn't have a firm alibi. He ran a couple of errands and then went to the club."

"When did he arrive at the club?"

"Around ten o'clock."

"What stops did he make on his errand run?" Mark asked.

"The drugstore, barbershop, and liquor store."

"What about Gigi's business partner?" I asked.

"Ms. Roth says she was home all morning. There's no one to corroborate it."

"Has anyone given you a helpful tip or lead? What about that woman Dusanka saw?"

"No one's come forward with information yet." Tracey checked her watch. "I've got to go. Remember, what I tell you in the church parking lot stays in the church parking lot." Heading for her car parked on the street, she gave us a wave over her shoulder.

"Good luck today," I called, sending up a silent prayer it would be a safe and successful day for the policewoman and her fellow officers.

A morose group gathered in my living room for the afternoon table reading. Iris, who had burst into tears the moment she crossed the threshold, sat at the end of the couch, taking an occasional dab at her eyes with a balled-up tissue. Kelsey and Erica were also teary and Jerome, normally in a jolly mood, sat silent in a corner chair. Nate was telling Peter how he had received the news from Sophie.

"I was up at Whiteface Mountain. I had just finished getting my skis on and was heading out to the lift. Almost didn't answer my cell."

"Have any of you talked with the police?" I gave the question a light phrasing so no one would think I meant interrogation instead of a simple information-gathering chat with the cops.

Nate raised his hand. "I spoke with Chief Price late yesterday afternoon. I wanted to know the status of our access to the office and barn. He said the barn will be clear for tomorrow night's rehearsal. He also asked me a few basic questions about Gigi. How long I knew her, if I knew of any problems she had with anyone. He asked me for everyone's contact information. I gave him your phone numbers, so an officer might be calling in the next day or so. Nothing to worry about."

"Of course not!" Iris exclaimed, affronted. "Not one of us would ever even think about harming Gigi."

"I think it's more to ask for help in the investigation." Nate's tone was soft and assuring.

"Can we get to the reading?" Erica asked. "It'll take our minds off the murder."

"We have a piece of business first." Nate sat up straighter on the chair he had brought in from the dining room and scratched his blond goatee. "We should take a vote on whether to continue with *Blithe Spirit*. Or at least whether we should put production on hold until the summer."

I don't know if Nate was serious about the vote or made the suggestion to shake the troupe from its gloom, but his words had an instant effect on the group.

"You can't be serious!" Lucy said, alarmed.

"Of course we're going on with the show!" Jerome bellowed. He stood, dragged his chair from the corner into the circle around the coffee table, and sat back down with a huff. "We're not quitting on the production, each other, or Gigi!"

"She'll haunt us if we do." Iris's frown of sorrow turned into a grin.

Nate sat back, satisfied. "I'll take this as a unanimous vote to continue." He paused, his gaze landing on Sophie. "There's one more matter. The BCT's bylaws state that if a director cannot fulfill the responsibility of the job, the stage manager assumes the duties. Sophie, I know you're ready. Do you accept the job of directing *Blithe Spirit* and this motley crew?"

I looked across the coffee table at Sophie. She swallowed hard, her eyes becoming moist. "I accept." A cheer went up and a pair of tears rolled down Sophie's cheeks. She acknowledged the group's ringing endorsement with a nod.

"We'll need a stage manager," Lucy said.

"I'll take over," Nate said.

With the new backstage responsibilities officially assigned, Sophie made her first directing decision. "Let's move to the dining room for the reading."

"We should discuss one more issue first." Peter shifted in his seat, his somber expression an indication the topic was not a light matter.

"The floor is yours," said Nate.

"I'm concerned about the BCT's future. I don't expect the Townsends will cut the cord before we stage *Blithe Spirit*, but what about the next production? Gigi struck a terrific deal with Zach and her in-laws. Will we still enjoy it, or will we need to find a new office, rehearsal space, and production venue? Are we going to have to scramble with every show?"

The tension, cut by our "show must go on" vote and Sophie's directorial installation, settled over us again. "I'm worried about this, too," Iris said. "We might be a painful reminder to the Townsends."

Nate shook his head. "I don't think we should worry about losing their support and use of their facilities. It wouldn't look good for them if they pulled the rug out from under a community organization their beloved daughter-in-law founded."

I kept my mouth shut about Gigi's thought of tugging the rug out herself. Was Nate aware of her desire to find a new home for the BCT or was that an impetuous idea Gigi had after her pre-rehearsal, tear-inducing meeting with Donna?

"But what if . . ." Erica pressed her lips together, hesitant to finish her sentence.

"What if what?" Sophie pressed.

Erica went for it, finishing her thought in a rushed blurt. "What if Zach killed Gigi?"

We were silent for a moment until Iris broke it. "That's the other thing I've been worrying about."

"The husband is guilty ninety percent of the time," Kelsey said.

No one questioned the accuracy of Kelsey's pronouncement and it hung over us for a minute.

"I don't think Zach would hurt Gigi," Nate finally said.

"When it comes to a marriage, only the two people in it really know everything going on." Jerome spoke the words of wisdom.

Sophie stood and dismissed the gloom with a clap of her hands. "All right, everyone. Chat time is over. Time for the reading."

Everyone filed into the dining room and for a minute there was a flurry of selecting seats and opening scripts. Nate brought up the rear, carrying his chair and setting it at the corner of the table's head where Sophie was sitting. I lingered in the doorway, considering Jerome's words. It wasn't always correct that only a husband and wife know the full truth of their marriage. Spouses kept secrets from each other all the time.

Infidelity, for example. A loaded gun, for another.

Chapter Ten

Claire and I swapped details on our weekend activities at our usual Monday morning meeting spot: the All Things' candy counter. The rest of the staff flitted around the sales floor, preparing for our nine o'clock opening.

"Tracey Brody asked me to act as an informant. Since I'm in the show and will be spending a lot of time with the cast and crew, she thinks I will learn something useful to the investigation."

"You're moving up in the world. You're a law and order insider now." Claire, who had been my sidekick the previous fall when I played sleuth in the murder of a young architect, beamed with pride.

"I think my insider status is temporary. I'm worried I'll be more of a snitch. What if I raise a red flag on an innocent person and the police turn his or her life upside down?"

"Tracey would figure it out soon enough."

"I'd hate myself for putting someone through the drama. I should make sure before I blow the whistle." I slid a tray of chocolate-covered cherries into the display case.

"You're going rogue, aren't you?"

"Semi-rogue. I will pass along information to Tracey, but I'm not going to jump to conclusions willy-nilly. I don't want to waste her time."

"If you want company following a suspect, give me a call." Claire popped a chocolate into her mouth and appreciated its taste with a slow chew. She referred to an adventure we had in our autumn sleuthing. One evening, we followed a suspect, ending up the pursued when the person tricked us and tailed us for miles.

"You're on my speed dial." I gave Claire's hand a playful slap. "Don't eat the merchandise."

"Life's short. We should enjoy every minute, and all the yummies, when we can."

I thought of Gigi. "Life can be short. But in case we're here for the long haul, we'll need money to pay for it."

I took an afternoon break and walked to the barbershop two blocks down Orchard Street. Tony Spiatto had been my dad's barber for many years before Dad passed; if anyone asked, my visit was social.

Tony was alone when I arrived. The white-haired, stocky barber greeted me with great fanfare and a peck on my cheek. "Here for a buzz cut?" he teased when I climbed into one of his barbering chairs.

"It's too cold for peach fuzz, but I'll consider it when the thermometer hits ninety." We chatted for a few minutes before I asked, in a casual tone, "Are you Zach Townsend's barber?"

"Yeah, I am." Tony's face darkened. "He was here Saturday morning. A terrible morning, yeah? Officer Nicholstone came by my house late that afternoon and asked about Zach's visit."

"What time was Zach here?"

"I can set my watch by Zach. He's here nine o'clock, the second Saturday of the month."

"How long did he stay?"

"I'd say he had to wait about five minutes and was in the chair twenty-five."

"What was his mood?"

"Fine. Cheerful. You know, Nicholstone asked me all this. Are you checking his work?" Tony laughed.

"No. I found Gigi's body."

Tony's expression sobered. "I'm sorry about that, dear. Of course, you're curious about what happened to the poor thing. I confess I thought about it myself when I heard the news. It's always the husband, right? But I can't say Zach was in a brooding, black mood. He was the way he always is. We talked about the weather and the holidays, sports, who'll play in the Super Bowl. He's always good about asking about my family. He's a nice kid."

I didn't know if men unloaded their romantic woes on barbers the way women do on hair stylists, but I ventured the question, "Did he say anything about Gigi? How they were doing?"

"All he said was Gigi was well and starting work on a new show at the theater."

An older gentleman entered the shop, ending our conversation.

"Zach Townsend is either an innocent man or a great actor," I mumbled on my trot back to All Things. "Though maybe he's both. Only time will tell."

Chapter Eleven

We were back in the barn for the night's rehearsal. I was the third arrival, after Jerome and Sophie. Both were on the stage studying their scripts, Jerome on the sofa of his alter ego's living room and Sophie sitting cross-legged on the floor. Both gave me a subdued hello when I joined them, taking the Queen Anne chair beside the sofa.

"I just remarked on how ironic this play has suddenly become," Jerome said. "Life imitating art, without the comedy part."

"I'm definitely feeling Gigi's presence," Sophie said. She gave a wary glance at the table where Gigi always sat and watched rehearsal.

I read her thought. "You're going to have to sit there, sooner or later."

"The idea of directing the show wasn't so daunting yesterday when we were all huddled around your dining room table. Now, when I look at how huge this place is, and how big this stage, I get scared."

"It's a converted barn and this stage isn't so big," Jerome said, his manner assuring. "Don't let it get in your head."

They went back to their scripts and I pulled mine out to study the scenes scheduled for the rehearsal. From my position on the stage, I could observe each cast member's arrival. There was a look of apprehension mixed with curiosity on each face. Everyone looked over the barn as if entering it for the first time. Iris's expression conveyed a struggle with her emotions; I was sure she had come half-expecting to see Gigi. A natural assumption despite the truth, for Gigi had been present at every other of the hundreds of rehearsals Iris had attended.

When Nate, the last through the door, had flung his coat over one of the chairs at the director's table and joined us all on stage, Jerome beckoned us to form a circle and join hands.

"Let's say a prayer before we start rehearsal. For Gigi, a peaceful passage to her new life. For Sophie, confidence and wisdom to lead our production. For us all, a renewed dedication of our talents."

We all bowed our heads for a moment of silence that Jerome broke with, "Now let's pay a visit to 1940s England. Passport not required."

Jerome's prayer didn't soothe Sophie's nerves. She filled the rehearsal's first hour with tentative directions, beginning each statement with "maybe."

"Maybe you should enter more slowly," she said to Kelsey.

She told Erica, "Maybe you should be standing more center stage."

"Maybe you should speak louder," she advised Peter.

Lucy received the suggestion, "Maybe you should say that in a lower voice."

Iris and I received the meek recommendation, "Maybe you should come on stage faster."

Nate finally addressed Sophie's diffidence in a calm, encouraging manner. "Maybe you should relax and stop doubting yourself, Soph. If you want something done a certain way, just say it."

Sophie bore a momentary, wounded-deer-caught-in-the-headlights expression. "I want to give the actors room to find their characters and express them." Her remark came out in a halting manner.

"I don't know if we have time for that," Nate said, laughing. "How about this. Why don't we run through a scene and you watch and take notes, and when we're done, you can share your observations and recommendations."

"Good idea," Iris said.

Sophie gave a shy nod. "All right."

Jerome did his part to lighten the tension. "Notice Sophie didn't give me any direction." Letting us in on the joke, Jerome made an exaggerated wink that someone standing at the far end of the barn would have seen.

Sophie's confidence grew with each passing minute and was complete when Lucy's cell phone, tucked in the back pocket of her jeans, started trumpeting in the middle of a scene with Jerome and Erica.

" '*If this is a joke dear, it's gone—*' " Erica, in the middle of her line, stopped and glanced at Sophie for direction.

"I'm sorry! I'm so, so sorry!" Lucy yanked the still blaring phone from her pocket and silenced it.

Sophie's response was patient but firm. "Okay. Don't let anything distract you when you're in the middle of a scene. Never break character! If someone drops a glass, or forgets a line, act like it was supposed to happen. If a cell phone goes off in the audience, as one inevitably will, *at every show*, ignore it. If it's really loud and people won't hear you speaking, everyone just freeze and stop talking until the phone is turned off."

Erica and Lucy, attentive to every word, nodded. Jerome beamed at Sophie like a proud father watching his child graduate from medical school.

Sophie had a final statement. "And remember! Turn your phones off before rehearsal!" There was nothing timid about her pronouncement.

Sophie, Nate, and I, the last to leave rehearsal, walked together to the parking lot.

"Thanks for the directing advice, Nate."

"My pleasure, Soph. All you have to do is believe in yourself, because everyone else already does." Nate pressed his car remote, setting off a beep from the 4Runner next to my car.

"I want you both to know I'm still fully committed to the capital campaign." I said.

Sophie and Nate exchanged baffled looks. "*What* capital campaign?" Nate asked.

"The major fundraising project. Gigi told me about it Thursday night." I felt as if I had spilled the secret on a surprise birthday party. "She said you haven't had a big fundraising campaign in a few years and she wanted to build your bank account. And she mentioned possibly moving to a new home if enough money was raised."

"Gigi's never said anything about moving to a new building," Sophie said. Thanks to the mix of light from the moon and the lot's halogen lamps, I saw the side-eye she gave me.

"We'd be in perpetual fundraising mode," Nate said. "We can't afford a mortgage or rent on some other place. Thanks to the Townsends' generosity, we don't have to worry about bills for heat, water, and electricity."

"What came first, Gigi and Zach's relationship, or the theater's deal with Townsend's?"

Nate allowed Sophie to tell the tale. "Gigi and Zach met at a business association meeting and started dating. At that time, the club used the barn to store maintenance equipment. When Zach gave her the *grand tour* of the club and grounds, Gigi mentioned barn weddings were becoming very popular and Zach should consider renovating the barn to hold various events.

"Gigi also had the wisdom to ask if the BCT could use the barn for productions. The theater didn't have a permanent home at that point. We had to hold shows in any school gymnasium that was available. Gigi promised the set guys would build the stage and the BCT would foot the bill. That was five years ago. The first production in the barn was also my first one with the theater."

"Gigi was a shrewd businesswoman," I said with admiration.

Nodding in agreement, Nate finished the narrative. "Zach loved the idea and loved Gigi, too, so he offered the BCT rent-free use of the barn for all shows. When Gigi saw that the old caretaker's cottage was empty, she secured it for our office, also rent-free."

"Sweet deal. Does the club get a cut of the ticket sales?" I asked.

"No," Sophie answered.

"May I ask what the typical amount of a donation is?"

"Two hundred, three hundred dollars. Once in a while a Townsend friend with deep pockets will throw us a check for five hundred or even a thousand." Nate, who was not only our production manager but also the BCT's treasurer, raked his fingers through his dirty-blond hair. "I do like the idea of a capital campaign. We need to build our coffers."

We talked about how the weak economy had affected the theater's influx of donations for a few minutes. After bidding us good night, Nate climbed into the 4Runner and drove from the lot.

"If Gigi was thinking of giving up our rent-free digs, something *must* have gone on between her and Zach."

"Or with Donna." I told Sophie about Donna's pre-rehearsal visit. "Gigi was definitely upset. The fundraising idea might have come to her that night. Maybe Donna wants the BCT to start paying rent."

"Or worse. Vacate the premises." Sophie allowed herself a dramatic sigh. "If directing this show isn't enough pressure. Now we might lose our stage!"

"You're jumping to a dire conclusion, Madam Director." I did my best to ease Sophie's worries, but I could tell from her weary tone I hadn't succeeded. We parted and I followed her car out of the lot.

Sophie's suggestion that Gigi's capital campaign plan had to do with Zach held more merit than my idea that Donna had inspired it. Considering the sweetheart deal Zach gave Gigi for use of the barn, would Donna have held any sway in changing the agreement? If all was fine in their marriage, Zach would have put the kibosh on any plan that would hurt the BCT.

It could be one more sign, along with Gigi's Friday melancholy and Saturday flower purchase, of discontent in their marriage. Was Gigi plotting to sever the BCT's connection with the club at the same time she terminated her relationship with Zach?

Chapter Twelve

The cast and crew took up three pews halfway up the aisle of Saint Paul's Lutheran Church Wednesday morning. I sat on the end, on the center aisle, a good position for observing the mourners attending Gigi's funeral. Sophie, sitting beside me, proved an excellent seatmate. Every few moments she would lean in, whisper a name and tilt her head in the person's direction.

"There's Gigi's business partner, Whitney Roth. The stork-like blonde in the red coat."

I held my gaze on the mid-thirties blonde, watching her settle across the aisle in the third pew's end seat. Whitney shrugged off her coat, showing off a snug-fitting black pantsuit over a silky white blouse.

"Do you know her well?"

"Not really. I've only dealt with her at our opening-night shows. She makes a big fuss over Gigi and the actors, but makes sure she does it in front of the Townsends and their rich friends. She doesn't talk to us otherwise. She's a phony."

Iris, who sat on Sophie's other side, leaned over and whispered, "She's the kind of woman who doesn't give a bleep about you unless you can do something for her."

We watched Whitney take a tissue from her purse and dab her eyes. "I bet those are crocodile tears," Sophie said.

Jerome and Nate, sitting in front of us, turned and gave us amused looks. "Hey, you're in a church," Nate said. "You were supposed to check your self-righteousness at the door."

"Sorry, Reverend Kelton," Sophie replied.

45

Nate smirked and faced the altar. Whitney reclaimed my attention. She was no longer drying her tears. Her purse was open on her lap; I could see her holding her iPhone in the mouth of the bag, her finger sweeping over the screen. It was a moment I had seen plenty of times before in church and it angered me every time. No one is that important, or busy, that she can't stop texting for an hour and have a one-on-one with God in His house.

I was shouting, "Put your damn phone away!" in my head when Nate turned around again and said, "Will one of you go tell that fraud to put her phone away?"

"Amen to that," I said *sotto voce* in unison with Sophie's and Iris's similar declarations. The five of us focused our peeved gazes on Whitney for at least thirty seconds until she dropped the phone in her purse and zipped it.

"Victory," Jerome said.

Sophie took a casual glance at the pews behind us. "There's Ariana. Ariana Costas," she added for my benefit. "She works for Gigi and Whitney."

"She *was* their assistant," Iris said.

Sophie gave me a conspiratorial look before asking Iris, "What happened? Did Gigi tell you?"

"I saw Ariana at the Farley Inn when my husband and I had brunch there on New Year's Day. Ariana was working at the front desk. I thought she was moonlighting, but she said she no longer worked for Gigi."

"Wow." Sophie dragged out the one syllable for several seconds. "Was she fired?"

"She didn't say. She was busy and couldn't talk, so I didn't get the full story."

"Huh." Sophie twisted around, sneaking another look at Ariana.

"Where is she?" I whispered, making a slow turn in my seat.

"The last pew, on the right. She's in a black turtleneck. Curly dark hair."

I located the young woman among the mourners. She wore a disconsolate expression, staring straight ahead for a moment before studying her copy of the service's program. She sat with Maura Stern, the Farley's manager. I was turning when Tracey and fellow officer Ron Nicholstone entered the church. Ron wore a dark suit, Tracey a navy pantsuit. She took a seat in Ariana's pew while Ron walked up the side aisle and slid into a pew two rows behind mine.

Sophie also noticed the law enforcement presence. "Taking seats in the back, I see. The better to watch us." We swiveled around. "You should check out Ariana, Veronica. Along with Miss Whitney."

"I will," I murmured.

We shut up and became reflective until the service began a few minutes later. With the choir singing "Amazing Grace," the funeral procession took its slow march up the aisle. Zach, flanked by his parents, with his mother's arm linked through his, kept his somber gaze on his wife's casket. Behind them were Gigi's parents and sister. Tears streamed down Mrs. Swanson's cheeks. Her husband maintained a stoic expression in the face of his massive loss. Gigi's younger sister, Blair, looked into the eyes of the mourners she passed. Was she, too, looking for her sister's killer?

Sophie and I stood outside the church after the service, watching the pallbearers slide Gigi's casket into the hearse. There would be no cemetery caravan; cremation had been Gigi's final wish.

Blair, heading for the limousine hired for the Swansons, stopped and gave Sophie a kiss on her cheek. "We'll talk soon, Soph."

"Aren't you going to the lunch at Townsend's?"

"No." Blair glanced at the limo and then slid a furtive look toward the limo Zach shared with his parents. "Mom can't be anywhere near the place where Gigi was killed. She just couldn't bear it. I think under the circumstances, it's best we stay away. Our family's gathering at our house."

Blair touched my shoulder. "I hope we can talk soon, too, Veronica."

"Whenever you'd like," I replied, puzzled by her comment.

With a "Thank you for coming," Blair made a dash for the limo. Sophie and I trailed her at a slow pace.

"This is the saddest day ever," Sophie said, forlorn.

"Are you up to going to the lunch?"

"Yeah. I'm not ready to go back to work. And I want to see if anything happens during the lunch."

"What do you think will happen? Everyone will be on their best behavior."

"You should know better," Sophie said with a sly turn. "Something *always* happens at soap opera funerals."

True. One time my character's arch nemesis pushed her into an open grave. I reminded Sophie, however, that we were in the middle of real life and she shouldn't have high hopes for a melodrama in the Townsend's dining room.

We said temporary good byes and parted. Sophie had parked across the street and my car was in the lot behind the church. I trailed behind a few mourners, my glance wandering the area, looking for nothing in particular.

I spotted Nate standing near a brown pickup truck, talking with a man. It took me a moment before I recognized the man Gigi met in front of the bakery the day before she died. He wore an unbuttoned black wool coat over a dark suit. A feature I didn't notice at the bakery, thanks to the cap he wore, was the man's thick red hair.

I walked to my car, keeping Nate and the man in my peripheral vision. I couldn't overhear their conversation, but from their expressions, I guessed the chat warmer than what I had witnessed between Gigi and the man. I plotted a delayed departure by holding a pretend phone conversation in my car while observing the pair, but the handshake and mutual backslap that preceded Nate's move away from the pickup canceled my opportunity for improvisation.

"See you at the lunch, Veronica?"

I turned and saw Jerome approaching a car across the aisle from mine. "Yes. See you there."

I let my car warm and watched both Nate and Mr. Redhead leave. "So who is this mystery man?" I mused aloud. I thought I had met *Blithe Spirit's* entire crew. Was the man a former volunteer with the theater? Someone they knew from the club?

I recalled the scene I saw outside Rizzuto's window. Something about Gigi's and the man's posture told me it was a confrontational meeting. The next opportunity I had for a private chat with Nate, I'd ask him the man's identity. He wasn't a suspect, yet, but he was definitely a person of interest.

The post-funeral lunch was held in a dining room overlooking a stone terrace and the eighteenth hole. A wall of windows afforded an excellent view of the tranquil grounds. The sparkling place settings, white votive candles, and cylinder vases filled with pink roses atop round tables for eight offered elegance and comfort.

Sophie and I stood by the window, observing the group of mourners. Not everyone who attended the church service joined us at Townsend's; besides the Swanson family, a few of our cast and crew had skipped the lunch, having only taken the morning off from their jobs. After scanning the black-clad group, I noted Ariana was also not there.

The crowd had divided into small conversation groups. Zach stood in one corner, talking with three men. Donna and her husband, Wayne, circled the room shaking hands and accepting condolences. Whitney, a glass of white wine in her hand, also made the rounds. In one moment, I spied her giving Zach's arm a squeeze and his shoulder a pat. He ignored her.

"Do you see Whitney working the room?" Sophie mumbled. "I won't be surprised if she starts handing out business cards."

"Let's give her some sense of decorum." We fell silent, watching Whitney chat with three women. Whitney maintained steady eye contact, her head bobbing in agreement with everything the other women said.

Sophie snorted. "Merry widow. Like I said, something always happens at funerals."

We fell into silence for a minute. Zach broke away from a group and approached us. "Thank you for coming." He shook my hand, holding it in both of his warm hands for a few seconds.

I introduced myself and gave my condolences. "I'm sorry I didn't have more time to get to know Gigi."

Zach, a black-haired guy with the lanky build of a track-and-field athlete, put on a smile that brightened his dark eyes. "Gigi was very grateful to you for joining the *Blithe Spirit* cast. I think she was afraid you'd be a diva and make all sorts of crazy demands before you agreed to take the role." His smile widened, revealing a perfect set of gleaming white teeth that reminded me of the dental work my fellow soap actors possessed.

Zach gave Sophie a lingering embrace. "How are you doing with this, Sophie? I haven't yet wrapped my head around this new reality."

Sophie, who had pointed an accusing finger at Zach all week, treated him like a helpless puppy. "I'm just heartbroken for you and your whole family. If there's anything the BCT can do for you, please let me know."

His parents joined us, initiating another round of sympathetic greetings. Seeing Zach at Wayne's side, it was obvious he had inherited his looks and bass tones from his father. Wayne's hair was more salt than pepper, though, and he wore wire-rimmed glasses and was several inches shorter than his son. With their penetrating, dark-eyed gazes, both Townsend men had the effect of making one feel like the most important person in the room.

Despite their wealth and power, the elder Townsends were a down-to-earth couple. Wayne asked me about All Things and praised it as a model of a successful small business. "We're lucky to have a number of large companies in the county," he said, "but our small businesses, rooted in the community and established by life-long residents, are our building blocks to a strong local economy." I wondered, uncharitably, how many times he had used that line in speeches.

Donna adjusted her silver-rimmed, half-frame glasses and addressed Sophie. "We'll have to meet to talk about Showcase Night. And I have an idea on a way to honor Gigi."

"All right," Sophie said.

"How about we talk about it over lunch on Saturday? Veronica, will you join us? You might have some fresh ideas for the evening."

Sophie and I joined Nate, Erica, Peter, and Iris at a table. A busboy making his rounds with a pitcher of ice water filled glasses for Sophie and me.

Iris pressed her shoulder against Sophie and said in a disdainful tone, "I overheard Whitney trying to schedule a meeting with one of Gigi's clients. She might have style, but she has no sense of taste."

"Better take back that sense of decorum you gave her," Sophie whispered near my ear.

Jerome joined us, taking a seat next to Nate. "I saw you talking with Kenny in the parking lot. How is he?"

Thank you, Jerome! The innocent question had me rapt; were I a dog, my ears would have twitched and my head cocked to one side.

"He's okay," replied Nate.

"Oh, I wish I had seen him," Iris said. "Why isn't he working on *Blithe Spirit?*"

Moving his water glass to his lips, Nate said, "He's got a lot going on." He took two gulps of water and shifted the conversation to the weather.

Was there a reason for Nate's abrupt response and chatter about the temperature (a classic diversionary tactic), or was I making a mountain out of a molehill where this Kenny fellow was concerned?

I'll ask Nate at rehearsal, I promised myself.

For a few minutes, our group made small talk and people watched until Donna and Wayne approached the table.

"I desperately need your help, Nate." Donna came up behind him, placing her hands on his shoulders. "I am lost in *the cloud*." Her shrug and headshake conveyed faux exasperation.

"I want in on this meeting," Wayne said. "Yesterday afternoon I tried to share a document with a guy in Parks and Rec, but Trevor said he couldn't access it."

"Don't worry. I'll get you straight on it," Nate said.

"Veronica, are you and your staff in *the cloud*?" Donna asked. I got the sense that, though she was lost in *the cloud*, Donna derived great delight from saying it.

"I'm a Virgo. We earth signs keep our feet firmly planted on the ground."

"There's a bit of a learning curve, at least for some of us, but it's worth the effort to keep your business up-to-date with the latest technology. Thank goodness we can rely on Nate for our hardware and software needs." Wayne patted Nate's shoulder and he and Donna made their way to their table across the room.

"You should send a bill to the county for the consultation," Jerome quipped.

Nate gave a good-natured chuckle, but said no more because Wayne had called for everyone's attention. While he offered words of welcome and thanks, Sophie gave me a whispered explanation about Jerome's remark.

"Nate is the IT guy for the club, but he didn't win the contract with the county for supplying all their computer-related needs."

"Too bad. Having the county for a client would give his business a big boost."

Sophie, her attention on Wayne's speech, gave a tight-lipped, "Hmm-hmmm."

I snuck a glance at Nate. He didn't seem bothered by Jerome's tease, though it must have smarted when he lost out on the county contract when he had an established business relationship with the club. Perhaps it was a simple matter of Nate's business not being large enough to accommodate the county's needs, or he just didn't present a strong offer for the contract.

Not my worry. I turned my attention on Wayne, forgetting all thoughts of clouds, contracts, and business deals.

After lunch, Sophie and I walked together to the front entrance. "I'm glad that's over," Sophie said, her voice low. She pulled on her gloves and slung her bag over her shoulder. "We can start getting back to normal."

"Normal won't happen until Gigi's killer is brought to justice."

"Veronica. Sophie." We turned at the call of our names. Donna and a man were descending a staircase from the upper floor. "I want you to meet Bret Foster, our event planner."

Donna made the formal introductions, with the fair-haired Bret greeting Sophie and me with a firm handshake. "Bret is available to meet on Saturday, so why don't we set our lunch for noon?" Donna asked.

"Sure. We'll be here," Sophie said.

The boyish-faced Bret grinned. "I'm excited to help you celebrate *Blithe Spirit*."

"Where's Julia?" Sophie asked.

"Julia left us to pursue her dream of running her own event planning business."

"Really? When did she leave?"

"October. We miss her, but we're so happy to welcome Bret to the Townsend family." Donna linked her arm through Bret's and gave him a proud look. "We'll see you Saturday."

We watched the pair continue along the hall toward the restaurant. "Gigi never said anything about Julia leaving the club. Weird," Sophie said. "I would have liked to have said goodbye to her and thanked her for all the great parties she put together for the BCT."

"You didn't see Julia at the funeral, did you?" I held the door open for Sophie, allowing her passage and then following her outside.

"No. And she wasn't at the lunch. You're not thinking she—"

"No. I'm not thinking anything other than she's someone who worked with Gigi and Zach and might have some insight into their relationship."

I'd place Julia on my growing list of interviewees. Top of the list, though, was Kenny. What history did he share with Gigi that made their Friday morning meeting a less-than-friendly encounter?

Chapter Thirteen

Wednesday's rehearsal was another subdued practice. Emotionally and physically drained by the funeral, we hit the stage after giving perfunctory greetings. Despite our fatigue, the scenes were sharp and pleased our director.

"Terrific rehearsal, everyone," Sophie said at nine thirty. "Why don't we call it a night?"

We welcomed the early dismissal with a collective sigh of appreciation and made a hasty retreat from the barn. When Nate told Sophie, "I'll close up," I lagged behind on the pretense of checking phone messages.

He followed me out the door, flipping the switch on the overhead lights. We began a slow trot over the well-trodden path.

I wasted no time on small talk. "Did Kenny and Gigi have a friendly relationship?"

Nate stopped. "Kenny Pangborn?"

"Yeah. The guy you met in Saint Paul's parking lot."

Nate, whose height fell two or three inches short of the six-foot mark, looked at me with a cheeky grin. "Are you asking if they had an affair?"

"No. But did they?"

Nate enjoyed a hearty laugh. "No way. Why are you asking?"

"I saw them together the day before Gigi was killed." I described what I saw through the bakery window.

Nate's cheer faded. "Why don't we go get a drink? Hot or cold, your choice. I think there's something I should tell you."

I ordered a ginger ale, Nate a beer, from the bartender at Connolly's Bar and we snagged a corner table. From our perch, we could watch the rowdy game of pool happening in the adjoining room and view the hockey and basketball games showing on the two large-screen televisions on the opposite side of the pub. The place wasn't packed, but there were enough patrons to create a cheerful din.

I started the conversation after Nate took a few pulls on his beer. "Was what I saw Friday morning a continuation of some difficulty between Gigi and Kenny?"

"Yes." Nate paused for a moment and gave me a severe look. "This stays between us. You can't tell Sophie or anyone at the BCT."

"I won't." I almost crossed my heart with one hand and "zipped" my lips with the other.

Nate braced himself with another gulp of beer. "In October, Gigi caught Kenny pocketing money during a fundraising bingo night in the barn."

"How much?"

"A couple hundred. But when she confronted Kenny, she asked if he had taken money on other occasions. He admitted he had."

I repeated my question.

"Roughly five thousand. Kenny had taken it over a period of a couple of years, stealing small amounts from money set aside for sets, from budgets on shows where he was the production manager, and swiping cash at fundraisers like the bingo night."

"What did Gigi do? What's the theater's protocol for dealing with theft?"

"Gigi first asked me to do an audit of the budgets of productions Kenny had managed so we would know the extent of his embezzlement before we told the trustees. I didn't find anything missing beyond what Kenny said he took."

"That's good. Did you then take it to the trustees?"

"Gigi didn't want to. She believed if we told them, the embezzlement would become public knowledge. Someone on the board would tell someone, and that person would tell someone. She feared the BCT's reputation would be tarnished. Donations would dry up and we might lose a portion of our faithful audience. Gigi was also concerned it would reflect poorly on her management of the theater. And I worried the trustees would think I failed in my responsibilities as treasurer."

A loud crack and cheer from the trio playing pool distracted us for a moment.

"So we told Kenny we wouldn't press charges if he returned the five thousand. He did, within a month. Gigi dismissed him from the BCT. That was the end of the story. I thought."

"You and Gigi were very kind to Kenny, sparing him from facing charges of embezzlement. He should be grateful and yet, it looked as if he wanted to throttle Gigi on the sidewalk. Was he angry when you talked with him this morning?"

"More passive-aggressive. Kenny's had a rough time the last couple of years. He runs his family's hardware store in Penny Woods. The Houseman Home and Yard store that moved in just a couple of blocks away has put a big dent in his business. And now he's going through a divorce and custody battle. Kenny cheated on his wife and he has a drinking problem. All this is to tell you that paying back the five thousand put Kenny deeper into the hole."

When I started a protest that Kenny put himself in the hole, Nate made a hand gesture indicating his agreement. "I know. He only has himself to blame. Today, when I talked with him, he told me he's behind in payments to his wife because he had to pay off a debt a couple of months ago. He didn't come right out and say it was the five grand he owed the BCT, but I know that's what he meant."

"Was he looking for a loan from you?" I asked, half in jest.

"It'd be more of a gift than a loan," Nate said. "I can't do it."

We sat quiet for a minute. Nate watched the hockey game while I processed the new information. If only I could read lips, I lamented, I would have understood what Gigi and Kenny were saying on the sidewalk outside Rizzuto's. Did Kenny unload his woe-is-me diatribe and Gigi wasn't having any of it? I wondered if her own marital woes fueled her anger at adulterer Kenny and whatever she said pushed him over the edge.

"Did you tell the police about the embezzlement?"

With an agonized look, Nate shook his head. "I didn't. Because Kenny returned the five grand, I didn't even consider he was involved in Gigi's death."

When Tracey asked for my help on the case, I didn't imagine embezzlement would be the bit of key information I would overhear.

"I hate to think Kenny killed Gigi. It would be tragic for his son if he did." Nate pulled his fingers through his hair and his eyes took on a sudden fatigue. "I consider Kenny a friend. I don't want to sic the police on him if he's innocent."

"How about I try to find out if he has an alibi? You said he manages a hardware store in Penny Woods?"

"Yeah. Bond Hardware on Main Street."

"All right. I'll pay a visit. See if he was at the store last Saturday morning."

"I hope it's as easy as that."

"Me, too. If I can't verify an alibi, we need to tell the police."

"Okay."

A couple of minutes passed before I asked, "Is there anyone else at the BCT who had disagreements with Gigi? Sophie said you're a big happy family, but that's obviously not true with this business with Kenny."

Nate gave the question a minute's thought. "Other than Kenny, I can't think of anyone who had problems with Gigi. We all do get along well."

"Are you close with Zach? You have a business arrangement, but do you socialize with him?"

"A bit. We're not best buddies, but I consider him a friend."

I told him about my impression of Gigi's mood when we met Friday morning and of her flower purchase. "Did you ever get a sense, from Gigi or Zach, of trouble between them?"

"I can't say I have. I don't think they spent much time together. Zach's devoted to the family business, and Gigi had her design business and the BCT. They both worked days, nights, and weekends. I guess that could have caused issues, or been the result of a problem."

"How well do you know Gigi's business partner, Whitney?"

Nate's tight expression relaxed. "Not well. I've met her only a few times. She's come to our last few opening nights and is very vocal about how proud she is of Gigi at the receptions. It was sort of a pick-up line to snag new clients. Did you see her in action at the lunch today?"

"Oh, yeah. It was obvious to Sophie and me that Whitney was trying to drum up business. Did it ever bother Gigi, watching her partner try to bag clients on Gigi's big night?"

"Gigi's usual reaction was a shake of the head and a 'There's Whitney being Whitney again' crack." Nate turned thoughtful. "Do you think Whitney might have—"

"Romantic and business partners are always eyed in murder investigations."

"It seemed Whitney was always trying to keep up with Gigi. Insecure, I think. It would be a shame if she were involved. Whitney's ambitious, but I've always thought she had a good heart."

Nate and I talked for a few more minutes before heading out into the frosty night. "See you tomorrow night, Veronica," he said, pressing his car's remote.

A few moments later, I buckled my seatbelt and gave him a wave goodbye. Nate pulled his 4Runner from the next spot; he tooted the horn, and made a left out of the parking lot.

The glacial temperature in my car sent a jerking shiver through me. I hugged myself and stamped my feet, impatient for the engine to warm. Waiting for a blast of heat through the vents, I contemplated whether Kenny had a role in Gigi's death. Was his bitterness toward Gigi so extreme, and his refusal to accept responsibility for his problems so rigid, that Kenny exacted revenge on Gigi by killing her?

The thought gave me another shiver the warm air coming through the vent could not relieve.

Chapter Fourteen

I called Gigi's business partner first thing after All Things opened for business Thursday morning and before the day grew hectic. I had a visit to Kenny's hardware store scheduled, along with a stop at a ceramicist's studio, and an in-store visit from our chocolate supplier.

Whitney's cheerful demeanor and attempt to mix business with grief at the lunch left me cold. I was stunned when Whitney answered, saying, "Roth Interiors. This is Whitney Roth."

Gigi's gone and forgotten, I noted.

"Veronica! Gigi was over the moon when you took the part in her play," Whitney chortled after I introduced myself. "I hope you're not calling to ask me to take over as director. Ha-ha."

"You're off the hook. Sophie has assumed the directorial reins. I'd like to meet and talk with you—"

"Are you finally getting around to redecorating your home since moving back to Barton? Gigi never mentioned you were a client."

"I—" I started to correct the misunderstanding when I realized I could use it to my advantage. Why not meet her on her "turf?" "I'm not a client, yet. I'm so busy with All Things and *Blithe Spirit* that I can't even think about redecorating until the spring or summer. But I want a pro's suggestions and an estimate of the cost."

"Smart woman," Whitney said in an agreeable tone. "Get all the particulars upfront."

We scheduled a meeting at my house for the next day. Shaking my head, I went downstairs.

I found Claire at the back of the shop, dusting a shelf of ceramic pieces made by a Barton resident. The original owner of All Things established the shop under the name *All Things Adirondack* and exclusively sold the handcrafted items of local artists. His widow dropped "Adirondack" from the name and replaced the work of resident talent with high-end, more expensive merchandise. When I purchased the shop, I struck a balance between one-of-a-kind goods and manufactured inventory. It's a point of pride that made-in-the-Adirondacks products line the shop's shelves.

I told Claire about Whitney's opening salutation. "Are you worried that if something happens to you, I'll try to wrest control of the shop and never let go? Because you know nothing of the sort happened after Anna died."

"I trust you completely. I don't think this was some innocent slip of the lip on Whitney's part. I answer the phone here with 'All Things' so many times a day, sometimes I say it when I answer my cell phone. It's a habit that would take more than a day to break if I changed the name of the shop. Whitney sounded as if she's always been the sole business owner."

"It was more of a Freudian slip, then. That Swanson comes first in the business name indicates Gigi had more power in the partnership. Whitney finally has the power and she has no shame in showing it. Mourning period be damned."

"The question is, is Whitney merely an ambitious, cold opportunist or a murderer?"

"How are you going to find out which she is?" Claire asked.

"I have an appointment with her tomorrow to discuss redecorating my house."

"Don't write her a check, in case she's guilty. But she could be innocent, so get some ideas for new furniture. Your home is lovely, but you should ditch the living room set you bought in the last century. You've started a new life here, time to give your house a facelift, too."

"A valid point, so I won't dock your paycheck for insulting the boss's couch. Or for that oblique insinuation I should get a facelift."

Chapter Fifteen

I had an excellent cover story for my appearance at Kenny's hardware store: I needed paint chip cards for my meeting with Whitney the next day. Walking into Bond Hardware, I gave myself a mental pat on the back and sent up a prayer my plan wouldn't go off-script.

A woman in her early twenties stood behind the checkout counter to the left of the door. "Good morning," she said in a sweet voice. "How may I help you?"

"I'd like to look at paint chip cards. I'm redecorating my house." I could see down two of the store's four aisles; both were empty and I couldn't hear anyone else in the store.

"Right behind you." The woman pointed at the front wall, where a wall rack held hundreds of paint chip cards in colors from one end of the spectrum to the other. "What's your color scheme?" She came around the counter and stood in front of the display, regarding it as if it was the *Mona Lisa*. The nametag pinned to her blue flannel shirt indicated she was Lori.

"I'm not sure. I'm getting ideas. This is a fact-finding mission." Not a lie, though the facts I was seeking had nothing to do with paint.

"No problem," Lori said, smiling. "A lot of folks aren't sure about what color they want when they come in."

"Kenny Pangborn's the manager here, right?" I kept my tone casual.

"Yep. He's not here right now, though." Lori plucked a paint chip card with shades of green on it. "This is a popular color." She tapped her finger on a square labeled *Sage*.

"I like it." I took the card and glanced at the color. I really did like the shade. Darn, my pretend act was turning into a real reconnaissance mission for paint. "I'm a part of the BCT's new production."

"I thought I recognized you. You're Veronica Walsh, right? I saw your picture in the newspaper. There was an article about you being in the new show."

"That's me. When I mentioned I was going to paint a few rooms, a couple of people recommended I come here for supplies. They said Kenny used to build sets and was a production manager."

"He was." Lori gave me a sympathetic frown. "I was sorry to hear about Gigi Swanson's death. The poor woman. Kenny's taken her death hard."

"He has?"

"I think so. He's been particularly quiet the last few days. He went to her funeral yesterday. He said it was very sad. He feels real sorry for her husband."

"We all feel for Zach and Gigi's family. It's a terrible loss for them."

"It's so sad. I feel bad for them, too." Lori selected a card of orange hues. "How about this? Too bold?"

I made a show of studying the card. "Maybe. But I should be bolder." I held onto the card, leading Lori to think I might really paint my walls Halloween orange. "We'd love to have Kenny back at the BCT. We're doing *Blithe Spirit*."

"Kenny's got a lot going on, so he's taking a break from the BCT."

I selected a few cards in shades of blue, pink, and yellow. "You won't think I'm boring if I take something in ivory, will you?"

"Not at all. A lot of people go with the white or beige. Do you want to take a small can or two of paint home? You can slap a few streaks of each on a wall to see which you like best. They're only four dollars each."

"Um, okay. Good idea." If Whitney had any doubt about my renovation intentions, a couple of paint cans strategically placed in my front hall would help convince her I was serious about the redo.

"I'll be right back." Lori dashed down an aisle. "I'll give you a can of that sage you like and one of the starfish orange. Is it okay if I throw in a blue blush and, oh, a periwinkle, too?" Her voice grew louder the further into the store she went.

"Ah, okay."

"All you do is paint a square of each side-by-side on a wall and just live with them for a while."

"Great. Thank you."

"No problem."

I wandered over to the counter and noticed a few business cards standing in a plastic holder. I picked one up and studied the card that had Kenny's name and phone number in black lettering over an image of stacked firewood. On the back of the card was a list of towns where Kenny made deliveries. Barton was on the list.

"Kenny's got a firewood business, too?"

"Yep. It's a way to earn extra cash. Every bit helps."

I hooked a lure on my invisible fishing pole. "It sure does. Does he have many clients?"

"Yeah. Mainly restaurants with wood-burning ovens and a couple of inns."

I cast my line. "I see he delivers to Barton."

"Yep. The Hearth and Farley Inn are two of his customers."

A bite! I slowly started to reel in my catch. "Terrific. You know, I think I might have seen a brown pickup loaded with firewood going down Orchard last Saturday morning."

"That was Kenny. He delivered to the Hearth that morning. And he was over there the day before delivering to the Farley."

A beautiful catch! Not only did I establish Kenny was in Barton on Saturday morning, now I also knew what brought him to the bakery Friday morning. I tucked my paint chip cards and Kenny's business card into my purse.

"Does he unload all that wood on his own?"

"No way! That would take too long. A couple of guys help him."

I moved away from the counter and was standing at the top of an aisle, staring at a display of smoke detectors and fire extinguishers, when the door swung open and Kenny charged into the store.

I found myself in a stare down with the unshaven, tousle-haired embezzler. Knowing I couldn't intimidate the broad-shouldered man with a penetrating gaze, I tried disarming him with a cheery, "Good morning."

"Morning." There was no warm welcome in Kenny's deep-voiced reply.

Maintaining eye contact with his cool stare, I said, "I think I saw you at Gigi Swanson's funeral yesterday, right?"

"Yeah. And I saw you talking to her outside Rizzuto's last week."

I paused, pretending I didn't immediately remember seeing him at the bakery. "Yes. That's right."

"Can I help you?"

"No, thank you. Lori's getting a few sample cans of paint for me."

Lori appeared on cue, holding four small cans and a few paint sticks. "Hey, Kenny." She went behind the counter and scanned the bar code on each can. "This is a good selection to start with." She grabbed a brown bag from under the counter and stacked the cans in it.

After forking over my cash and dropping the change in my purse, I grasped the bag, anxious to flee the hardware scene. "I hope you didn't give me too many choices. I'll never make up my mind."

Lori folded the top of the bag twice. "Then you'll just have to paint every room a different color," she said with a giggle.

I smiled and took the bag. "Thanks for your help, Lori." I took several steps toward the door.

"Did you tell Kenny you're working on the latest BCT production? This is Veronica Walsh."

Drats! Two more steps and I would have been outside and making a dash for my car.

I turned around. "Nice to meet you, Kenny. I've heard great things about you at the BCT. Everyone says you were a great carpenter and production manager. They miss you."

"Yeah, well. I'm busy. No time for that stuff."

"Maybe the next show. Bye." I yanked open the door and speed-walked to my car. I flung myself into the front seat and exhaled after locking the doors and buckling my seatbelt. It was then I realized I had a knot in my stomach from the stress of my brief one-on-one with Kenny. The guy's menacing quality made me nervous.

I had a vision of Kenny tearing out of the store carrying an ax or chainsaw. "I better get out of here." I backed out of my parking space and drove out of the stand-alone hardware store's lot. Once on the road, I considered Kenny's opportunity to kill Gigi.

Like Zach, Kenny was out and about Barton on Saturday morning. Did his wood delivery occupy him during the window of opportunity in which Gigi's killer acted, or did his route include a stop at the BCT office?

Chapter Sixteen

We were an hour into rehearsal, and in the middle of the séance Madame Arcati holds with the other characters, when three unexpected guests arrived. Wayne carried a large carafe in each hand, Zach a canvas tote and a plastic-wrapped platter. Donna followed with another platter. The trio placed their goods on a table at the back of the room and watched until we finished the scene. They rewarded our end with applause.

Donna came forward with her platter. "That was wonderful!"

The trio lay their offerings on the table where Sophie and Nate sat. "We brought coffee and hot chocolate." Wayne gestured at the carafes.

Donna unwrapped the platters, which held an assortment of cookies, while Zach unloaded napkins, plastic plates, and large paper cups from the tote.

After we gave thanks for their generosity, Wayne said, "We don't mean to interrupt your rehearsal. Donna, Zach, and I just wanted to visit with you for a minute and express our thanks for your support in this difficult time."

"You were Gigi's family, too," Zach said, any emotion he might be feeling under tight control. "I know you're grieving and I'm so glad you've decided to continue with *Blithe Spirit*. I think this production will help us all come to terms with Gigi's death. I know she'd be happy that you're going on with the show."

Donna spoke next. "If there's anything you need from us, anything we can do, please don't hesitate to ask."

Wayne put his arm around his wife's shoulder. "We want to

assure you the BCT has the full support of our family and Townsend's. We want our relationship to continue for years to come. The Barton Community Theater will have a home here as long as the Townsends are, well, at Townsend's."

We applauded and spoke more words of gratitude.

"Dig in, please!" Wayne said.

Sophie and I stood at the side, watching everyone snatch up the treats. "I guess they didn't get a memo from Gigi declaring her independence," she mumbled.

"Or maybe they did and they want to pretend they didn't," I whispered.

Wayne joined us, offering us each a plate of several cookies. "I hope you're not angry we burst in here, Sophie. Gigi would have kicked us out."

"No problem, Mr. Townsend. We were ready for a break. It's a sweet gesture."

"It was Zach's idea. People have been unbelievably kind to him. He's feeling almost suffocated by the love. He wanted to give a bit of comfort to others. And it takes his mind off the police investigation." Wayne lowered his voice. "He understands why he's a suspect, but he knows he is innocent and will be fully absolved. Until then, though, he will be under considerable stress."

"We all hope the case is closed soon," Sophie said.

I murmured agreement and surveyed the group. Nate and Zach stood apart from the group, talking. Zach was bobbing his head at whatever Nate was saying and watching everyone. His gaze moved my way and settled on me. It wasn't a blank stare, I knew Zach *saw* me, but he made no sign of notice. I held his glance for a few seconds before turning to Wayne.

"The Barton PD will catch Gigi's killer very soon, I'm certain."

The Townsends left a few minutes later and we returned to the stage, our bellies full from the unexpected treat. The murmurs of my castmates, who moments ago had been vocal in their gratitude, surprised me. They were terrific actors offstage, too.

"Are they trying to bribe us to stand behind Zach?" Erica asked under her breath.

"That was uncomfortable," Peter said.

"Wayne sure was spinning you away from Zach," whispered Iris, who had been standing nearby when Wayne was talking with Sophie and me.

"I think politicians are required to be spinning something at all times. They don't know what to do with themselves otherwise."

"Okay, folks. Let's get back to work. What's the next scene, Sophie?" Nate asked.

Sophie announced the scene and the principals took their places. I wasn't in the scene, so I moved off stage and sat with Iris, Peter, and Kelsey in a row of chairs against the wall.

I considered Iris's remark. Here was the consequence of being a successful sleuth: everyone knew I was a successful sleuth. Suspects put their guard up higher and relatives overcompensated in their declarations of their loved one's innocence. Zach's cool stare and Wayne's assertion were two examples of the effect of my new claim to fame.

I considered operating under a disguise. I owned a few wigs from my soap days and had used a black, bob-styled piece on a surveillance mission the previous October. I could also borrow from the BCT's small inventory of costumes.

I closed my eyes, exhausted by my thoughts, the day, and the sudden sugar rush from the cookies and few sips of cocoa I had drunk. For a few minutes, I entertained the idea of relinquishing the sleuth part of my identity. Actress-businesswoman hyphenate was plenty.

" *'To hell with Ruth.'* "

My eyes popped open at Elvira's exclamation that closed Act One. Lucy nailed her delivery to Coward's specification of gentle and sweet.

"I know we just had a break, but I need to make a pit stop. Everyone back in five minutes." Sophie got up and dashed into the backstage hall.

I caught Nate's attention and tipped my head toward the front door. He accepted the invitation for a private chat in the vestibule.

"Did you find out anything about Kenny's alibi?" he asked, looking concerned.

"I went by the hardware store and had a chat with an employee and a short exchange of words with Kenny. I learned he was in Barton Saturday morning delivering firewood to the Hearth. I'll check if he has an alibi when I'm there for dinner tomorrow night. Maybe Kenny was too busy unloading wood to go to the BCT office."

"I hope so."

"If I can't account for his whereabouts before eleven a.m., I'm going to tell Tracey Brody. She'll have questions for you about the embezzlement, so we should talk with her together."

"I really don't want anyone knowing about the embezzlement. If the trustees find out . . ."

"The Barton PD will keep it quiet. Are you around on Saturday morning to meet with her, if we need to?"

Nate pulled on his goatee. "Um . . . yeah. Sure."

"Not a great way to start the weekend, but we should tell Tracey sooner rather than later. If we have to." I glanced through the open doorway and saw Sophie at the table. "Time to get back."

"Thank goodness," Nate said, his face relaxing. "I've been relishing these visits to the Condomine household a little too much. It's a great stress reliever. Makes me want to take up acting so I can make a full escape."

"Tell me about it, my friend. I escaped to make-believe land twelve hours a day, five days a week for over thirty years."

Chapter Seventeen

Whitney stalked up my front walk like a hunter tracking a bear, and I was the bear. Suppressing an urge to spin on my heels and escape into my backyard, I opened my front door and greeted Gigi's business partner.

Whitney yanked off one of her black leather gloves and put such a strong grip around my hand I almost dropped to my knees and cried, "Uncle." "What a pleasure to meet you, Veronica." She displayed two rows of gleaming white teeth framed by lips coated with a glossy red lipstick. "I'm looking forward to working with you to make your beautiful home even lovelier." I caught a voracious glint in her steely sapphire eyes. I ditched my hunter analogy; Whitney was more like the wolf stalking the Three Little Pigs. You won't blow my house down, lady!

I hung her knee-length, down coat in the hall closet and followed the red pantsuit-wearing Whitney into the living room. So much for business-widow's weeds, I snarked in my head. She produced a large binder and a stack of brochures from her red leather tote and set them on the coffee table.

"Let's get to know each other before we talk shop," she said, settling on my couch as if we were old friends getting together for a long session of girl chat.

"Terrific," I said. I offered coffee and went to the kitchen for the pot I had brewed. I set the carafe on a tray with cups, the milk pitcher, and sugar bowl, eager to do some getting-to-know you digging of my own.

Breezing past the dining room's doorway, I caught a movement in the corner. I stopped and observed Whitney peering into the china cabinet.

She became aware of my presence and said, without a hint of embarrassment, "You should display your Emmys more prominently instead of hiding them behind the gravy boat. Show them off! Be proud of what you earned."

I was proud of my two statues and wasn't hiding them, the position of the gravy boat notwithstanding. The pair need not be the centerpiece of a room, nor the subject of conversation.

"Seen, not heard, is how I like them," I cracked.

Whitney smiled and didn't press the matter. "It saves you from constantly having to wipe off the fingerprints of all your admirers."

We returned to the living room for our coffee klatch. Whitney peppered me with questions about my career and life in Barton for a few minutes before I maneuvered the conversation to satisfy my ulterior motive.

"How did you and Gigi get into business together?"

"We met a few years ago when we were working for different design firms. We met at all the trade shows. Gigi went out on her own first. When I got the itch to do my own thing, be my own boss, I gave her a call and proposed we hang out a designer shingle together. I brought in a number of clients from Albany and Saratoga Springs."

Should I be impressed? I wondered. Was that a shot at Barton denizens, as if we were less sophisticated than the city folks?

"So it was just the two of you in the business? Do you have an assistant or supporting team?"

"I'm in between assistants right now." Whitney let out a woe-is-me sigh. "We had issues with our last girl and had to fire her."

"I'm sorry to hear that."

"When it rains it pours. It's a challenge finding someone who is strong with both right brain and left brain stuff, plus has a strong aesthetic."

"Well, I hope you find someone soon to help you manage your workload."

Whitney rolled her eyes. "It's been crazy. Gigi's clients are all in a panic. Some have big parties coming up. Spring events. One's having her daughter's wedding in her backyard in June and wants her whole house looking fabulous. I have lots of hands to hold."

Enough with the litany. "Did Gigi have conflict with any clients? Anyone unhappy with her work?"

"Gigi worked hard to keep her clients happy. Some people are impossible to please, but there is no one who would kill her because the paint didn't dry in the color they expected."

"Can you think of anyone who would want to hurt Gigi?"

Whitney's eyes widened and she made a fuss of protest. "I cannot think of one person who did not like Gigi. I am still in utter shock over her death. It must have been some random act of violence. Someone looking for money for drugs or guns or something."

"But there's no evidence of robbery. Gigi's computer wasn't taken and there was money in her desk drawer."

Whitney shrugged with an "I have no idea" look. "Then maybe someone shot her for the thrill of it. There are sick people in this world."

I agreed with her. "Maybe Gigi didn't know her killer, but I have a sense she did."

"She may have met someone picking *something* up. If you know what I mean." Whitney gave me a leading look.

I couldn't ignore Whitney's implication that the something wasn't a house key or a Pyrex dish left behind after a potluck supper. "Do you have evidence that Gigi was involved in something not on the up-and-up?"

"I don't. I really have no reason to believe she did. She was the kindest person I knew. But how many times have we heard about a great person everyone adored being arrested for dealing drugs or blackmailing someone or running a brothel?" Whitney finished her coffee. "What I don't like is the rush to blame Zach. The poor man's already been convicted in the court of public opinion. He doesn't deserve it. He's contributed so much to this community and it's turned on him."

Whitney pulled a pen and leather-bound book from her tote. With an eager look, she handed me several of the glossy brochures that had Swanson and Roth Interiors written in gold script on the cover. I held back a comment of surprise she hadn't crossed off "Swanson" from the brochure.

"Now let's talk about your vision for your home. What do you think about knocking out your back wall and installing french doors out to your backyard?"

I cut Whitney off before my amateur investigating became an expensive enterprise, using the "just looking" excuse I frown upon when delivered by visitors to All Things. "I think I'll just start with paint colors. Let me show you the samples I picked up at the hardware store yesterday."

If looks could kill (and french doors talk), I'd be *mort* from the sneer Whitney flashed at me.

Chapter Eighteen

I scooted past the Farley Inn's front desk, slowing for a few seconds and stealing a peek at Ariana, who was assisting a telephone caller with a reservation. From the smile she wore, though no one was looking, I judged her pleasant demeanor genuine. A good sign, I thought, picking up my pace on the route to the manager's office.

"I've been wondering when you were going to show up with your questions," Maura Stern, the inn's manager, said a minute later. She gave me a knowing wink.

"You couldn't pick up the phone and call me? What do you know that I don't?"

"Let's have coffee."

Maura and I dispensed with small talk while a server poured the inn's popular vanilla coffee into white china cups. We had ample privacy for our conversation; the dining room's only other occupants were two businessmen having their own chat at a table across the room.

"So, your new employee, Ariana Costas, used to work for Gigi Swanson." I savored my first sip of the aromatic coffee.

"She did, and Ariana had nothing to do with Gigi's murder. She was at the front desk the entire morning. From eight until her lunch break."

"Okay. I'm glad that's cleared up."

"Did you really suspect Ariana?"

"Gigi hadn't told anyone at the BCT she no longer had an assistant. One of my castmates saw Ariana working here over the holiday and I thought maybe they had a difficult parting of the ways."

Maura, swallowing a gulp of coffee, made a stop signal with her hand. "Ariana didn't lose her job at Swanson and Roth. She quit. But yes, Ariana has some lingering sour feelings about her time there."

"Did she have issues with Gigi?"

"No. Her problems were with Whitney. Ariana thought Gigi was a terrific boss. Poor girl is heartbroken over Gigi's death. Well, many of us are. Gigi was my favorite vendor. She did an exquisite job decorating the inn for the holidays."

"Will you retain Whitney for all your design needs?"

Maura's response was swift. "No. I'm going to save money and have my new hire handle the seasonal décor. Gigi taught Ariana well, and Ariana's tastes match mine."

"Terrific. Have you informed Whitney?"

Maura's amber eyes flashed. "I'll wait until she comes a-calling."

I entertained Maura with a few details of my meeting with Whitney. "What went on between her and Ariana?"

Maura snorted. "I'll let Ariana tell you."

"Is she available for a talk?"

"Sure. She's due a break soon. I'll give her a few more minutes to fill you in and answer the questions I know you have."

"Maura told me you're doing a fantastic job."

"I appreciate the opportunity she's given me. My last job was . . . difficult, and I left it without having another position lined up. A dumb move. I'm lucky the inn had an opening."

Ariana and I sat in the wingback chairs in front of the reception area's fireplace. Dressed in a black pencil skirt and black blazer over a baby-blue turtleneck, Ariana sat with her hands folded in her lap. She wore a minimal amount of makeup on her smooth olive skin.

"You worked for Gigi Swanson and her partner, Whitney."

Ariana pushed a strand of her dark Grecian curls behind her ear. "Yeah. I worked for them for a year. Gigi was a fantastic boss."

"And Whitney not so much?"

Ariana shook her head, a glint of ire brightening her dark eyes. "No. Gigi was a mentor while Whitney treated me like a grunt. I don't know how she ever earned her design degree. She couldn't even take correct measurements. And Whitney would always blame me for every mistake *she* made."

I was glad I hadn't signed a contract with Whitney. I might have ended up with a crooked bay window or french doors three sizes too small.

"Plus, Whitney's an uninspired decorator. Most of the time, she just gave clients what she saw in magazines and on television."

"Really?"

"Yeah. She was nailed for it in September. She gave two clients the same living room she saw in a spread in *House Beautiful*."

"The *same* living room?"

Ariana nodded; it was obvious from her smirk and the gleam in her eye she enjoyed sharing this Whitney gossip. *Schadenfreude*, thy name is the ex-assistant. "The exact same living room. The paint. The rug. The throw pillows. The lampshades. Everything."

"Wow."

"Whitney didn't know the women were friends. Mrs. Appleton invited a few of her pals for lunch. When Mrs. Ferrari walked into a carbon copy of her new living room, she ran to the bathroom and called Whitney. I answered the phone and got an earful before Whitney got off another call."

"Did Gigi find out?"

"Yeah. She overheard me talking with Mrs. Ferrari, trying to calm her down, and asked me what was going on."

"And did Gigi talk with Whitney?"

"I think so. But I wasn't there when she did. I would have loved to have been a fly on that wall."

"So what happened that you quit your job?"

The muscle in Ariana's jaw twitched. "I went on a client call with Whitney. The woman had an unfinished basement she wanted to turn into a family room. Whitney wanted to measure the square footage, but she forgot to bring her laser measuring tool. Of course she blamed me for that. So she asked me to clear away all the stuff shoved against the walls so she could use the client's measuring tape. There was *a lot* of stuff in that basement. Like everything the family ever owned.

"I told Whitney I wasn't dressed for cleaning a basement. I was in a skirt and heels! Whitney just snapped and pointed her finger and told me to go do it or I'd lose my job. So I sucked it up and went down to move the boxes and other junk. Within five minutes, a *huge* spider crawled out of the pile of crap and a rat ran out."

I clucked my tongue in sympathy.

"That was it. I went upstairs, told Whitney I quit, and walked out."

"Did Gigi try to convince you to stay?"

"Yes." Ariana's voice faltered. "I told her I just couldn't put up with Whitney anymore. Gigi understood. And she gave Maura a stellar recommendation for me."

"Sounds like you deserved it."

"I felt bad about leaving Gigi, but now I'm so glad I did. I couldn't bear working for Whitney without a Gigi buffer."

"Did Gigi ever indicate she might dissolve her partnership with Whitney?"

"No. Never. Gigi was very professional. She'd never complain about Whitney to me."

I welcomed the gust of cold air on my face when I walked outside a few minutes later. "Quite a download of information," I muttered, unlocking my car door with a press on the remote button. "Whitney is certainly a drama queen. Maybe she should watch her back."

I had one question. Did Whitney take her show on the road to the barn Saturday morning?

Chapter Nineteen

"Here's one of my theories on Whitney. She knew there was trouble in Gigi and Zach's marriage, maybe she overheard Gigi talking with Zach on the phone, and worried that all the Townsends' rich pals would find a new interior decorator when Gigi and Zach separated."

"A twist on who gets the friends when a couple splits."

"Exactly." I took a swig of ginger ale and a bite of pizza. Mark and I were at the Hearth, enjoying a pie cooked in the restaurant's wood-fired oven.

"But, if their relationship was with Gigi," Mark said, "the clients could decide to go with a new decorator with her gone. It would be a big gamble for Whitney to kill her. A double gamble: keeping the clients and not being caught."

"Whitney has a great deal of self-confidence. She probably believes she can convince the clients to stay with her, play on their sympathy to keep them from bolting."

"And she quite possibly can. They'll want to stay with the familiar. Whitney will have to buy out Gigi's share of the business, though."

"I wonder if she has the funds to do that."

"Usually business partners will hold life insurance policies with the partner named the beneficiary. The payout would cover the agreed buyout price with maybe something extra to run the business during the transition."

I considered the information. "Lucky Whitney would have a successful business all to herself. I wonder if the insurer will withhold payment until the case is solved."

"I'm sure."

"I bet Myrtle will have some information for me at our canasta game tomorrow night." My friend Myrtle Evans was an insurance agent who often knew the confidential details of village business.

"She certainly has her finger firmly on Barton's pulse." Mark chuckled. "What else did Whitney have to say?"

"She sent out mixed messages. Gigi was loved by all and the most amazing person ever, but who knows, she could have been selling drugs or guns or cloned puppies."

"Is cloning puppies illegal?" Mark asked, his gulp of beer washing down the dry comment.

I shrugged, my mouth filled with a large bite of pizza crust. "Here's another Whitney theory. Maybe she didn't kill Gigi because Gigi was leaving Zach, but because she was about to leave Whitney. I can see that happening. It must have made Gigi furious hearing Whitney treated both their clients and assistant with such disrespect. I wouldn't be surprised. She erased Gigi from the business fast, if the way she answered the phone was any indication. *Roth Interiors.* How offensive."

Mark calmed me down by taking the conversation on a lighthearted turn. "So what new décor did you select? Gold gilding on everything or wall-to-wall floral?"

"I haven't agreed to anything, yet. From what Ariana told me, I'd probably end up living in a replica of my soap character's house. But if I do update my digs, I'm thinking one color for everything. Carpet, walls, furniture. Maybe black or white, but I'm leaning to lime green or fuchsia."

"How beautiful. I think we'll be spending most of our time at my house so we don't go cross-eyed."

I swiped another slice from our pizza order. "Maybe Whitney can redecorate your house first and I'll see what I think of her work."

"I never agreed to be your guinea pig."

Mark and I ate in comfortable silence for a minute until I broke it with, "This pizza reminds me I have to ask Dan about Kenny Pangborn."

"How does it do that?" Mark asked, amused.

"Kenny supplied the wood used in the wood-fired oven that cooked this delicious pizza."

"Aha."

My opportunity came a few minutes later when Dan Miller, the Hearth's owner, strolled into the dining room. When he looked our way, I wiggled my fingers to get his attention.

"Are you enjoying your meal?" he asked, leaning his hands on our table.

"It's delicious. Do you have a minute to talk?" I asked.

Dan pulled a chair from the empty table beside ours and sat. "What's up?"

"Was Kenny Pangborn here Saturday morning?"

Dan stared at me for a beat. "Why do you need to know that?"

"I'm trying to figure out who killed Gigi Swanson."

"And you think Kenny is a suspect?" Dan's eyebrows shot up.

"*Maybe.* He worked with Gigi at the BCT and he might have had a dispute with her. Let's keep this between us."

"Sure. Well, yeah, Kenny was here with our monthly wood delivery."

"What time?"

"He got here around nine fifteen."

"He has a couple of guys who help him unload the wood, right? Did they come with Kenny?"

"No. Jorge and Xavier came in another truck. They all had come from a delivery in Warrensburg."

"What was Kenny's mood?" Mark asked.

"He was the way he always is. He said things were going okay at the hardware store. We talked football. Kenny seemed fine to me."

"How long were he and Jorge and Xavier here?" I asked.

"Um . . . about an hour. They left just before my meat guy

pulled up at ten fifteen."

"Do you know where Kenny went after he left here? Did they have more wood to deliver?"

"If they did, they had to reload their trucks. Kenny didn't say anything about his next stop. Does this help?"

"Every piece of information does. Thanks, Dan."

Dan and Mark talked sports for a minute before the proprietor left.

Mark studied my expression. "You're pensive. What are you thinking?"

"If Kenny was so bitter about having to give back the five thousand he stole, if he blamed Gigi for his troubles, why did he go to her funeral? If he's a busy guy with a lot going on, why would he give up a morning for the funeral of someone he was so angry with?"

"Because he didn't want people to suspect him, perhaps?" Mark said. "He might have thought Gigi had told someone about their Friday morning confrontation and wanted to show he held no hard feelings toward her. You want the last slice?"

"No, thanks."

Mark lifted the pizza from the tray, folded it down the middle, and took a generous bite from the saucy, cheesy slice. While he enjoyed the food, I took out my cell and texted Tracey.

Are you available to meet tomorrow morning? My house 10:00ish?

"You're not going to track down Jorge and Xavier and question them, are you?"

"How would I do that without letting on I'm suspicious of Kenny? Go back to the hardware store for some nails and say, 'Oh, by the way Lori, can you give me the last names, telephone numbers, and addresses of the two guys who deliver wood with your boss?' I'm going to hand it over to Tracey. I hope tomorrow morning. I just texted her."

"Good." Mark tipped his glass against mine and washed down the pizza with beer.

Tracey responded: *Will be there.*

I texted Nate with the meeting place and time. Within a minute, he replied. *All right. See you then.*

I put the phone back in my purse. "We're all set." I took a nibble from my slice, a gulp of soda, and mulled over a common thread in the case.

Kenny seemed to have the same blasé attitude the morning of Gigi's murder as Zach held. Was it a mark of innocence or cold-blooded indifference?

Chapter Twenty

Nate arrived a few minutes before ten a.m. We sat in the living room, our conversation light over coffee and fresh danish from Rizzuto's until Tracey arrived. I sat on the couch while Nate sat in a chair opposite me.

"How long have you been with the BCT?" I asked him after he had swallowed a mouthful of black coffee.

"Three years."

"How did you become involved?"

"It was soon after the club became a client. Donna asked me to do some work on the BCT's website and to recommend a software package for its donor database and bookkeeping. I caught the theater bug, started doing various jobs behind the scenes, and then became a production manager. And now I'm also the treasurer. I took over the books from Donna."

We talked about his IT company and how he started it, and then went on to discuss his frequent visits to the ski slopes and his passion for the great outdoors.

"Do you enjoy these activities with anyone in particular?" I asked, prying a wee bit.

"No." Nate, a good-looking fellow in his late thirties, shrugged. "Not since my retriever, Cookie, died last year."

I offered my condolences over the doorbell's ring.

A minute later, I led Tracey into the living room. With a hand wave I gestured at the faded jeans, green turtleneck sweater, and sneakers she wore. "I'm sorry to bother you with business on your day off."

Tracey settled on the couch. "We're always on duty. And I have a shift later. So what's up?"

"We think you should take a look at someone who used to work at the BCT," I said, pouring her a cup of coffee. I gave Tracey an account of the bakery meeting between Gigi and Kenny and of spotting him with Nate after the funeral. I looked over at Nate and gave him an encouraging look.

"Last fall, Gigi discovered Kenny had embezzled from the BCT."

Tracey produced a small spiral-bound pad and pen from her back pocket. "How much?"

"Five thousand dollars." Nate told of how he and Gigi had confronted Kenny and made the deal for him to pay back the money. He then related his conversation with Kenny in Saint Paul's parking lot after the funeral. "I got the feeling he was blaming Gigi and me for his troubles. As if it was wrong for us to ask him to return the money he had stolen."

Tracey and Nate went back and forth for a few minutes, with Tracey asking questions in her objective manner and Nate answering.

"Why didn't you tell Officer Nicholstone about the embezzlement when he interviewed you about Gigi's murder?" she finally asked Nate.

"I frankly didn't think about it, since Kenny returned the money."

"Hmm-hmmm. Have you had similar issues with anyone at the theater? Anyone else help themselves to bingo money or set funds?"

"No. And please, can we keep this incident quiet? If Kenny's embezzlement becomes public knowledge, we'll lose the trust of our donors and audience. And of the BCT's trustees. They'll want to go over the books with a fine-tooth comb and will probably ask me to step down as treasurer."

"If Pangborn has an alibi, there will be no reason for the Barton

PD to mention the embezzlement."

Tracey turned and bestowed on me a leveling look. "If you found this out on Wednesday, why are you only telling me now?"

Before I could answer, Nate said, "I asked Veronica to check out if Kenny has an alibi. I didn't want to bring the matter to your attention and cause him more trouble if he's covered for that morning."

"The police checking his alibi wouldn't cause him trouble if he has an alibi."

I piped up with, "All I did was strike up a conversation with the young woman minding the hardware store when I went there to get paint chip cards."

Tracey's brows shot up. "Paint chip cards?"

"I'm thinking of painting some rooms."

"Have you hired an interior decorator, per chance?"

"No." I ignored Tracey's sidelong look. "Lori, she's Kenny's employee, told me he delivers firewood to earn extra cash and made a delivery to the Hearth on Saturday morning. I had dinner at the Hearth last night and asked Dan Miller about the delivery. Dan said Kenny and two guys who help him arrived at nine fifteen and were there about an hour."

Tracey's piercing stare conveyed a "You broke our no-sleuthing agreement" message. I gave her a one-shoulder shrug and a silent reply of, "You knew I would."

Tracey regarded Nate for a moment. "Do you have any other *friends* who might have a motive for murdering Gigi you haven't wanted to tell us about?"

"No ma'am."

"All right."

When Tracey rose from the couch, Nate popped up from his chair, a beseeching look on his face. "So you'll keep the embezzlement quiet? Like I said, this would be a particularly bad time for it to go public."

"Of course." Tracey allowed a hint of compassion into her tone. "We don't name or discuss suspects with the press and I'm sure you've observed we're a watertight department. No leaks from us. Especially when no one is telling us anything." She delivered the sharp remark with a withering look at me.

"I told Nate we can trust the Barton PD to keep it quiet." I was emphatic, hoping for a return to Tracey's good graces.

"Thank you for your confidence. I can't wait to see your paint job."

Nate's and my exhalations created a wind tunnel in my front hall after Tracey departed.

"I never want to undergo a real interrogation," Nate said, his face pale and expression stunned. "I'm sweating and my heart's pounding."

"Would you like some calming chamomile tea?"

"No, thanks."

"It's early and I don't recommend doing this on a regular basis, but would you like a shot of something harder than herbal tea?"

Nate gave me a blank look for a second and then chuckled. "No, thanks. I'm okay. I'll have a drink or two when I get home." His wink indicated he wasn't serious about boozing it up before noon. He grabbed his coat and left.

I brought our mugs and plates to the kitchen and poured the remaining drops of coffee into the sink. Opening the dishwasher, I reflected on the uncomfortable conversation.

I knew Tracey wouldn't chide me (too much) for my visit to the hardware store. We had an easy rapport and I bet she had already shrugged off my rogue operation. Tracey and Nate, however, had no history, and she seemed peeved by his neglect in telling the police of Kenny's embezzlement. I prayed it wasn't a grievous oversight.

I wanted Gigi's killer caught and I didn't want the BCT damaged in the process. I hoped my wish wasn't a mutually exclusive proposition.

Chapter Twenty-One

Sophie, when she spotted my car turning into the club's parking lot, waved and directed me into the space next to her Jeep.

"Is valet parking your weekend gig?" I cracked, climbing from my car.

"I thought we could make a dramatic entrance together."

"Because we're the ladies of drama." We fell into matching strides on our trot across the lot.

"Yep. I can't wait to see you in super-sleuth action."

I gave Sophie a warning look. "The goal is to give the impression we're *not* in detective mode."

"Got it. I won't stare at you in gaping awe." Sophie held the club's front door open for me, the corner of her mouth twitching in amusement.

We crossed into the elegant circular foyer. A vase of white roses stood on an oval table under a magnificent crystal chandelier. On the cream-colored walls hung candle-style sconces in gold finish and a few portraits of the Milton family, the mansion's original owners. A hall on our right led to a sitting room and the banquet room. Down the center corridor were three offices and a kitchen entrance. A passage on the left took guests and club members to the west dining room and the dining area at the back of the building where the post-funeral lunch had been held.

Donna entered the foyer through the west wing's arched passageway, greeting us with open arms and air kisses. "I'm so glad you could join us, Veronica," she said, giving me a light touch on the shoulder. With murmurs of "How are you, Sophie, dear?" "I know this is a difficult time for you, too," and "I'm so proud you're taking over for Gigi," Donna guided us to the west dining room.

The room, the smaller of the club's two restaurants, overlooked a grassy expanse and a row of firs that concealed the swimming pool and, beyond that, the tennis courts. We passed several occupied tables on our way to the corner table where Bret sat. Standing, he greeted us with handshakes and then acted the perfect gentleman by pulling out our chairs for us.

Once we had given our drink and food orders, Donna chattered about *Blithe Spirit*, asking Sophie and me questions about the production and sharing memories of a revival she saw in New York City a few years earlier.

"We have a high standard to meet, then," Sophie said.

"You'll be my favorite production," Donna promised. "Are we still welcome at the dress rehearsal?"

"Of course," Sophie replied. "Gigi always invited Wayne, Donna, and Zach to our dress rehearsals," she explained to me. "Bret, you're welcome, too."

Bret, who was sending a text message, looked up. A blush rose in his cheeks. "Just answering a nervous bride's text. Thanks. I'd love to watch your dress rehearsal."

"Do you have a reception today?" I asked him.

"Yes. We're hosting a reception for three hundred and fifty at six o'clock."

"Wow. That must take the planning skills of a five-star general."

"That is exactly what Bret is," Donna said. "Our five-star planner. Townsend's is very fortunate to have him."

"I was really surprised when you told us Julia had left the club. Gigi never mentioned it. Where did she set up her business?" Sophie asked.

"Bolton Landing," Donna said in a clipped voice.

Sophie asked Bret, "When did you start here?"

"Early November."

"It was a baptism by fire," Donna said. "We had a wedding every weekend through New Year's. Plus two bar mitzvahs, five bridal showers, and three baby showers."

"And a partridge in a pear tree," I quipped.

The server brought our meals and we dug into the food with gusto. After a few minutes, Donna brought the conversation back to *Blithe Spirit* and the opening-night reception. After briefing Bret on past celebrations she said, "I'd like to do something different, to honor Gigi and bring something positive from her death."

Sophie, her knife poised over a steak fry, froze. "What do you have in mind?"

"I want to turn *Blithe Spirit*'s opening-night performance into a gala benefit for the Gigi Swanson Townsend Memorial Scholarship fund." Donna, delighted by her announcement, surveyed the table for reaction.

I kept my attention on Sophie, attempting a bit of mind reading. She patted her pursed lips with her napkin and then folded her hands in her lap. "What do you mean by a gala benefit?"

"We'll hold it in the banquet room. A three-course dinner, followed by the show, and then cake, champagne, and a presentation afterwards. I know Wayne and Zach would like to say a few words."

"It should be held in the barn. That's where we do all our performances. We're comfortable on the stage, we know the acoustics of the room, and why move the sets? And remember, it was Gigi's idea to convert the barn."

"The banquet room has a higher seating capacity and it's more elegant."

"It will be embarrassing if we don't fill the room. I think the cast will prefer the barn."

Donna relented. "All right. The barn it is."

Sophie fiddled with her fork. She wasn't finished with her protest. "The audience will get a three-course dinner, champagne, and cake all for the price of a twenty-five dollar ticket?"

"Well, no, dear. We would raise the ticket price to one hundred dollars. Twenty-five would go to the BCT, twenty-five to cover the cost of the dinner, Townsend's will underwrite the rest of the cost of the food, and the remainder would go to the scholarship fund for an Arden theater student. We hope to make it an annual award."

"But we've already sold a good number of tickets to opening night. What do we do about those people?" Sophie asked. I wondered if I was the only one to detect her growing ire.

"They can pay the difference and attend the gala, or switch their ticket for another performance."

Sophie, ignoring her food, dug into her position. "That's not fair. Some of our audience can't afford one hundred dollars for a fancy dinner and the show."

"Then they are free to attend another evening."

I spoke up. "I have a friend who is very excited to see the *opening-night* show. I'd hate to ask her to pay more." I knew Dusanka would shell out the extra seventy-five dollars for a seat at the gala, but her job didn't earn her the big bucks. I agreed with Sophie; it wouldn't be fair to force her to break her budget.

Bret offered a compromise. "We could sell tickets for the dinner and show, and tickets for the show only. People who have already purchased tickets can have a choice of upgrading to the dinner package."

From Donna's and Sophie's sour looks, I knew the suggestion wasn't acceptable.

"Everyone at the BCT is working hard to make opening night special," Sophie said. "I feel like this will take some of the glory away from them."

"I certainly don't mean to do that." Donna's reply didn't drop the temperature at the table, but it certainly didn't give me a warm, cozy feeling.

"Why don't we hold the benefit on another evening?" Bret was working hard to secure a nomination for the Nobel Peace Prize.

"Perhaps you could add an evening at the end of your run. A closing night gala would be a fitting end to your production."

"I like that idea." I gave him a grateful smile.

"I think Nate and the cast would agree to that," Sophie said.

Donna didn't accept Bret's counter proposal at once. "Gigi should be honored at the start of the run, not its end."

Sophie retorted, "*We* will honor her on opening night. And I like the idea of a big finish. It will be something to look forward to."

Bret opened a portfolio lying next to his plate. "The barn is available the evening of Friday, April fifth. We could serve cocktails on the terrace, weather permitting."

"That's the Friday after Easter, right? That's better. It wouldn't be appropriate to have a gala during Lent." Sophie finally put the knife to her steak fry, sliced it in half, and popped the piece she speared with her fork into her mouth.

Donna, conceding defeat to the religious argument, turned her attention to her Caesar salad. Relieved the debate was resolved without a brandish of cutlery, I ate my turkey club and listened while Bret explained the menu choices and table arrangements for the gala.

Talk about Showcase Night arrangements carried us through our dessert of coffee and cheesecake. When we parted from Donna, she said a remark that seemed a throwaway line but would soon come back to haunt me.

"If the gala is the success I think it will be, it might be the start of a whole new chapter for the theater."

Before we left the club, Sophie made a stop in the ladies' room. Waiting in the entry hall, I met Wayne coming down the stairs.

"What do you think of Donna's gala benefit?" he asked, offering his hand.

"It will be a fine tribute to Gigi."

"Gigi meant the world to us. We want to remember her in a meaningful way."

"A scholarship endowment is a wonderful way to do that."

"And did you enjoy lunch?"

"I did. My compliments to the chef."

Wayne said he'd pass along the praise. "I don't believe you're a club member, Veronica. Though I'm no longer running the place and haven't seen the membership roll in a while. I could be mistaken."

I didn't believe Wayne's claim he didn't know whether I was a member. Of course he knew the who's who of the Townsend's membership roll, everyone's social security number, and the names of everyone's pets. "No, I'm not a member." I prayed he wouldn't launch into a pitch to buy an expensive membership and learn some secret handshake.

"We'd love to have you. If you'd like a tour, let Donna know. She'd be happy to show you around the place. And please, accept a complimentary dinner for two, anytime you like. I'll have the reservation office put you on the guest list. Just give them a call when you'd like to visit and tell them Wayne sent you." He winked. "I still have some pull around here."

I thanked him for the invitation and we talked about the local economy and its impact on small businesses until Sophie joined us. We said goodbye and Sophie and I left the club.

"Donna really has a lot of nerve trying to rearrange our performance schedule," Sophie griped the moment our feet hit the parking lot.

"She didn't succeed," I said in a placating tone. "A gala is a special way to honor Gigi."

"I don't think the profit should go to a scho—" Sophie's arm shot into the air, almost knocking me in the head. "Hi, Heather!"

I looked to the next aisle and saw a young woman return Sophie's wave. She was pacing between the cars, talking on her cell phone.

"I spy a potential informant," Sophie said under her breath.

I followed her into the next aisle where Heather, a college-aged gal, had ended her call and was walking toward us.

Sophie introduced us after the pair exchanged a hug. "You probably know Veronica's in *Blithe Spirit*. Heather was in *The Sisters Rosensweig* last summer."

"I'm sorry I can't be in the new production. Between classes and work, I'm busy and stressed." The fresh-faced young woman gave Sophie a regretful look.

"Heather's a junior at Arden and she works here on the weekends." Sophie gave me a ten-second stare, making sure I understood the implication of Heather's part-time gig.

Duh.

After showing interest in her studies, I asked Heather about the mood at Townsend's. "Everyone must still be in mourning."

"Yeah, we're still sad, but things are pretty normal today. I didn't work this week, though. I heard it was really depressing around the club for a few days. Understandably." Heather glanced at her phone. Checking for a message or the time?

"You worked last weekend?" Sophie asked.

"Yeah. I was here all day Saturday and I worked Sunday brunch."

Sophie and I swapped knowing looks while Heather glanced at the club. I followed her gaze, expecting I would see Donna watching from one of the windows, or standing outside the door, tapping her watch and foot with a "You're late!" scowl.

"Did you see Zach Saturday morning at all?" Sophie inched closer to Heather, eager for her answer.

"Um . . . yeah. You know, I need to get back to the kitchen."

Drats. Did Heather sign some confidentiality agreement when she accepted her club job?

"Oh, sure. Sorry."

Heather's attention moved between Sophie, me, and the club. "I can talk with you later. My shift ends at three thirty. I can meet you around four. Maybe Rizzuto's?"

Gloria!

"Rizzuto's at four!" Sophie's exuberance might have been a tad much. And loud; several crows cawed and fled the tree at the parking lot's entrance. "I'm buying the sugar and caffeine."

We watched Heather hustle into the club. "Nice girl," I said.

"I bet she has dirt on Zach."

"Be careful with your assumptions." It was a teasing remark, but I fervently hoped she was right.

Chapter Twenty-Two

Sophie and I regrouped at the bakery at three forty-five. When I arrived, I found her seated at a window table, snacking on a large chocolate chip cookie and hot chocolate. I picked up a cup of black tea at the counter and joined her.

"I'm still thinking about Julia leaving Townsend's," she said. "Gigi worked closely with her. It's surprising she never mentioned Julia left. I'm wondering if something happened." Sophie's brow made a suggestive arch.

"Between her and Zach?"

"Yeah."

"Maybe Heather can shed some light on the matter."

"I hope so. You haven't told me about your meeting with Whitney." Sophie snapped a chunk from her cookie, offered it to me, and popped it into her mouth when I declined the piece.

"Well, she's utterly shocked by Gigi's death, but she's still managing to run the business and hold every client's hand. And Whitney implied Gigi was doing something illicit, like selling drugs or guns, and got herself killed." I relayed everything Ariana had told me about working with Whitney.

"What a lovely person to have as a business partner. How did Gigi ever end up with her?" Sophie rolled her eyes and took a slurp of cocoa.

"That's one thing I'd like to ask her sister. Do you think Blair would be agreeable to a chat? Would she share anything Gigi confided to her?"

"Didn't she say she wanted to talk with you when we saw her at the funeral? It's worth asking," Sophie said. "I know if I were her, I'd be as helpful as I could be to anyone who wanted to find my sister's killer." She watched the light traffic going along Orchard Street for a few moments. "We should hire a medium to help us."

My mouthful of tea went down in a hard swallow. "A what?"

"We should consult a real life Madame Arcati." Sophie's eyes gleamed with the spark of her idea. "We should have a séance to talk with Gigi."

"And you think Gigi's spirit will come right out with her killer's name?"

"It's worth a try."

I'm a staunch skeptic on all matters clairvoyant. "If so-called mediums could really talk with the dead and get such specific information from them, every police investigation would be an open-and-shut case. They'd be solved in an hour."

My gaze fell on my purse and then drifted to the spot outside the bakery where I had stood with Gigi a week earlier. I replayed the action of Gigi handing me Agnes Steinert's business card.

Uh-oh. I may not be a believer in talking with spirits from the beyond, but I can get behind the "everything happens for a reason" philosophy. What if Gigi handing me that card was some sort of providential act?

I considered whether I wanted to open that can of worms for a moment before snatching up my purse and digging through it for the card.

"What are you looking for?" Sophie mumbled through a mouthful of cookie.

I located the card at the bottom of the bag. "Madame Arcati Incarnate's phone number." I recounted my sidewalk meeting with Gigi.

"Wow." Sophie took the card and studied it. "We're meant to call her."

I hesitated. "Are you sure about this?"

"Yeah. We have nothing to lose but an hour or two of our time and a few bucks. I'll pay the woman."

"All right." I took the card back from Sophie. "I'll call her and set up an appointment."

Satisfied, Sophie took another nibble from her cookie. "Here comes Heather." She nodded at the window.

Heather was jaywalking across Orchard, her cell pressed against her ear. She was inside seconds later, still chattering into the phone. She dropped her knapsack on the floor next to her chair, placed the iPhone on the table, and tore off her jacket.

"If I was twenty-one, I would have told you I'd meet you at the Hearth's bar." Heather tossed her jacket on top of her knapsack.

"What would you like?" Sophie grabbed her wallet from her bag and pushed back her chair. Heather gave Sophie her order and me a shy smile when Sophie left for the counter.

"Did you work breakfast and lunch at the club today?" I asked when Heather covered her yawning mouth. I noticed she still had a few faded childhood freckles on her nose and cheeks.

"Yep. And I have a ninety-minute break before I head back for a wedding reception tonight." She tugged out the black scrunchie holding her long, light-brown hair off her face, ran her fingers through her hair, and pulled it into a ponytail, fixing it in place.

"Wow. Maybe I should buy you a second coffee to get you through the night."

Heather giggled and asked a few questions about my career until Sophie returned with Heather's treats.

We allowed the college student a few minutes to savor her coffee, red velvet cupcake, and time off before easing into a stealth interrogation.

"So," Sophie began. "You said you worked last Saturday. It must have been intense around the club."

Heather nodded, her mouth full of food and drink. "The cops were all over the place."

"Were they searching the club?" I asked.

"Not inside, though I saw a couple of officers hanging around the first floor while the police chief was up on the second floor with Mrs. Townsend and Zach. There was also a bunch of cops outside, going over the golf course and grounds. Someone said they were looking for the murder weapon. Then a rumor spread that they had cornered a suspect in the woods behind the tenth hole. Obviously, that was wrong."

"Was the club on lockdown?" Sophie asked.

"For a half hour or so."

"Where do you work in the club?" I remembered Heather mentioned she had to return to the kitchen when we met in the parking lot. "Are you a food preparer?"

"No. I'm a server in the dining rooms, and I work a lot of events like weddings and bar mitzvahs. Sometimes, if they don't need waiters, I'll work the coatroom. I've even done valet parking."

I admired the young woman's work ethic. "Did you happen to see Zach arrive at the club Saturday morning?"

"I did. Well, I assume he had just arrived when I saw him. Mrs. Townsend was having breakfast with a friend. Zach came in to say hello. He still had his coat on."

"What kind of mood was he in?" asked Sophie.

"I didn't talk with him. He said hello when he walked by as he left the dining room, but that was the extent of our conversation."

Sophie pressed. "Well, how did he look? Worried? Relieved?"

"I can't say that Zach looked any different than usual. He did seem in a hurry to get to his office."

"Hmm."

I didn't wait to hear how Sophie would twist that tidbit. "Did Gigi spend a lot of time at the club on weekends?"

"Not a whole lot. She and Zach would have brunch with his parents one Sunday a month. Other than that, she wasn't around much, except for BCT rehearsals and shows. I'm sure she had errands to run on the weekend, like everyone else. And work for her own business."

"I'm sure. Is Zach usually at the club on Saturday mornings?"

"Yeah. He's in and out on Saturdays and usually takes Sundays off. He'll work in his office for an hour or two on Saturday mornings. In warm weather, he'll play golf with his dad or friends, or oversee a tournament on the course. Then he'll be around at night to mingle with the members who come for dinner. And to check in on whatever party's going on."

Add it up and Gigi and Zach did not spend much time together, an observation Nate also shared at Connolly's. Absence doesn't always make the heart grow fonder.

Sophie asked, "What's the deal with Julia Rogan leaving so suddenly?"

Heather grew quiet and stared at her coffee cup.

"Did something happen?"

Heather hesitated, took a fleeting glance out the window. "Zach and Julia were very close."

"Like a 'let's get frisky' kind of close?" Sophie asked with a straight face.

"Well . . . last summer, they ate lunch together in Zach's office a lot. Behind closed doors. I was working here full time then and brought lunch up to them a few times. And a couple of times I saw them going out together, in Zach's car. I assumed they were going out for lunch."

"Who goes out to lunch when the club serves some of the best food in the village? And you're the owner's son so you can eat for free!" Sophie clicked her tongue. "They were having a little lunchtime hanky-panky. A nooner—"

"Stop!" I blurted.

"And with his mother in the next office. Did you see anything else, Heather?"

"I saw them get very close at a charity golf tournament

in September."

"Define *very close*." Sophie, impatient, shifted on her chair.

"I drove one of the beverage carts. It was late in the afternoon and I had just a couple of bottled waters left on the cart, so I headed back to the clubhouse. Most of the golfers were done for the day and there were only four or five groups left at the last few holes. When I approached the eighth hole, I noticed a couple at the tee. It was Zach and Julia. Zach was showing Julia how to hit the ball."

I glanced at Sophie, who gave an eye roll and sarcastic, "What a cliché."

"Zach was standing behind Julia, with his arms around her. He held her arms and guided her through the swing. Then he put his hands on her hips to show her how to move them."

Another derisive rejoinder from Sophie. "Yeah, right."

"Then Zach stood back and Julia hit the ball. A good shot. Zach slapped her on the butt, like baseball players and football players do. Then they hugged. And Zach kissed Julia on the lips."

Heather sure got an eyeful passing that eighth hole. She must not have been driving the cart too fast, or did she slow down to engage in some sporting voyeurism?

"So Zach did get frisky." Sophie was triumphant.

We lapsed into silence for a minute. "Was there a goodbye party for Julia when she left Townsend's?" I asked.

My question caught Heather with her mouth full of cupcake. "No. I heard she just walked around one day, telling everyone she was leaving and saying goodbye."

Hmm. "Did the police interview you last Saturday morning?" I asked.

"They asked me what time I got to the club and if I had seen any strangers hanging around when I arrived. That was it."

"Nothing about Zach?" Sophie asked.

"No."

"Sloppy."

We spent the rest of our visit talking about *Blithe Spirit*, Heather's winter/spring semester classes, and what it was like filming bedroom scenes with my soap character's many handsome love interests. My acting career might be over, but people were still more interested in that time of my life than in my current career, where the great excitement of the day is a new inventory of hand-carved animal statues.

I didn't let the "small" talk keep me from moving Julia Rogan's name from one column to another: an interviewee had become a suspect.

I walked with Sophie to her car parked in front of Orchard Street Books, the shop my parents opened when I was a child. My mother still owned and managed the shop and was probably spying on Sophie and me at that very moment.

"So this is why Julia left Townsend's in a rush without any fanfare. I bet Gigi knew! That's why she never said anything about Julia leaving. Oh, this makes me so sad." Sophie leaned against her car's hood. "I wonder if Donna knows about them. Imagine if she caught Julia and Zach together? Oh, Townsend's must have security cameras on the greens!"

"That tape has probably been destroyed and the security guard *told* he didn't see anything on it. And who needs security cameras when you have golf cart-driving college students patrolling the grounds?"

"Unfortunately, there's no camera behind the barn, or we'd be spending our Saturday afternoon doing something far more pleasant." Sophie reached into her jeans pocket and pulled out a tube of lip balm. She continued talking while applying the protectant. "Let's consider the possibilities. Julia and Zach had an affair, broke up, she left Townsend's, and Zach killed Gigi to be with Julia. Or they're still having an affair, Julia left so they could be more discreet, and she killed Gigi to have Zach all to herself. Or nothing happened between the two except for that moment on the golf course, highly unlikely, and now Julia really is just living her dream. So how do we find out what the truth is?"

"I'll pay a visit to Julia at her new place of business on Monday. Bolton Landing, Donna said?"

"Yeah. Are you going to pretend to be someone else? Pose as a mother-of-the-bride? Too bad Julia knows me, or I could pretend I'm your daughter. 'Hey, Mommy, who's my daddy?' "

"Ah, all the joy of motherhood without the labor pain, teen angst, and college expense. Just don't expect me to pay for the wedding."

"Don't worry. It will be a low key, backyard affair."

We shared a laugh. "I'm not going to pose as anyone but myself. I know what my excuse for the visit will be. Courtesy of Donna."

Chapter Twenty-Three

"Zach Townsend did it. No need for discussion." Myrtle Evans pulled a chair away from the dining room table, plopped herself in it, and lunged for a cracker and cheese slice on the plate in the center of the table.

"Do you have evidence to support your conclusion?" I asked Myrtle, my fingers crossed she would have a tidbit of insider information to assist my sleuthing. Perhaps she'd have more facts to bolster the case against Zach than the material I had on his golf liaison with Julia.

"It's always the husband," she replied, her mouth full of a large chunk she had chomped from the cracker.

"What about Gigi's business partner, Whitney Roth? She might have killed Gigi to hang onto the clients the business might have lost if Gigi divorced Zach."

"That's a lot of mights."

"Just two. I thought you'd know if Gigi and Whitney had insurance policies with each listed as the other's beneficiary."

"Neither is a client."

"Darn it, Myrtle. I was counting on you to have something I could use."

"Sorry about that. It's an interesting theory, but considering Gigi was murdered behind her husband's barn, I'm calling Zach the killer. Maybe he killed his wife for the insurance money, though he certainly wouldn't need it."

"It's unlike you to make such hasty pronouncements." Madeline Griffin came into the room, followed by her sister Ella.

Myrtle shrugged and snatched another cracker. "I'm going with the percentage." Myrtle, who had quit smoking a few months earlier (but clung to an unopened package of cigarettes for weeks after taking her final puff), had apparently reentered the irritable, "stuff your face" phase of nicotine withdrawal.

"Not so fast," bellowed Dotsie Beattie, who was sitting across from me.

"Here comes the conspiracy theory." Our hostess, Sandy Jenkins, charged behind my chair. She carried a tray bearing tall glasses filled with alcoholic beverages.

We had gathered for our weekly canasta game, the first of the new year. We were supposed to meet the previous Saturday, but when I begged off due to Gigi's murder, the get-together was cancelled. Madeline had invited me to join the group soon after my Barton return, and after one of its members had died. We take turns hosting and, besides playing cards and enjoying a pre-game dinner, have a lot of laughs and share a bit of gossip. The best part is I'm the youngest of the group. Ella and Madeline are in their eighties, Dotsie is in her late seventies, Myrtle hasn't disclosed exactly where she is in her sixties, and Sandy is two years my senior.

Usually held on a week night, the five agreed to play on Saturday nights during the *Blithe Spirit* rehearsals and we all approved Sandy's suggestion to eliminate the dinner part of the evening for a couple of weeks. It was a temporary cancellation of the meal until we all recovered from the cookies, pies, turkeys, and roasts we had prepared in November and December. Some of us (not me), were also cutting back on the calories after feasting on all that food.

Dotsie waited until we all had a drink and then shared her thoughts on the murder case. "I think the police need to look for a bridezilla," she pronounced before taking her first gulp of Seven and Seven.

"*What* is a bridezilla?" Ella asked. The eldest Griffin sister, Ella was made of stern stuff. She brooked no nonsense, a trait that made her maintenance of a decades-long friendship with Dotsie a mystery.

"A gargantuan creature that wears a wedding dress and terrorizes everything in its path to the altar," Dotsie said in a nonchalant tone that implied such a creature really did exist.

Madeline, whose sunny demeanor softens Ella's sharp edge, laughed. "What a funny image!"

"A bridezilla is a woman who micromanages every detail of her wedding and drives everyone around her insane," Sandy said.

"Some of them can be unbelievably nasty," Dotsie said, "even to the groom. The police should check out all the brides who wanted to hold their receptions in that barn the opening night of *Blithe Spirit.*"

"You think a woman would kill because her preferred reception venue was booked?" Myrtle, looking doubtful, asked.

"Some women start planning their weddings before they've even met the groom. They know what designer gown they will wear, the color theme, the maid-of-honor's dress size, the first dance song, *and* where they want to hold the reception."

"Dotsie's right." Sandy gave me a look that suggested I take Dotsie's theory seriously. A professional housekeeping whirlwind, Sandy was a dynamo of organization. I bet she could relate to brides who had every second of the wedding day scheduled. "Townsend's hosts beautiful receptions. A lot of couples want to hold their weddings there."

Dotsie gave a knowing nod. "A woman who had her heart set on strutting into the former cow house as the new Mrs. Whomever that first Saturday in March may have lost her mind when she was told she couldn't have the barn because Veronica Walsh was staging a career comeback."

"Now you're blaming me!"

"Just saying."

"Watch your back." Myrtle swiped another cracker-cheese combo.

I refrained from making a sharp retort about how easy it was for Myrtle to chortle because she hadn't twice been in the crosshairs of a murderer.

"Ridiculous. Who might have actually killed your director?" Ella asked. She might scare me at times, but I could count on Ella having my back.

"Besides Zach, there's Gigi's business partner." I told them about my meeting with Whitney.

"Her ambition might have gotten the best of her," Ella agreed.

"It's curious Gigi was killed outside and not in the barn. You'd think the killer would have worried about someone hearing the gunshot," said Madeline.

"Zach didn't want to mess up his barn and lose business," Myrtle said. "Who'd want to get married in the place where a woman was shot dead?"

"Yep," Sandy agreed. "I sure wouldn't want to dance with my groom in a former crime scene. Any other suspects?"

I mentioned Julia. "And Zach might have had, or still have, something going on with the club's former event coordinator."

"The wedding planner!" Dotsie exclaimed, smacking the table with her fist. "If it's not the bride, it's her accomplice."

"Time to play!" I declared, reaching for the stack of cards.

I visited the kitchen during our canasta break. Mark; Myrtle's husband, Merv; and Sam, the man of the house; sat around the breakfast nook's banquette playing poker. The fellas usually aren't present at our canasta nights, but with the game on Saturday night and at Sandy's and his house, Sam invited Mark and Merv over for five-card draw.

Mark slid over, making room for me on his side of the table. "Good night," I said, pointing at the large pile of quarters next to Mark's beer bottle.

"It's not over yet. Don't jinx me," he teased.

"Maybe I'll tell the ladies we should play for money."

Merv's belly shook with mirth. "I'd be shocked if you got Ella to play for anything more than a penny."

"You've got yourself in the middle of another murder case." Sam laid his cards face down on the table and placed his hands over them.

"Are you folding?" Merv asked, his eyes growing wide with hope.

"No. I'm putting the game on hold for a second." Sam returned his gaze to me, his round face showing concern. "How does that always happen?"

"I don't know. It's a knack I'd rather not have."

Merv rubbed his fingers against his cheek. "Myrtle is positive Zach Townsend killed his wife." He took a sip from his glass of Scotch.

"She told me. I guess the odds are in her favor of being right."

"He's a good looking, rich guy. He probably does have a woman on the side. Or two or three." Merv set his cards down and crossed his arms. "Have you heard any whispers about that?"

"Maybe, in not so many words."

"Well, I've heard talk that Zach's preparing for a run for the county legislature," Sam announced.

I sat up straight, intrigued by the new gossip. "When did you hear that?"

"A couple of my guys were talking about it this morning." Sam owned an appliance store.

Merv said, "I figured he'd follow in his pop's footsteps."

"I suppose he'll self-finance his campaign, just as his father did," said Mark.

"Good guess," Sam agreed.

Mark tapped his cards against the table's edge. "Call me cynical, but I bet he'll win a lot of votes playing the grieving widower card."

"Cynical, but correct." Merv took the last mouthful of his Scotch.

I wanted to wrap my brain around the new information, but Dotsie's sashay into the kitchen prevented any intellectual thought.

"What do you fellas say we merge our card games into a group round of strip poker?"

Merv hid his face in his hands while Sam shouted, "Sandy, let's go to bed so these folks can go home."

"Strip poker. Can you imagine?" Ella uttered those words two seconds after Mark closed the car door and buckled his seatbelt. "And a bridezilla? Where does Dotsie get these crazy ideas?"

"At the crazy idea dollar store in Lake George." Mark's guffaw at my reply put a schoolgirl smile on my face. If Ella and Madeline weren't in the back seat, I would have leaned across the front seat and planted a ten-second kiss on his lips.

Mark glanced in the rearview mirror. "Would you ladies care to stop at the Hearth for an after-canasta beer?"

"I think I'd rather go home, crawl into bed, and erase from my mind the images Dotsie's suggestion put there." Looking over my shoulder, I caught Ella, who was sitting behind Mark, shaking her head over the wild and abrupt end to the evening. I also saw her amused smile when Mark said, "A beer might help you do that."

Madeline took the conversation on a serious turn. "Veronica, do you have any evidence to support Myrtle's conclusion that Zach Townsend killed his wife?"

"It's all circumstantial." I didn't share the possibility of an affair with Julia Rogan. It was gossip at that point and, though I knew Ella and Madeline would keep their lips sealed, I wouldn't mention a potential scandal when I had zero proof of it. What Sam told us of Zach's nascent political career was a different matter.

"Sam heard Zach's planning a run for a seat in the county legislature."

Ella's hum lasted several seconds. "What came first, the political campaign or the wife's murder?"

"Maybe he'll put the run on hold to mourn for Gigi," Madeline suggested.

"Oh, he'll run. Play the grieving widower, dedicating his campaign to his late wife." Ella harrumphed. "A sort of protestation of innocence. Only the most cynical would think a man would kill his wife right before he declared himself a candidate for office."

"Usually it's the mistress who's *disappeared*."

My mouth dropped open at Madeline's uncharacteristic remark. I had never heard her voice such a dark thought. "Talk about cynical."

"I suppose I've watched too many true crime stories on the television. I think I'll skip *48 Hours* tonight."

After a short silence, I said, "It's like what you said last weekend, Mark, about Zach maybe killing Gigi on the Townsend's property because no one would believe he would be dumb enough to murder her there."

"Though his reasoning might have been to hide in plain sight," Ella said.

Mark turned into the Griffins' driveway a few minutes later. We got out and helped the sisters from the back seat. With Mark holding Ella's arm and Madeline clasping my hand, we made our way along the short path to their front porch. A line of light shone through the parlor's drawn curtains. Ella unlocked the door and stood aside for Madeline to go in the house.

Ella crossed her hands in front of her, her purse dangling from her fingers. "Here we are, assuming Zach Townsend committed adultery, and no one has suggested Gigi was less than angelic in her marriage."

I considered asking Ella if she were a Whitney acquaintance. "You think she might have been the one with a lover on the side?"

"Anything is possible."

"It is," Mark agreed. "This hypothetical affair could have gotten messy and the lover killed Gigi. Or his wife did."

"I don't think Gigi was having an affair. There's not an iota of evidence she did. She was so busy with her design business and the theater, I don't know where she would have found the time for it."

"You're probably correct, Veronica," Ella said. "It's something to consider, that's all."

Mark and I said good night and walked hand-in-hand down the path.

"Let's recap the night," I said. "Myrtle believes Zach killed Gigi. Dotsie is sure it was a bridezilla. And Ella suggests Gigi is guiltier than her husband."

"Or it could be none of the above."

"The dreaded 'E' in multiple choice questions." I disliked the option on my school exams. I hated it more in my sleuthing.

I tightened my hold on Mark's arm and leaned my head against his shoulder. "Is that invitation for a beer still open? Let's go have one and entertain Dotsie's party-ending suggestion."

Chapter Twenty-Four

Mark and I met my mother in Saint Augustine's vestibule when we arrived the next morning for the nine o'clock Mass. We sat together halfway up the aisle, me sitting between the two.

"Who was that young woman you were talking with outside the bookstore yesterday afternoon?" Mom asked.

So she did spy on us. How well I know my mother. "Sophie Morrissey. *Blithe Spirit*'s director."

"Oh, did you have rehearsal yesterday? I thought you had Saturdays off. Do you need extra rehearsal or direction?" Mom gave me a teasing look. "Or did you just happen to meet on the street?"

"Obviously, you got your snooping acumen from your mother. Must be genetic," Mark whispered in my ear.

I acknowledged his remark with a squeeze of his hand. I told Mom about the lunch date with Donna and Bret and of the bakery meeting with Heather. "Zach might have had, or even still be in, an affair with his former employee."

"I'm not with the majority on this." Mom lowered her voice and leaned against my shoulder. "I don't think Zach killed Gigi."

"You don't?"

"Nope. I think he has more ingenuity than to kill his wife outside in broad daylight, even if it was behind a barn where no one could see him."

I nudged Mark's elbow. "Another supporter of the 'Zach isn't dumb' theory."

"Zach would have killed Gigi in a spot where there was no chance he'd be seen and dumped her body miles away. Perhaps a few miles up Lake George, in a remote section."

I shivered at the suggestion of a cold, watery grave for Gigi. The knowledge my mother had channeled the mind of a killer elevated the goosebumps creeping along my arms.

"You've given this much thought."

"I just finished the latest James Patterson. Sorry, it's where my head is at the moment."

"You should read some soothing, heartwarming Jan Karon."

"I just might." Mom opened her missal. I did the same for a minute before letting my glance drift over the congregation.

The pews in our Adirondack-style church are divided into four sections. We sat in the leftmost section, next to the spectacular stained-glass windows of the Last Supper and the Wedding at Cana. I spotted Dotsie near the front of the far-right section, sitting with Sister Patti, who was principal of Saint Augustine's elementary school when I was a student there. The pair was talking with Father John.

Tracey slid into the empty pew in front of us. This Sunday, she was dressed in civilian garb: black pants, a purple turtleneck, and black boots. Her hair hung loose on her shoulders. She knelt in prayer for a couple of minutes and then relaxed against the antique-oak bench, turning and giving us a cheery good morning.

After asking about the well-being of one of Barton PD's finest, Mom leaned forward and inquired, "How's the murder case coming along? Any leads?"

Tracey gave me a side-eye. "Like daughter, like mother."

"You should have heard what she said two minutes ago," I said.

"We're working hard on the case, Mrs. Walsh."

"Any new news?" I asked.

Tracey didn't indicate if she understood my cryptic query concerned Kenny. Her response offered nothing. "No."

I considered asking if she had knowledge of Julia and the nature of her relationship with Zach, but she probably wouldn't be happy I got a juicy bit of gossip out of Heather when the police asked only perfunctory questions of the college student. Since her observation was gossip and not a cold fact like Kenny's embezzlement, I decided not to spread the word yet. I'd ask in a roundabout manner.

"Do you have any leads on whether Zach had an affair?"

"We're still gathering evidence."

"Do you have evidence of a mistress?"

"Veronica, the investigation is ongoing. We're still gathering facts and interviewing people."

"So there is a woman!"

"I didn't say that."

"Any evidence Gigi had an affair?"

"No." Tracey swiveled and faced the altar.

I'd have made another attempt at information extraction if I wasn't surrounded by holy water founts and religious statuary. I would check out Julia myself before dropping her name into a conversation with the lady cop. It might not even be necessary, depending on what the police uncovered on Kenny.

I sat back and relaxed. My gaze wandered across the pews and landed on Dotsie. What the hell. Heck! I mean heck! I cast a beseeching glance at the crucifix on the wall behind the altar. Please forgive me.

I tapped Tracey's shoulder. "Sorry to keep bothering you. Are you considering wedding parties that were denied the Townsend barn the first Saturday in March, *Blithe Spirit*'s opening night?"

"You think an angry bride killed Gigi, thinking that would force the show's cancellation?" Tracey asked, mystified.

"Out-of-the-box thinking. Shrewd."

I appreciated Mom's display of maternal pride and hated shifting credit to the notion's true originator. "Dotsie Beattie thinks there's a bridezilla on the loose in Barton. Lock your doors, folks."

Mom laughed. "I love Dotsie."

Tracey, relishing the theory, grinned. She did need some comic relief. "We haven't thought of that angle, but it's worth asking."

The organist called for our attention, inviting the congregation to sing a verse of the new offertory hymn. Tracey turned her back on us and Mom and Mark opened their missals to hymn number seventy.

I blessed myself and begged for understanding and forgiveness for the less-than-sacred conversation. "You know it's for a good purpose," I whispered. "I'm only trying to help." I blessed myself again and grabbed a missal, promising the Mass my full attention. Indeed, it was thanks be to the Lord I was still alive, sleuthing my way through a third murder case.

I didn't have a chance after Mass to ask Tracey about Kenny. She didn't return to the pew after receiving Communion. From my seat, I could see her standing in the vestibule during the final prayer. When I looked again, when the congregation had said, "Thanks be to God," and Father John was recessing down the aisle, Tracey was gone.

Did she have to get to the station or was she avoiding me?

Chapter Twenty-Five

I arrived for Sunday afternoon's rehearsal twenty minutes early, not for time to slip into character, but for a check of the road behind the barn. The gravel drive fed into the parking lot near the barn and theater office. Passing through the lot and onto the private road, I was glad there were no other rehearsal early birds there to observe my move.

An unsettling eeriness filled me on the short journey between the lot and barn. The beauty and calm of the adjacent woods couldn't erase from my mind the image of Gigi lying on the ground, her body soaked in blood.

I doubted this was a well-traveled path, save for the BCT crew delivering lumber and other materials for sets and club employees bringing supplies for events in the barn. I was curious about the length of the road and the points of interest dotting its course. A satellite image from Google Earth gave me a clue, but traveling the route in person was imperative.

I passed behind the office, the back of the cottage visible through a sparse patch of trees, and stopped the car when I reached the barn door. At ten miles per hour, it took me a little over a minute to reach the barn. If the killer had escaped in a car, he (or she) would have been gone from the scene in a flash. If only there had been snow on the ground the morning of the murder, the police might have ascertained the make of the killer's vehicle from the tire tracks.

I continued down the road and was soon on a section bordered on both sides by fir trees. Through small gaps in the trees, I saw the golf course on my right. The road stretched along the golf course in a straight path for about seven-tenths of a mile before a gentle curve signaled I was rounding the eastern boundary of the course and approaching the club. A few yards more, the road made a sharp left turn and I was on a short stretch that gave onto Club Lane. I passed through an open iron gate and two stone pillars and pulled onto the lane.

I increased my speed from ten to the road's limit of twenty-five and arrived at Townsend's parking lot. My journey had taken seven minutes. Someone making a getaway could have cut that time in half with a lead foot on the gas pedal.

I drove past Townsend's and down Club Lane, making the right on Old Bridge Road. I made another right turn and drove the short distance to the barn's lot. There were now three cars there, Sophie's and Nate's two of them. I pulled beside Sophie's car and turned off my engine.

"So."

I contemplated a possible sequence of events the morning of the murder. I guessed the killer arrived on Townsend's property through the Old Bridge Road lot and parked behind the office or barn, or in the tunnel of trees beyond the barn. Did the person go to the office and ask Gigi outside for a walk, or was Gigi on her way to the barn when her killer confronted her? Or, if Whitney was correct and an illicit deal had taken place, had a meeting behind the barn been prearranged?

After killing Gigi, I guessed the killer took the longer route away from the scene. If the killer had exited via the lot on Old Bridge Road, someone could have seen the car and later reported the sighting after the murder became front-page news. So the killer took the road around the golf course, knowing no one would be playing a round on the frigid morning and pulled onto Club Lane. If Zach were the murderer, he then drove into the main parking lot for his ten o'clock public arrival.

"This could very well be what happened," I murmured, sliding from my car and pressing the remote's door lock. Even if Zach didn't kill Gigi, I was sure the killer had escaped on the route I had just driven. With a sense of dread consuming me, I quickened my pace. I looked forward to slipping into the mind of Madame Arcati for a couple of hours with more eagerness than usual.

"We have a piece of business to discuss before we start." Sophie paused and looked over the expectant faces of the cast assembled on the stage.

"They've caught the killer!" Kelsey said.

"Sorry, no. Veronica and I had lunch yesterday with Donna Townsend and Bret Foster. He's the club's new event planner who will organize Showcase Night and the opening-night reception." She explained Julia's new business venture in response to an inquiry from Iris. "We discussed plans for the parties. But Donna also presented an idea for honoring Gigi. She wants to hold a gala performance, dinner included, with all proceeds going to a scholarship for an Arden theater major. The Gigi Swanson Townsend Memorial Scholarship."

"A scholarship?" Jerome asked. From his puzzled look, I could tell he wasn't fond of the idea.

"Yeah. I don't like it. I like the gala performance part of it, but I think the evening should benefit the BCT." Sophie also shared her disagreement with Donna's original plan of holding the gala on our opening night.

"You were right to say no to that," Nate said. "It wouldn't be fair to the folks who've already purchased tickets and can't afford a higher-priced seat."

"Do we all agree to do the gala performance after our original run ends?" When the enthusiastic expressions of agreement subsided, Sophie asked, "And what about this scholarship deal? I think the proceeds should benefit the theater Gigi founded and nurtured. We should fight for that."

Everyone but Nate gave ready consent. "I don't know if we should fight Donna on this, Soph. After the huge support Townsend's has given us, maybe we should give them this one thing. Gigi was their son's wife."

A silent minute followed. "I agree with Nate," Iris said. "We can do something special later on. Maybe over the summer."

"We could get actors from past shows and do a revue or something," Jerome said.

"What about music? Perhaps local musicians, maybe kids from the high school band, can join us," Peter said.

"We can do show tunes!" said Lucy.

Nate urged Sophie toward a change of heart. "We can do an outdoor performance. You always tried to push Gigi to do a Shakespeare in the Park type deal. We can start there."

Sophie, not yet fully convinced, caught her lower lip between her teeth. "I thought this gala could kick off the capital campaign Gigi wanted to hold."

"What capital campaign?" Jerome led the chorus of surprise.

Nate pulled a face—not another tangent!—while Sophie filled in the group on Gigi's fundraising idea. After a few minutes of discussion on moneymaking events (suggestions included a casino night at the Elks club and a carnival in the firehouse parking lot), Nate popped the bubble.

"Folks, the board of trustees has to approve this campaign first!"

"I don't think there will be a problem convincing them the BCT needs more money," Iris said.

"Yeah, well." Nate ducked his head and grinned. "Still, we need to make it official before we rent a dunk tank and Ferris wheel."

"Okay everyone," Sophie said, "it's rehearsal time."

"I have a question." Erica claimed the floor. "I just thought of this last night. Should we be doing English accents?"

Over the laughter and groans, Sophie said a brusque, "No way."

Chapter Twenty-Six

I like to think I have an open mind, but there are some things I can't get behind, and talking with the dead is one of those things. My eight hundred page Catholic Catechism contained a hearty warning against consultation with mediums, astrologers, and psychics. I also had a tiny worry Agnes really did have the *gift* and would establish contact with one of my deceased loved ones, who might mention some embarrassing tidbit about me.

Having convinced myself that Sophie had twisted my arm on the idea, on Monday morning I sat in my office at All Things, said three Hail Mary's, and dialed the phone number on Agnes Steinert's business card. She answered on the third ring.

"I'm Veronica Wal—"

"The latest Madame Arcati," Agnes said, her voice modulated and warm. "I've been wondering if Gigi Swanson told you about my offer of a consultation. May she rest in peace."

"She did." I fumbled for my next words. I should have written a script. "The director and I would like to meet with you." I couldn't bring myself to say séance.

"I'd enjoy that," Agnes said.

We set a date for Friday evening. When I inquired about her fee, Agnes replied, "Consider it a contribution to the theater."

I hung up, wondering if her *contribution* was tax deductible.

I received a text from Tracey a half hour after my chat with Agnes.

Do you have a minute?

I caught my breath. Was she going to share insider information?

Was there a break in the case thanks to what Nate and I had told her?

I sent a reply in the affirmative and waited for her next message. *I'm in the alley.*

The urgency I inferred from Tracey's summons sent me through the stockroom and out the back door without grabbing my coat from my office. A row of cars owned by the proprietors and staff of the stores along the block between Sycamore and Maple lined the alley. Tracey's cruiser was double-parked next to Claire's Civic.

I dashed around the cruiser and slid into the front passenger seat. "Did you crack the murder case?"

Tracey placed a steaming cup of coffee in the cup holder on the console between us. "No."

"Have you interviewed Kenny? Do you know where he went after he left the Hearth?"

Tracey held up her hand, stopping my flurry of inquiries. "Ron Nicholstone paid him a visit Saturday afternoon. Pangborn has an alibi."

"What is it?"

"He was in Penny Woods."

"At his hardware store? What time did he arrive?"

"Veronica, Kenny Pangborn didn't kill Gigi."

"What's his alibi?"

Tracey was stone-faced for a few seconds before she answered. "He has an ATM receipt from a bank in Penny Woods. The time stamp is ten thirty-five."

"Kenny still has a receipt from a week ago?" I was incredulous; Kenny seemed the kind of guy who would crumple a receipt and throw it on the ground. Though perhaps he kept it when he learned of Gigi's murder, believing he would be a suspect.

Tracey's response was a stare I met for a few seconds until I blinked. Darn cops and their steely resolve. "Well, I'm glad, for the sake of his son. Why didn't you just call or text me with the news?

Or tell me at church yesterday?"

"I thought you would enjoy a covert meeting in the alley. But I'm disappointed. You said you'd wear a trench coat and yellow rose behind your left ear." Tracey dropped her amused expression to take a drink of coffee.

"*You* said we weren't going to turn this into a CIA operation. Next time, I'll need more than a minute's notice if you want props."

"A *next time* is the last thing I want." After another gulp of coffee, Tracey finished with, "Seriously, thank you for sharing the information on Pangborn. This is the kind of information I was looking for when I asked for your help."

I grumbled a "You're welcome" and a "Have a nice day" and got out of the car. I stepped back, leaned against Claire's car, and signaled for Tracey to move first. She waved and pulled the cruiser straight ahead, moving at a snail's pace down the alley and stopping for a few seconds before making a right turn onto Maple Lane.

"Darn it," I muttered. I would have bet good money the surly, embezzling Kenny was Gigi's murderer. The revenge motive I had assigned him and his presence in Barton on that Saturday morning had me contemplating what I would wear when I took the witness stand against him.

I started back to All Things, considering how Kenny could have a receipt from a bank in Penny Woods and also be Gigi's murderer. It was possible he had stopped at the barn on his way out of Barton, killed Gigi, and then floored the gas pedal and cut the fifteen-minute trip to Penny Woods in half. A tight timeline, but doable, I thought. Dan said Kenny left the Hearth "just before" the meat guy arrived at ten fifteen. "Just before" could mean five, seven, or ten minutes. More time for Kenny to take out his anger on Gigi.

I quieted my skepticism with the reminder Tracey wouldn't lie to me. Or would she?

Was Kenny deep on the police's person-of-interest radar and Tracey fed me a line to knock him off my suspect list?

Chapter Twenty-Seven

Julia Rogan's event-planning business was located on a tree-lined street in Bolton Landing, a Barton neighbor to the south. Her office was on the end of a row of three other shops: a hair salon, florist, and travel agent. Scrawled on the shop window in elegant script was her new venture's name: *Soirees by Julia.*

I took a glance at the window display before going inside. A vase stuffed with a giant arrangement of assorted flowers stood in the center of the bay window. I wondered if Julia had paid for it or if the floral shop two doors down had loaned it to her in an entrepreneurial act of synergy (I bet all four businesses were in a constant state of mutual recommendation). An opened white album beside the vase displayed a photograph of a bride and groom standing under a tree, a large swath of grass surrounding them. In the window's right corner a placard held on a small easel announced in elegant script the nature of Julia's enterprise. Whether the celebration was a wedding or vow renewal, baby or bridal shower, retirement party, corporate event, or birthday party, Julia's talent would make the day beautiful. One item in her list caught me by surprise: Julia was available for divorce parties, too.

"I suppose that's a cause of celebration for some," I muttered.

I stepped into the shop, soothed at once by a blast of warm air and scent of lavender and vanilla. Along the right side of the shop were shelf and table displays of candles, photo albums, and guest books. Right near the door was a selection of reading material, including books of poetry for weddings, verses for vows, and toasts for every occasion. There was an oak table to my left and behind it a shelf of white binders. I noted the label on one binder's spine: *Destination Weddings*. At the back of the room were a desk and three cushioned chairs around a coffee table.

Behind the desk sat a woman in her early thirties. She acknowledged me with a smile and held up a finger, signaling her phone call would end in a moment.

Julia ended her call and greeted me. After shaking my hand, she brushed aside a long strand of the auburn hair that had fallen across her brow and rested her wide, green-eyed gaze on me. "What type of event are you planning, Veronica?"

"I'm not planning a party."

"Oh?"

"No." I felt compelled to apologize. "I'm here about a mutual friend. Gigi Swanson. I understand you recently left your job at Townsend's."

Julia pressed her hand against her heart and her eyelids fluttered. "I'm heartbroken over her death." She paused for a beat. "That's right. You're starring in the BCT's latest production. Is it still going to go on?"

"Yes. Sophie Morrissey is now the director."

"Good for Sophie. Are you here selling tickets to the show?"

"Not exactly. Though . . ." I filled her in on the gala benefit and asked if she would attend.

Julia pouted in dismay. "Oh, I'm so sorry I can't make it. I have a wedding that evening."

"Maybe you can come to another performance." I took in her noncommittal shrug before continuing. "Do you have a few minutes to talk about Gigi?"

Julia hesitated before gesturing to the table of sample binders. "Let's sit."

I noted the table's proximity to the door and formal seating. We would have a quick chat, I guessed. Customers get a seat around the coffee table, and probably champagne and chocolate-covered strawberries. I get the business world's equivalent of the kid's table.

We took seats at the end of the table, Julia across from me. "I'm very sorry I couldn't attend Gigi's funeral. I had a meeting."

I bit back a snarky comment that Julia's business must be thriving with all these meetings and events. She couldn't move it back a couple of hours so she could attend the funeral of her former boss's wife? Gigi was also a former colleague, having worked with Julia on BCT events. "When did you last see Gigi?"

"Gosh, I think it was the opening night of the BCT's show last summer. I didn't have an opportunity to say goodbye to her when I left in October."

"Have you had any contact with her since you left?"

Julia shook her head. "No. Gigi and I weren't close, but I admired her greatly. She had such talent. I only dealt with her on the receptions for her opening-night shows. And Showcase Nights. I enjoyed working with her, though. Those evenings were fun."

Long answer to a yes or no question. "Have you talked with Zach recently?"

Julia's gaze focused on the table; she smoothed her hand over the bleached wood for a few seconds before she answered. "No, I haven't. I've been so busy getting my business going, I haven't been able to keep in touch with anyone from Townsend's. I haven't talked with anyone from the club. And I haven't been to Barton since leaving. I did send Zach a condolence card. Why do you ask?"

"I'm talking with everyone who knew Gigi, asking if they knew of anyone who would hurt her. I was just getting to know her."

"Gigi was a very sweet woman. Very poised and smart. A Renaissance woman. I always enjoyed working with her."

Yeah, you've said that already. "Do you know anyone who had a problem with her?"

"No. Like I said, I didn't know Gigi very well. But in my time at Townsend's, I never heard anyone say a bad word against her."

I remembered Dotsie's bridezilla theory. What the heck, I'll ask.

"When you were planning events at Townsend's, was there ever anyone who wanted to book the barn but couldn't because the BCT had reserved it? Perhaps someone recent, who wanted to hold her reception at Townsend's on our opening night in March?"

Julia shook her head and gave me a mystified look. "No. There were no conflicts in scheduling the barn."

"This is embarrassing to ask." I put on an abashed look that suggested I was going to ask Julia something very personal. "I heard a rumor Zach was having an affair with a Townsend's employee."

Her cheeks colored and she glanced out the window. "I never heard that rumor. I don't think Zach would ever cheat on Gigi."

"You know him better than I do. I heard between their careers, Gigi and Zach didn't get to spend much time together."

Julia looked at her desk. I imagined she was willing her phone to ring. "That was true. But it didn't make Zach cheat on her. He loved Gigi very much. And I'm sure Gigi was faithful. She was a wonderful wife."

"I'm sure they were committed to each other," I said, agreeable. "I'm sorry I never got to know them as a couple."

Julia nodded, but made no further comment on the state of Gigi and Zach's marriage. She checked the time on her wristwatch. "I'm sorry. I have an appointment in a few minutes."

I stood up, extending my hand. "I won't keep you. Thank you for the talk. The Swansons and her BCT family are trying to make sense of her death. I'm just trying to help them do that."

"I'm sure the police will make an arrest soon and then everyone can be at peace."

"I'm sure." I asked how she was doing in her start-up business. "You probably have a lot of contacts from your Townsend's days."

"I'm doing well, thank you. And yes, my work at Townsend's has certainly prepared me."

I wished her good luck and left. "First Whitney throws shade on Gigi, and now Julia pours sugar on her," I muttered on the way to my car.

Whitney had suggested Gigi was devious and Julia overcompensated on how wonderful and perfect she was. The two were guilty of something. Was it murder? Adultery? Greed? Plain old envy?

I buckled my seat belt and started the engine. Giving the car a minute to warm, I took my phone from my purse and checked my messages.

Turning to look for traffic before pulling from the curb, I spotted a black Lexus pass and maneuver into the empty space ahead of the car in front of mine. The slow movement of the Lexus afforded me a glimpse of its driver.

Donna Townsend.

I slouched down in my seat, flipping the sun visor down to give myself extra cover. I watched Donna get out of her car and push the remote button to lock the Lexus's doors. She wore a pair of wide sunglasses and a knee-length, white parka with a fur-lined hood.

I slipped on my sunglasses and held my breath, waiting for visual confirmation of Donna's destination. I doubted she had made the trek to Bolton Landing to have her hair done, buy a bouquet of flowers, or plan a winter getaway.

"Yep," I murmured, my gaze following Donna to the door of Soirees by Julia. A white envelope in her left hand caught my attention. Hmm.

I waited a couple of minutes, hoping Donna and Julia would conduct their business near the window. Too bad secretive meetings take place in the wide open only in the movies and on soaps; Julia must have led Donna to the cozy conversation cluster at the back of the shop.

A sudden panic filled me. What if Julia was recounting my visit, telling Donna every syllable I had uttered?

"I should have worn a disguise and used an alias!"

With a jolt I checked for oncoming traffic and then jerked the car from the parking space, hitting the gas pedal so I could make it through the intersection before the yellow light turned red.

My heart rate slowed and my breathing became normal in a few moments. Whatever dealing Donna and Julia were doing in the little shop on the corner, Donna would sure as heck never breathe a word of it to me.

I did, however, have an inkling of what was in the envelope.

Chapter Twenty-Eight

"So you think Donna Townsend is bribing Julia to keep her away from her son and not ruin his political career before it even begins?" Claire took a drink of hot chocolate and set her mug on my desk.

"I do." I had shared my inkling with Claire upon my return to All Things. We sat in my office, the door closed. "I'm certain there was hush money in that envelope. I think something went on between Julia and Zach. Julia was nervous and adamant she absolutely, positively hasn't seen, talked to, or even thought about Gigi since she left the club."

"The lady doth protest too much."

"Yeah. And she had a quick excuse for not attending our benefit performance. She was also too busy to attend Gigi's funeral. She had a *meeting*."

"Maybe she did."

"Meetings can be rescheduled. She wasn't doing emergency brain surgery."

"You've gathered a few interesting suspects. I thought this was an open and shut case of the husband did it. But you've uncovered a possible mistress, a jealous business partner, and an embezzler."

"And when I joined the production, I thought Gigi had the perfect life. There was a lot going on, and she apparently kept it from almost everyone."

"People do that when they're trying to hold up that perfect façade."

I picked up my cell phone and stared at it. I had delayed making contact with Gigi's sister long enough, despite her post-funeral mention of having a chat. I had held onto the hope the police would make an arrest, making questions I had for Blair unnecessary. I feared she would think me a busybody looking for gossip material. I understood, though, she might be the one person in whom Gigi confided all her woes.

"I'm going to call Gigi's sister. See if she can offer any helpful information."

Claire stood and picked up her mug. "I'll go mind the store."

"Stay away from the edible inventory," I warned before she opened the door.

"I've reached my chocolate limit for the day." Claire slipped out the door, closing it behind her.

"Please may I not look like a fool," I said, calling the phone number Sophie had given me.

Blair answered on the third ring. After I announced myself, but before I could begin my spiel about why I was calling, or even ask how she was, Blair said, "I've been waiting for you to call."

"You have?"

"Oh, yeah. After you accepted the *Blithe Spirit* role, Gigi and I had a long conversation about your many talents. Irony of ironies, she joked that she hoped you wouldn't be distracted by another murder in the village." Blair was quiet for a moment. "Now I'm the one who's praying you have been distracted."

"I have been, and have my own hope you'll talk with me about your sister."

"I'll be in Barton on Saturday to pick up some of Gigi's things at her house. Are you available in the afternoon? I'll come to you."

"I'll be home."

I hung up, my heart heavier from Gigi's joking words. And instead of feeling relief that Blair wanted to talk with me, I felt greater pressure to crack the case for the sake of Gigi's family.

Irony, I hate you.

Chapter Twenty-Nine

The rest of the week proceeded with surprising calm and quiet. I didn't hear from Tracey again and there were no articles in the *Chronicle* concerning the murder case. The Townsends, too, kept out of sight. Our rehearsals continued on a steady course without any discussion about the case, save for me telling Nate about Kenny's alibi. I didn't share my doubts and he didn't appear to hold any of his own.

"I'm sorry I wasted your time and Officer Brody's."

"It was no waste. Tracey's thankful we told her about Kenny and the embezzlement."

"Let's just hope Kenny gets his act together." Nate gave my arm an affectionate squeeze and returned to the rehearsal.

Friday morning brought an interesting visitor to All Things.

Claire and I were in my office discussing Valentine's sales when Haley, one of the staff, darted through the open doorway, her face filled with worry.

"There's a woman downstairs, taking photos of the miniature animal woodcarvings."

"Do you think she's casing the joint?" Claire asked, her tone droll.

Haley's cheeks turned pink. Passing her in the doorway, I gave her arm a pat and led the pair to the first floor. The delightful woodcarvings, all crafted by a local artisan, were located on the wall behind the stairs. I took the sharp turn around the bannister and caught Julia Rogan in the act of snapping a shot of two bowler hat-wearing brown bears with her iPhone.

"Julia. Hello."

Julia twitched, the hand holding the phone dropping to her side. "Veronica! I'm—"

"Casing the joint?"

A snort came from Claire, who was hovering in the Christmas corner on the other side of the staircase.

Julia tittered. "In a way. I'm planning a fiftieth anniversary party. The couple would like to give every guest a small gift. Your visit the other day reminded me of the beautiful items you sell."

"A fringe benefit of my drive to Bolton."

"I'm just taking photos of things to show Mr. and Mrs. Fegan."

"Make sure you also take photos of the blown-glass pieces over there and our selection of ceramics. We also just received an order of beautiful votive holders."

Claire, still eavesdropping, rewarded me with an approving hum.

"I will." Julia gave a self-conscious smile. "How are rehearsals for *Blithe Spirit*?"

"Going well."

"How's everyone? Sophie? Nate? Jerome? Iris?"

"They're all well. I'll tell them you said hello."

"I miss working with the BCT. It was a particularly fun part of the job." She paused for a minute and fingered a figurine of a giraffe with a red scarf tied around its neck. "How's Zach? And his parents? I keep meaning to call them . . ."

Oh, I see what you're doing, Julia Rogan. You're doubling down on what you said the other day. You know you didn't give a convincing performance on Monday and are now trying for a stronger second act.

"It's a difficult time. You should stop by the club while you're here. I'm sure Donna would be delighted to see you. And Zach."

Julia turned to the shelf and held up her phone to take another photo of the figurines. I spied a flush filling her cheeks. "Have you heard anything about the murder case? Are the police close to making an arrest?" She took a photo and made a show of examining it on the phone's screen.

I drew closer to Julia. "No. The Barton PD is working twenty-four seven to solve it. Have they interviewed you?"

"Yes," she said, still staring at her phone. "I'm sorry I couldn't help them. But like I said, I hadn't seen Gigi since I left the club." Julia put on a toothy smile. "Where's the blown glass?"

I spent ten more minutes guiding Julia around All Things, playing businesswoman giving excellent customer service and not amateur sleuth digging for clues.

I stood by the window, watching Julia walk across Orchard to her car. Claire came up behind me. "You messed with her head."

"She lied through her teeth."

"Just don't bust her before she places that order for the anniversary party."

I lingered at the window for a few minutes after Julia drove down Orchard. Was the anniversary party a cover story for coming here to . . . what? Ask after Zach? She could have asked Donna during their Monday visit, unless Mama Donna put talk of her son off-limits. Did Julia think I would give her confidential information from the police investigation? Or mine?

I had a difficult time envisioning the sweeter-than-apple-pie-a-la-mode young woman confronting and killing Gigi. Though she could have, I knew, the expression "It's always the quiet one" popping into my head. Julia was a nervous Nellie about something. Simple guilt over harboring an attraction to a widower? Or shame over a darker matter?

Sooner or later, I hoped, I'd put my thumb on the reason for Julia Rogan's troubled conscience.

Chapter Thirty

I swiveled the knob on my dining room wall, trying to decide how bright the room should be for the gathering. Would Agnes bring candles to create a setting conducive to spirit talking? Would we sit in total darkness, with the only illumination being the moonlight coming through the windows? Or would we sit like normal adults in a well-lit room?

I twitched my head to clear it of these images influenced by television and movies. I turned the knob so the chandelier was at its brightest. "The Long Island Medium doesn't turn the lights off," I muttered, taking my cue from a reality show.

The doorbell chimed, signaling the beginning of what I was sure would be a surreal evening. I paused in front of the hallway mirror for a final check. I tousled my hair, picked a piece of fluff from my black turtleneck (I thought I should wear a somber color), and pressed my hand against the silver cross I wore under the sweater.

Agnes was the first arrival. I expected a woman in heavy eye makeup and flowing clothes in vibrant colors, with many rings on her fingers, a long strand of beads around her neck, and hoop earrings the size of salad plates dangling from her earlobes. Instead, I found a slim woman of about sixty in a knee-length black coat with a Burberry scarf wound around her neck. She wore her hair, white strands tipped with silver at the ends, in a pixie cut.

"Veronica? I'm Agnes. A pleasure."

Shrugging off her coat, Agnes complimented my folk-Victorian home and declared her delight that it was Friday.

"What is your work?" I asked, hanging her coat in the closet. I

135

noted Agnes had also chosen subdued tones for the evening; she wore a gray turtleneck, black slacks, and pearl stud earrings.

"I'm a wealth advisor at the Bank of the Adirondacks."

A money-managing medium? Agnes's ordinary occupation stunned me. I fumbled with the wooden hanger, mumbling "Oops" when I dropped it. It clattered against my vacuum and bounced into the hall. "That must be interesting work." I picked up the hanger, embarrassed by my pedestrian reply.

Agnes, declining my beverage offer, followed me into the living room. "Gigi mentioned she got your name from her Pilates instructor."

"Yes, her trainer is one of my clients. I've had a few meetings with Yvonne. When Gigi told her the BCT's latest production was *Blithe Spirit*, Yvonne gave Gigi my card. I had a terrific conversation with Gigi a few days before she passed. She thought it would be fun if you and I met. She also was considering having the whole cast for a meeting."

"She mentioned something about a séance."

Agnes offered an amused laugh and settled in a chair. "I don't call my meetings séances. The term scares some and it gives others expectations of materializing spirits, like Elvira in your play."

"That won't happen?"

"Of course not."

"That's good to hear. I'd act the good hostess and offer it a drink. Who knows what would happen to my carpet."

Agnes studied the framed photograph on the end table. It was a photo of my parents and me at my graduation from Fordham. Agnes ran her finger along the lower edge of the black frame and studied the photo for a moment. "Has your father passed?"

"Yes. Nineteen ninety-seven."

"He's a strong presence in this house."

"Dad told me about the house the moment it went on the market. He took a tour with the realtor, checked the sockets, looked for dripping faucets, and checked every board on the front and back porches."

"He's ever present. He's still looking out for you."

I didn't need a woman with a "gift" to tell me that. The doorbell rang, thank goodness, before Agnes could tell me Dad was sitting in the other chair.

I opened the door to Sophie standing on my porch, looking like a specter. She wore a black beret, black pea coat, and black jeans.

"Nice get-up," I cracked. "It's a good thing you put on red lipstick or whatever spirits show up might mistake you for one of their own."

"I hope you haven't started without me," Sophie said, stepping into my front hall and working on her coat's buttons.

"Agnes was just telling me some things about my father I didn't know."

"Really?" Wide-eyed with wonder, Sophie put her coat in the closet.

"No."

Sophie disregarded my comment and charged into the living room, introducing herself and exclaiming how eager she was to witness Agnes's gift. I gave my hallway mirror reflection a final eye roll and joined the pair.

"Shall we get started?" Agnes asked, very matter-of-fact.

"Yes!" Sophie said. I was glad one of us didn't think this was a waste of time.

"Is the dining room a good place to . . ." My voice trailed off. To what? Watch this sweet-faced woman communicate with Gigi? ". . . talk?"

"Perfect."

I allowed Agnes to lead us into the adjoining room. She pulled out the chair at the head of the table and indicated that Sophie and I should sit at the end, next to her and across from each other.

"Should the light be dimmed?" Sophie asked. "Veronica,

do you have candles?"

"The lighting is fine." When Sophie did a poor job of concealing her disappointment, Agnes added, "But you may lower the lights, just a bit, if you like. Candles aren't necessary."

Sophie bolted from her chair and made a beeline for the light switch. Agnes's lips twitched. She leaned toward me and said in a soft voice, "I long ago stopped being offended by people who expect an experience similar to what they see in the movies."

"Or on stage, like in *Blithe Spirit*?"

"Poetic license, I've decided. I assume you wish to make contact with Gigi."

Sophie sat down, pulling her chair so her body pressed against the table. "We do."

"If she does choose to communicate with us, don't expect her to name her killer. You must understand that before we begin."

Her caution didn't surprise me, but Sophie looked like a kid who expected a drooling, woofing puppy for Christmas and instead found a stuffed toy dog under the tree.

"Let's start by closing our eyes and clearing our minds of all distractions."

Sophie squeezed her eyes shut, an intense look of concentration on her face. Agnes relaxed against her chair's back, folded her hands on the table, and closed her eyes. I suppressed a sigh and closed my eyes.

"Please focus on your breathing, in and out, and picture Gigi's face in your mind. In and out. In and out."

A minute of silence passed before Agnes spoke again.

"Now think of a memory of a happy time you shared with Gigi. Focus on Gigi's smile and her laugh. Remember the bond you shared with her."

I recalled Gigi's visit to All Things, when she offered me the Madame Arcati role. I replayed the scene in my mind, losing myself in it until Sophie broke the silence with a giggle.

"Wonderful," said Agnes. "I'm beginning to sense a new presence with us. Gigi, are you here with your friends Veronica and Sophie?"

I raised one eyelid a few centimeters. Agnes, her eyes still closed, was a vision of serenity. Sophie tilted forward, her ear cocked for the slightest sound of Gigi's presence.

Agnes opened her eyes and I snapped mine shut. "Gigi is here now. Please, open your eyes."

"Can you see Gigi?" Sophie asked.

"No, dear. I can't see her. But I feel her spirit here. It's a strong spirit."

"Can you ask her to move something, or knock something over, as a sign for Veronica and me, since we can't feel her spirit? Maybe move the vase a few inches." Sophie gestured at the arrangement of silk flowers in the center of the table. "Or maybe she can make some noise?"

"We should take Agnes at her word that Gigi is with us." Now be quiet and let's be done with this séance. Or "meeting." Thank goodness Agnes waived her fee. If she hadn't, I would have insisted Sophie pay for it out of the theater's petty cash or her own wallet.

"Thank you, Veronica. What would you like to ask Gigi?"

"Is she happy?" Sophie's voice cracked.

After a few beats, Agnes relayed a response. "Yes, Gigi is happy. She wants you to know she is in a beautiful place and not to worry about her."

I could have told you that, I said in my head. Was there a Better Business Bureau for mediums that keeps these folks honest?

"Did it hurt when you died, Gigi?" Sophie asked.

Another pause. "A sharp pain, but it went away quickly."

"I miss you, Gigi." Tears slipped from Sophie's eyes and made a slow slide down her cheeks.

Darn it. I realized Agnes, though she might not really be "communicating" with Gigi, offered us a moment of catharsis and comfort.

"She misses you, too, Sophie." Agnes rested her hand over Sophie's hand. "She's very proud of you. She wants you to know you're doing a terrific job directing the show."

Sophie hid her face in her hands and let out a sob. Agnes and I sat without speaking, allowing her grief full expression.

After a couple of minutes, Sophie wiped her face with a tissue. "Is Gigi still with us?"

"Yes."

"Gigi," Sophie said in a loud, determined voice, "did your husband kill you?"

I tossed her a warning glance. What did Agnes just tell us!

"Gigi can't answer that," Agnes said, patient. "The messages I receive have more to do with feelings than with what happened in the person's earthly life."

How ethereal, I thought, a cynic once more.

"She can't give yes or no answers?"

"No."

"Then ask her how she feels about Zach." Sophie was nothing if not persistent. "Does she hate him? Feel betrayed by him? Gigi, were you happy with Zach in the last moments of your life?"

Agnes was silent for a minute. Sophie kept her attention on the banker medium; I imagined her trying to influence Agnes's "discourse" with Gigi via mental telepathy.

"Gigi has only love and forgiveness for Zach," Agnes finally said.

Sophie's hum was drawn-out and suggestive. "*Forgiveness.*"

"She could be forgiving him for using the last of the toilet paper and not telling her they needed more," I cracked.

Agnes laughed; Sophie gave me a petulant glance.

"What about Whitney? And Julia? Let's throw in Donna and Wayne and Nate and Iris and Jerome while we're at it." Plus Kenny. I couldn't help myself. And the kitchen sink.

Agnes closed her eyes, inhaled and exhaled slowly to my count of ten. "Gigi has left us." She opened her eyes and offered us a solemn look.

Sophie put her head on the table, letting out a groan of frustration.

"I'm sorry. I wish I was able to give you the answers you seek. Those who have passed before us no longer have earthly concerns."

"Thank you for trying." My gratitude was genuine. "You've given me insight on how you share your gift." Those words were sincere, too.

"That medium on television. Many times a deceased person will give someone's initials to her. Do you ever get that?" Sophie asked.

"Yes. Often."

Sophie's despair dissolved. "What if you come to the theater office? Gigi spent a lot of time there. So she might have more to tell us. And the barn. Maybe she'd tell you the initials, or even the first letter of her killer's name."

"I'd be glad to visit Gigi's home away from home. I want to help you in any way I can."

Sophie's grin was wide. "Can you come tomorrow morning?"

"Don't you work Saturday mornings?" I asked Agnes.

"I work two Saturdays a month. Tomorrow I'm off."

"Fantastic!" Sophie committed Agnes to a meeting time and wrung the woman's hand, thanking her with gusto.

An odd look came over Agnes's face. She held Sophie's hand for a long moment. "You've lost someone very close to you recently. I'm getting the letter 'E.' "

Oh what a coincidence, I thought. Sophie asks if Agnes ever receives initials and all of a sudden, a big "E" shows up.

Sophie gasped and pressed her hand to her chest. "My grandmother's name was Evelyn! She died a year ago, Thanksgiving."

"She watches over you, constantly."

"She does?" Sophie's eyes watered again.

"She does. She's proud of the woman you have become. I'm getting the word "soapie." Does that have meaning to you?"

"Grandma called me Soapie. She's the only person I allowed to call me that."

"I'm also getting the message that she wants you to be careful."

Sophie's chin bobbed; she wiped her wet eyes. "Do you think . . . do you think *she* knows who the killer is? Is she warning me about him?"

Good grief. I couldn't wait to meet Mark at the Hearth's bar. I made a mental note to call him and have him order my drink so it would be ready for consumption when I arrived at the Hearth.

The two went back and forth about Sophie's grandmother for a few minutes. I took a mental inventory for my grocery list, hoping to squeeze in a trip to the Food Mart between the morning meeting with Agnes at the BCT office and Blair's early afternoon visit.

"Veronica, is there anyone you would like to contact, before I leave?"

"Your dad!" Sophie said.

"Um . . . no, thank you. Maybe another time."

Agnes left a few minutes later. "That was something!" Sophie declared, pulling on her coat. "Even though she didn't give us any clues about the murderer, I feel so much lighter knowing my grandma is in a good place."

"But you believed that anyway, didn't you? We good Catholic girls keep the faith, right?"

"Yeah. I knew Grandma was in heaven. But it feels so good to *know* it."

"You don't need Agnes or anyone else who claims to talk with the dead to prove your faith."

"Yeah, but it helps."

I pushed Sophie toward the door. "I'll see you at the office. I'm eager to hear part two of what Agnes has to say."

"It would be incredible if she sees a big 'Z' in her head, wouldn't it?"

"Yeah, 'Z' for Zorro. Good night, Sophie."

I waited until Sophie was in her car before closing the door. The frosty air helped me decide on my Hearth beverage of choice. I snatched my cell from the coffee table and called Mark.

"Order me an Irish coffee. Heavy on the Irish. I'll be there in five minutes."

Chapter Thirty-One

"We should have a cover story, just in case someone sees us." Sophie, noshing on a doughnut from Fortier's, leaned against the desk in the BCT's office.

"We'll introduce Agnes as your favorite Aunt Aggie." I sat in the visitor's chair, enjoying a cinnamon-powdered doughnut from the half-dozen Sophie had brought. Still bemused by the previous night's get together, we were awaiting Agnes's arrival.

Sophie, chomping a large bite from her doughnut, gave my suggestion a serious nod. "I hope you thought more about what happened last night. It really should have dispelled your doubts about Agnes's ability. I'm still amazed she talked with my grandma and Gigi."

"I don't think she really talked with either of them."

"But she knew Grandma's first initial."

"Lucky guess."

The door swung open, allowing in a bracing breeze and Agnes. "Good morning, ladies." She shut the door and took a survey of the office.

Sophie shoved the rest of her doughnut in her mouth and wiped her hands on the back of her jeans. I wrapped my doughnut in a napkin and dropped it in my purse.

"What a cozy room." Agnes gave an approving nod. She slipped off her gloves and stashed them in her coat pocket. Opening her purse and pulling out her wallet, she said, "Before I forget, I would like to buy two tickets for your opening-night performance, if it's not sold out."

"Not yet." Sophie sat down, opened the desk's bottom drawer, and removed a metal box. Her dull tone suggested disappointment with Agnes's mundane request, as if Sophie hoped the medium would make a pronouncement the moment she crossed the office threshold. The business transacted, Agnes took a turn around the room. Sophie, fidgety, watched closely.

"Gigi was very ambivalent about this space," Agnes finally said. "She was grateful for it, but she didn't like the sense of debt that hung over her."

Sophie gave me a look that screamed, *Bingo!* "A couple of days before she was killed, Gigi told Veronica she wanted the BCT to have its own home."

"Independence. That's what she wanted." Agnes walked to the window, staring out it for a minute.

My heart betrayed my brain by kicking up its beat.

"Are you seeing what Gigi saw her last morning here?" Sophie's eyes were wide with fascination.

Agnes shook her head. A few long beats passed before she answered. "No. I sense Gigi appreciated the peace of this view. The trees, the expansive lawn. And the way the light came through. That's all." She moved away from the window, reaching into her pockets for her gloves. "I'm ready to visit the barn."

Sophie snatched her coat and shoved her arms into it. I didn't move as fast, but I admit intrigue had replaced a portion of my doubt.

We followed Agnes out the door. "Maybe Agnes couldn't talk to Gigi last night because Gigi's never been to your house," Sophie whispered.

My remaining slice of skepticism reared its head. "That's ridiculous."

We walked along the path, everything quiet but for the birdsong and the distant sound of a car with muffler trouble.

Sophie, walking side-by-side with Agnes ahead of me, broke the silence after a moment. "Agnes, do you ever work with the police?"

"No. Though several times a family has asked my help on a cold case involving a missing loved one."

"Did you help find the people?"

"Sadly, no. The cases are still unsolved."

Sophie unlocked the barn door and held it open for Agnes and me. Agnes, not waiting for an escort, went through the vestibule and into the chilly main room.

Standing in the center of the room, she did a full turn in a square of dull natural light falling through the high windows. Sophie and I formed a triangle with her, making Agnes the top point.

"I'm feeling an overwhelming warmth."

Sophie, her eyes wide, mouthed "wow."

"Gigi was very happy here," Agnes said in a definitive tone. "She spent a great deal of time in this space."

Agnes's pronouncement prompted Sophie to relate the story of Gigi's convert-the-barn idea.

Agnes's head bobbed in slow time to Sophie's voice. "This was Gigi's sanctuary."

After a minute of silent remembrance, Agnes said, "I'm ready to see where Gigi passed."

Sophie opened the door next to the stage and led us through the back hallway. She didn't bother switching on the light, leaving us to make our way by a streak of light from the main room.

"I'm experiencing a growing sense of tension. Of dread." Despite her startling declaration, Agnes's voice was soft and calm.

Outside, a squirrel scooted across the gravel road and a male cardinal landed atop one of the trees, making its familiar "ticking" call.

"Gigi was lying over there." Sophie, her voice faltering, pointed to the ground near the barn wall. Agnes regarded the area for a minute. Knowing Sophie was giving me a suggestive look, I turned my gaze to the woods.

Agnes made a slow approach to Gigi's resting spot and stood over it for a few moments, her head bowed. "I'm getting a strong message of anger and fear. Surprise." Agnes's words jolted me and brought Sophie to tears. "I'm sorry." Agnes's condolence carried a double meaning: sympathy for Gigi's death and apology for stirring Sophie's sorrow.

"Does Gigi say . . . do you sense that she suffered?" Sophie sniffled and wiped a finger under her nose.

"Only in her soul. And only for a moment."

I drew close and put my arm around Sophie's shoulder. Unable to keep the image of Gigi lying lifeless on the ground, I closed my eyes and listened to the cardinal's call. Hearing the sounds of an approaching car, I opened my eyes and looked down the driveway.

A black Volkswagen was coming toward us from the direction of the Old Bridge Road parking lot. We moved toward the door, allowing the car ample room for passing. Instead, it stopped in the middle of the road, just a few feet from where Gigi had died. The car's door swung open and its driver climbed from the front seat.

Zach Townsend.

He raised his hand in greeting and started toward us. "Hi, ladies."

"Hey, Zach," Sophie said, no longer weepy.

"Are you taking a break from theater business?"

"Yes," Sophie answered. "This is Agnes. She's a medium. Agnes is advising Veronica in her role."

So much for Aunt Aggie.

"Oh, wow. That must be interesting." Zach's glance landed on me. "Are you learning to read palms? Tarot cards?"

"Fortune tellers read palms and tarot cards. Mediums communicate with the dead." To my ears, Sophie was challenging Zach, trying to drag an incriminating reaction from him.

"Is that what you're trying to do now?" Zach turned his assessing gaze on Sophie.

"Agnes doesn't have to try. She's always receiving messages."

"So what does my wife have to say? I hope she hasn't shared any of my secrets." Zach's crooked grin was unsettling.

"Are you hiding something?" Sophie wrapped her tease in ice.

"Just dirty laundry on the floor and a toilet seat perpetually left up."

Agnes, whose attention had been fixed on Zach, spoke. "Is there anything you would like to say to Gigi?"

"I don't need help communicating with my wife. I talk with her a thousand times a day."

"What are you doing here, Zach?" Sophie asked.

"A DJ is coming in a few minutes to set up for a wedding. I wanted to make sure you guys got all your stuff off the stage."

"We always do. You know that, Zach."

"Well, I always check. Have a nice day, ladies."

Once Zach entered the barn and the door shut behind him, Sophie snapped, "I guess he's not interested in hearing from his wife."

"Everyone's grief is unique," Agnes said.

"Did you get any messages from Gigi while he was standing here?"

"No." Agnes's gaze lingered on Zach's car. "Just an overwhelming feeling of sadness."

Sophie had the last word. "Maybe Gigi didn't have anything to say to him."

Chapter Thirty-Two

I did my weekly shopping at the Food Mart and headed home for lunch before Blair Swanson arrived. I pulled the car into my detached garage, my thoughts fixed on Agnes, Zach, Gigi, and Blair. I was oblivious to the brown pickup truck blocking my driveway until I turned away from my car trunk, two plastic bags of groceries in each hand.

Stomping up the driveway was Kenny Pangborn. I put the grocery bags on the ground and hurried down the driveway so we'd be in full view of my neighbors and passersby. I wanted witnesses to whatever was about to happen.

"Good morning," I said in my most pleasant tone.

"Keep your nose out of my business." Kenny's voice was gruff, his size intimidating.

I toughened my pose, though my legs were suddenly shaking. "What do you mean?"

"You snooped around my hardware store and then reported me to the police!"

I glanced at the house across the street in time to see a hand pull back the curtain in the living room window. Thank goodness for my inquisitive neighbor, Ellen. Anyone who resents a busybody has never feared being thrown into a brown pickup and never seen again.

"As I told Lori, people at the BCT recommended I get my paint supplies in your store. Trust me, I'll go elsewhere next time."

"Paint my ass. You wanted to find out if I have an alibi."

Kenny stepped closer, his threatening scowl worked like a charm, quickening my pulse and firing my adrenaline. I prayed Ellen was recording Kenny's license plate in legible print or, even better, taking photos of us with the digital camera she got for Christmas.

I maintained my innocent act. "Why would you need an alibi, Mr. Pangborn? For the morning Gigi was murdered? Weren't the two of you friends?"

Kenny huffed and slapped his hands. His padded gloves muted the smack. "Gigi told you I stole money from her stinkin' theater!"

Kenny obviously didn't think Nate was the snitch. Did he trust in some "bro" code?

"Yeah, she did." I sent up a non-verbal prayer for divine absolution for the fib. I didn't want to tell Kenny Nate was my informant, on the chance Kenny was innocent. It would ruin whatever friendship the two men had between them. "And she showed you a lot of mercy by not pressing charges."

Kenny called Gigi an offensive name and sent a ball of spit onto my driveway. "She could have given me a break and not demanded I pay it back at once. She knew I was having problems with my wife. She knew I had a kid to feed. All she cared about was her precious theater. Now I'm in the hole on child support because I had to give everything I had to her."

"Gigi didn't cause your problems. And that was the BCT's money you stole. Is that what you were arguing with her about outside Rizzuto's? Were you spewing your bitterness on her and blaming her for all your woes?"

"Yeah. And she threw it back at me and said she should have told the board and pressed charges, just to teach me a lesson. Gigi was no angel. She threatened to tell my wife and screw up my fight for custody of my son." Kenny muttered another derogatory name for Gigi. "I can't believe you called the police on me. They came by my store and questioned my employees!" His fury suddenly disappeared. "Look. I didn't kill Gigi. I made a delivery to the Hearth and then went right to the store. So lay off your snooping and pester someone else."

Did Kenny forget about his stop at the bank's ATM or did he simply not bother to mention it?

"You're an embezzler. Why should I believe you?"

"I didn't steal the money for kicks or to buy stuff." Kenny's ruddy face softened. "I've had a rough couple of years and I'm working hard to get back on my feet and take care of my kid. I didn't hate Gigi enough to kill her."

"Lovely. Your fury didn't rise to the level of murder. If you hated her, why did you go to her funeral?"

"Out of respect for her saint of a husband."

"Baloney bender. You figured the police would be there, counting heads. You didn't want anyone thinking your absence implied guilt." I wanted to end the conversation by walking away, but I didn't dare turn my back on Kenny until he and his brown pickup were gone from my street. "You should go now."

"Keep your nose out of my business."

Kenny walked to his truck, shooting me a last glower before opening the driver's door and climbing into the cab. I watched him drive away and gave Ellen an "everything's fine" wave. I couldn't see her, but I was sure she was still standing guard.

I carried my groceries across my back porch and into the kitchen. If the police accepted Kenny's alibi, why was he bothering warning me against snooping? Why try to convince me he wasn't Gigi's killer?

I grabbed my cell from my purse and called Tracey, not waiting for a hello when she answered. "Kenny Pangborn just accosted me in my driveway."

Tracey's response was quick and sharp. "Do you need help?"

"No. He's gone." I gave her a full account of the encounter. "He told me to stay out of his business and insisted he has an alibi for the murder."

"Well, he does." Tracey's voice was more relaxed once she knew she didn't have to speed to my house and subdue Kenny. "Veronica.

Forget about Kenny Pangborn."

I tempered my pique. "All right."

Though shaken by Kenny's appearance, I would put it out of my mind. For at least a while. With Blair Swanson's arrival imminent, I had other suspects occupying my thoughts.

An hour later, I opened the front door and greeted with an embrace the woman whose heart was heavy from loss and the task of collecting her deceased sister's effects. Blair held me close for a few seconds with appreciation for the solace.

"What may I get you?" I asked, leading her into the living room. "It's not too early for a good stiff drink. It's five o'clock somewhere."

Blair laughed. "A hot cup of tea would be welcome."

"I needed this," she said a few minutes later, swallowing a mouthful of still-scalding black tea. "It was a tough morning." She avoided eye contact, instead focusing on the crimson cloth covering my dining room table. She ran her fingers over one of the satin stripes on the cloth.

I studied her for a moment, noting the striking similarities between her and Gigi, who was older by two years. Blair had the same round face and brunette coloring Gigi had and the same medium height.

After offering my sympathy, I inquired about Zach. "I haven't seen much of him. How is he doing?" No way was I going to tell Blair I had seen Zach three hours earlier at the site of her sister's death.

"I haven't seen him, either."

"You didn't just see him at his house?"

"No. Donna was there. She told me Zach couldn't bring himself to go through Gigi's things, so Donna gathered up all her clothes and a few other things." Blair scowled at her mug of tea.

"What's wrong?"

Blair shook her head and rubbed her brow. Was she erasing an upsetting image or conversation from her mind? I wondered. "Nothing. Oh . . . I think it's too soon for any of us to be going through Gigi's things, boxing and bagging them up to shove in the attic or give away. I'm going to donate her winter clothes to our church for people in need, but I'm not going to go through Gigi's other stuff right now."

"When my father died, all my mother's friends told her to wait a year before making any decisions about the house and dad's effects."

"Did she follow the advice?"

"Dad's been gone almost twenty years and she still lives in their house, his basement workshop hasn't been dismantled, and his shoehorn, watch, spare change, and driver's license are still in the top drawer of his dresser."

Blair returned my smile. "That's lovely. I know Zach's going to move on, but I didn't expect him to take his first steps two weeks later. I wonder if it was his idea, or if his mother pushed him to clear out Gigi's closet."

"Donna might think she's helping her son with his grief."

Blair took a gulp of tea. "Pushing and dragging might be more like it."

"What kind of relationship did Gigi have with Donna?"

"They got along well. They were very fond of each other."

"So Donna didn't criticize every little thing Gigi did? Like her cooking, cleaning, how she folded the towels. Typical mother-in-law gripes."

Blair laughed. "Donna's in no position to criticize how anyone keeps house. She has a woman who does all that for her and Wayne."

"I met Donna outside the barn before our first Thursday rehearsal. When I went inside, Gigi was alone and she seemed upset. Did she say anything to you about their conversation?"

Blair's response came out in a hoarse voice. "The last time I

tea.
»"

e. They were happy
ey wanted to ki—"
her eyes for a few
ap each other silly
that grate on their

de Rizzuto's, her
at the office.

s widened a bit when I related the information I got
he flower shop and her lips slanted upward. "You've
rea   ur homework."

"   this I got the impression Gigi wasn't very content."

"I gu   ou caught her in one of her slap silly moments." Blair
took a bite t. m one of the Pepperidge Farm Milano cookies I had
put out.

"What do you know about Zach's relationship with Julia
Rogan?"

"Julia? The club's event planner?"

"Former event planner. She left in the fall to open her own
business."

"Good for her." Blair's countenance darkened when she realized
the weight of my question. "What have you heard about Zach and
Julia?"

"A rumor that they had an employer-employee relationship that
was a bit too close."

"Gigi never said anything about Zach cheating on her." Blair
became thoughtful. "I hope the rumor isn't true."

I decided to shut my mouth about my visit with Julia and her
telltale signs of guilt. I'd let it rest and, if Zach was unfaithful to Gigi,
allow Blair to learn it from someone else.

I let a few seconds pass before moving the conversation to Gigi's other partner. "How was Gigi's relationship with Whitney?"

"High maintenance. You know, they started off as equals, both working hard to build a client list. Then Gigi started the BCT, landed the decorating contract with Townsend's, and negotiated the family's patronage of the theater. When club members and Donna's friends saw Gigi's fantastic decorating and design work, Gigi soon had a full plate of clients.

"Gigi didn't change with her success, but Whitney did. She became very jealous and, at times, surly. She and Gigi had an argument not too long ago about Whitney's mistakes. Whitney tried to take Gigi down a notch, telling her the only reason she had her clients was because of her mother-in-law."

No wonder she was such a wretch to Ariana, I thought. Feeling powerless in her partnership with Gigi, Whitney wielded her authority over her subordinate. "I talked with their former assistant, Ariana. She doesn't think much of Whitney's talent."

"Ha! She's right. Whitney's taste isn't as refined or sophisticated as Gigi's was. Whitney's a good designer, but no decorator."

I decided not to tell Blair of how Whitney "worked the room" at the post-funeral lunch. "Did Gigi ever think about ending the partnership? Going solo? She would have been very successful on her own."

"Once in a while Gigi would say she made a mistake going into business with Whitney, or something like, 'If it weren't such a headache, I'd dissolve the partnership.' Don't think Gigi didn't like Whitney. Gigi cared for her very much. But I do think Gigi realized she shouldn't have gone into business with a friend."

Could Gigi have decided the headache was worth it and made a declaration of independence to Whitney?

I wasn't going to add to Blair's grief with gossip on Whitney's dark suggestions about the cause of Gigi's death. I moved on to the BCT, the third important part of Gigi's life. "Did you know Gigi wanted to move the BCT to its own building?" I told Blair of Gigi's nascent capital campaign and suggestion the theater might find a new home.

"I didn't. Though I know she sometimes wondered aloud, joking really, what would happen to the theater if she and Zach went splitsville. Her word. Zach would say they'd have to become street performers."

"Have you heard Donna wants to hold a special benefit performance of *Blithe Spirit* to raise money for a scholarship in Gigi's memory? In the barn, dinner and the show. She's calling it a gala." I paused a beat. "I hope you and your parents can come."

Blair grimaced. "We'll have to see how the case is resolved."

We were quiet for a minute. "How are your parents doing?"

"Slammed with grief. Dad's angry and Mom is in denial that Gigi was murdered. She thinks it was some random, freak accident, despite the fact that someone shot Gigi up close and didn't steal anything from her. Mom just can't bear the idea that someone who knew Gigi hated her. She can't fathom that anyone who knew Gigi would hold ill will against her."

My heart broke for Mrs. Swanson. What an awful thing to have mixed with the grief of the loss of your child, the knowledge someone didn't cherish her.

Blair and I discussed pleasanter topics for another twenty minutes. I caught her up on the production, and the goings-on of several members of the cast and crew, the folks who had been with the theater, and therefore Gigi, from the beginning.

She gave me a warm embrace when she left. Blair's parting words weren't about the murder case, but a plea to protect Gigi's legacy.

"I frankly don't care what Whitney does with the decorating business. That's just paint and fabric. Gigi worked hard at her career, but she put her heart into the theater. It was all about helping people realize their talents. Please don't let it be another loss."

By the end of the afternoon, I would wonder if Blair had a special power like Agnes, but in getting psychic vibes from the living, not the dead.

Chapter Thirty-Three

A while after Blair left, I walked to All Things for a surprise white-glove inspection of the staff. In other words, I needed to get out of the house for a few breaths of fresh air and the quality thinking time walking provided me.

The shop's mid-afternoon business was in a lull. There were a couple of customers perusing the hand-made quilts on the second floor and my weekend manager was helping a young man select chocolates at the candy counter. I had one foot on the stairs when a woman stepped away from the display of animal woodcarvings. It was not Julia Rogan.

"Veronica! What a treat!" With four strides Donna Townsend was in front of me, kissing my cheek and scenting the air with her oceanic perfume.

"Wonderful to see you, Donna."

"You have such lovely things here. This is the place to shop when you need *the* perfect gift. Or just want to browse and calm your mind for a bit."

I thanked her and put on a grin that kept me from making a snarky comment. I let them fly in my mind: "For whom do you not want to purchase the perfect gift?" and "We appreciate the 'just looking' shopper about as much as we enjoy having the flu for two weeks." That was too sarcastic—browsers often make impulse buys, which we love.

Donna gave my hand a squeeze. "Do you have time for a drink?"

It was only three o'clock and the tea I shared with Blair (I drank a second mug after she left) was still sloshing around in my stomach, but I said yes. I can spot a bad actor a mile away; Donna's exuberance told me she wasn't here satisfying a shopping itch. She came to All Things to see me.

My hope was that it wasn't to grill me on my visit to Julia Rogan.

Though Donna and I were only having drinks, Dan Miller escorted us to the restaurant's best table on a winter's afternoon: a cozy table for two beside the fire snapping in the eponymous hearth.

Donna took a sip from her dry martini and eyed me over the glass's rim. "I'm so pleased you'll be a part of our gala performance, Veronica. What a brilliant idea Gigi had to cast you."

"Thank you. I'm thankful for the invitation. It's felt good to exercise my acting muscles."

"How would you like to do that on a regular basis?"

"I suppose I'd have that opportunity with the BCT." What was she getting at? I wondered.

"I mean acting with other professional actors in more polished productions."

Oh boy, did I want to kick Donna under the table.

"I'm quite content with the talent I'm working with now and the high standards everyone associated with the BCT brings to productions."

"Of course you are. But with Gigi's passing, I think this is a good time to make a change for the better. I want to fold the BCT into the club and open a dinner theater for the enjoyment of both members and non-members."

"A dinner theater?"

"It's not too cheesy, is it?" Donna's grin was crooked; she was very proud of her idea.

"As long as you don't serve fettuccine Alfredo."

Donna's laughter lasted several seconds. She lifted her glass in a toast to my quip. "I'll be sure to tell the chef."

"Why dinner theater?"

"I've always loved it. Dinner theater offers couples, families, and friends a wonderful evening out. Dinner and a show, all in one place. And we can do special events, too. Shows for corporate retreats. School trips. Tourist groups." She took a drink. "We'd put on classic shows and newer productions that are wowing audiences on Broadway, with experienced directors and a mix of regional professional actors."

"What about the local amateur actors who shine in the BCT's shows? And all the volunteers who work so hard on the productions?"

"There would be a place for them. The actors could play supporting roles and there would be plenty of behind-the-scenes work for the backstage people."

I envisioned BCT veterans Jerome, Iris, and Peter in no-name roles in one of Donna's productions. The thought made me want to tear her hair out. "You're cutting the community out of community theater."

Donna's sigh sounded like one of a parent trying to explain to a toddler why he couldn't put his little sister in the dishwasher. "I think a dinner theater would combine the best of both worlds. You know the BCT struggles with fundraising. A dinner theater would provide steady funding for productions and attract a larger, broader audience."

"So that heartwarming support you gave us last week was just a crock. This is all about making money."

Donna's expression tightened. "Townsend's has lost a lot of money thanks to our generosity to the BCT. On any given night, we could have earned at least five times what a production earned in ticket sales. We should have received a percentage of the take. It was foolish of Zach to let Gigi have the barn and cottage rent-free. Foolish."

Donna finished her drink and pressed her lips together, giving me the impression she regretted her snappy remark.

I didn't point out the barn was a storage area for the club's maintenance equipment before the BCT started its run there. Nor did I remind Donna it was Gigi's idea to turn the old building into an event venue, a suggestion that brought the club a six-figure revenue (maybe even seven) each year. The image in my mind at the moment was of Gigi wiping away tears after her pre-rehearsal meeting with Donna.

"Did you discuss this plan with Gigi?"

Donna's eyebrows shot up and she hesitated. Did my question simply startle her or was Donna taking a moment to consider whether to lie or give me an honest answer?

She turned her head and stared at the fire. "It's something I have been contemplating for a while, but no. I had not discussed it with Gigi."

Veracity of the statement to be determined.

"Would she have had a role in the dinner theater? Artistic director?"

"Absolutely! She would have been integral to the dinner theater. If she wanted. She and Zach were starting to talk babies, so I'm not sure if she would have had time for her design career, theater work, and a growing family."

I doubted Gigi would have wanted a role in Donna's plan, new baby or not (I wondered if Gigi and Zach were really considering starting a family). Gigi loved the *community* theater she founded and wouldn't ditch it for productions squeezed in between the appetizer and dessert.

"Why are you telling me this, Donna?"

"I'd appreciate your support in convincing everyone at the BCT this is their best bet for a secure, bright future. It would be better if we don't have a war over this, though I know the trustees will side with me. They all possess good business sense."

"I will not participate in the dissolution of the theater. It would be traitorous."

"I won't present my plan until *Blithe Spirit*'s run is completed." Donna's tone was that of a cool businesswoman. "That will give you time to rethink your opposition. I know the gala will be a huge success and will convince everyone that a dinner theater in Barton will benefit us all."

I left the Hearth with renewed consideration for a niggling question. Was Gigi's notion to sever the BCT's ties with Townsend's because she was going to leave Zach or because her mother-in-law was about to stage a hostile takeover?

Chapter Thirty-Four

"She's the stereotypical mother-in-law. Supportive and generous to your face, then she undermines all you've done the moment you turn your back."

"I have a wonderful mother-in-law." Carol's voice filled my family room. I was using my cell's speaker to talk with my friend, who was driving home after a busy day at her flower shop.

"It's so unseemly that Donna is planning this now. Plotting to wrest control of Gigi's theater mere days after her funeral."

"She's like Lady Macbeth."

"Do not mention the Scottish play! It's bad luck!"

"I thought it was only bad luck if you say it in a theater?"

"In light of the circumstances, the prohibition extends to all of Barton."

Carol let out an amused huff. "Donna could sincerely be worried about preserving Gigi's legacy. Maybe she doesn't trust anyone else to do it."

"It's all about profit motive, my friend." I stared at the squares of sage, starfish orange, blue blush, and periwinkle paint I had brushed on the wall next to the television.

"Does Donna have an alibi? Do you know where she was the morning Gigi was killed?"

I repeated what Heather had told Sophie and me. "She had breakfast at the club with a friend."

Carol was quiet for a moment. "Do you think Gigi told Donna or Zach about Kenny Pangborn's embezzlement? Donna could have concerns about financial mismanagement and want to put the sound organization of Townsend's behind the theater."

"I understand your point, but if Donna is painting the whole team as incompetent, she's wrong." Speaking of paint, I gave the starfish orange two thumbs' down. It was too close to the color my soap character had on her living room walls in the late 1970s.

"Why don't you put this all out of your mind until you're done with *Blithe Spirit*? Then you can focus fully on fighting Donna."

I had a sudden inspiration. "Maybe I should tell my theater pals and suggest we cancel the benefit performance."

"What would that accomplish?"

"Donna wouldn't be able to use it as evidence in her case for a dinner theater. Why should we participate in our own demise?"

"Don't you think you would all look like wretches for boycotting a fundraiser in honor of your friend?"

I was quiet for a minute. "I suppose it would be a dumb move."

"And it wouldn't stop Donna from steamrolling the BCT."

I ended the call thankful I had Carol to confer with on Donna's "steamrolling." Despite my "light bulb" idea about thwarting the dinner theater, I would not share details of Donna's dinner theater plans with my BCT friends. Sophie would lead the freak out and not only would the gala benefit be in danger of cancellation, but I feared *Blithe Spirit*'s entire run would be placed in jeopardy. We'd need the calm Bret plus a UN team of mediators to broker a peace deal and save the production.

And a gallon of the blue blush paint. It was very soothing.

Chapter Thirty-Five

"One hundred and fifty thousand."

"Huh?"

"The amount of the insurance policy Whitney Roth had on Gigi Swanson," Myrtle explained.

That was Myrtle's greeting when Mark and I arrived for the Saturday night canasta game. The Griffins and Sandy were in the dining room, listening to Dotsie's account of her horse's bout with seasonal affective disorder.

"Whitney and Gigi had a cross-purchase plan," Myrtle added. "Whitney bought life insurance on Gigi and named herself as the beneficiary. And Gigi did the same."

"How did you get this information?" I asked, handing Mark my coat to hang in the closet. "You told me you weren't Gigi's and Whitney's agent."

"I'm not. But I know who is. An old pal I used to work with."

So much for agent/client confidentiality in the local insurance business. Not that I minded. "Thanks, Myrtle. Did your old pal tell you if Whitney has made a claim for the money?"

"She did. On Monday."

"Was it paid out?" Mark asked.

Myrtle gave us a coy smile. "No. My friend refuses to do so until Gigi's murderer is caught."

"What was Whitney's reaction?" I suddenly was hanging on Myrtle's every word. I noticed the chatter in the dining room had ceased.

"A full-throated hissy fit over the gall my friend had to imply

Whitney was a murder suspect." Myrtle turned toward the entry into the dining room. "Merv and Sam are watching the Rangers game in the family room, Mark. Grab yourself a beer from the fridge and join them."

"Enjoy the canasta." Mark started down the hall to the kitchen.

"A hundred and fifty grand," I murmured, following Myrtle into the dining room.

"One hundred to buy out Gigi's share in the business and fifty thousand to keep it going." Myrtle handed me a glass of Seven and Seven from the tray on the sideboard.

"That sounds like a motive for murder," Ella said.

I took a seat at the end of the table, next to Dotsie and across from Sandy, my playing partner.

"Especially if she was worried about the fallout from Gigi and Zach's divorce," Sandy said.

I took a taste of my drink and popped a few cashews in my mouth from the bowl on the table. Munching on the nuts, I considered another angle on the insurance policy.

"I can smell the smoke from the gears turning in your brain," Dotsie said. "Are you thinking about how you can nail the duplicitous designer?"

"No. I'm thinking about what Sam told me last week. He said there's a rumor that Zach is prepping a run for the county legislature and he'll probably self-finance his campaign. What if he killed Gigi for the insurance buyout money to fund his political run?"

"That would be a nice twist," Myrtle said. "He'd get the hundred thousand from her business plus the money from her personal life insurance policy."

"Why would he need the insurance money? He has plenty from the club." Sandy's tone held a tinge of disgust.

"Maybe he doesn't have access to all that money," Ella said.

"A divorce would have added to his financial burden," Madeline added.

"I wonder if they had an infidelity clause." Dotsie plucked a few cashews from the bowl. "Can you get a sneaky peek at the prenup, Myrt?"

"No. I *cannot* get a *sneaky peek*. You really think a Townsend lawyer would pull it out of the vault and let me have a look?" Myrtle riffle-shuffled the playing cards.

Sandy caught me staring at my drink. "What are you thinking, Veronica?"

I snapped out of my trance. "About this morning." I related Agnes's office and barn visit. "Zach showed up when we were behind the barn. He practically parked over the spot where Gigi died."

"Was he emotional?" Sandy asked.

"No. He was very calm."

Sandy's expression was thoughtful. "You'd think if he's guilty, he'd be shifty-eyed and nervous. And if he's innocent, he'd be distraught over being where his wife was shot dead."

I nodded. "That's what's bothering me."

"Remember," said Myrtle, "Zach's a budding politician. Not a one has a conscience. Politicians never show remorse or regret, so you can't judge this guy by the face he puts on." She dealt the cards.

Dotsie fanned her cards in her hand. "So Zach is either a grieving widower or a cold-blooded killer. Time will tell which he is."

I picked up my cards and glanced over them. "I just wish time would hurry up and answer the question."

Chapter Thirty-Six

January's days faded and soon we entered February. My responsibilities at All Things consumed my days, and rehearsals for *Blithe Spirit* kept me busy at nights. There were no breakthroughs in the murder case and I didn't learn anything more to pass along to Tracey. In late January, Sophie lowered the boom on the cast, ordering us "off-book," meaning we would no longer reference our scripts during rehearsal. Performing from memory struck fear in all our hearts, my own included, and led to several moments of uncomfortable silences, stutters, and salty utterances that were definitely not in the original text.

At the shop, our January lull soon turned into a bustle with the approach of the holiday of hearts. February fourteenth fell on a weekday, giving Mark and me little time for celebration thanks to our work responsibilities. He had a breathtaking bouquet of red, white, and pink roses delivered to me at All Things and that evening I gave him three bottles of his favorite merlot. We had a quick dinner at the Hearth before I hurried off to rehearsal, and then on the Friday evening we enjoyed a longer, more romantic meal at Giacinta's, Barton's excellent Italian restaurant.

We capped off the week of love with a Saturday night dinner at Townsend's. I wanted to take advantage of Wayne's invitation sooner rather than later. I had a simple philosophy. Why delay a free meal or a sleuthing opportunity?

Townsend's reminded me of a piece of silver, stashed in a cabinet for months, and then brought out, polished and buffed, and put on proud display. A soft yellow glow emanated from every first floor window. The parking lot was at full capacity, keeping the two valets busy. A dusting of snow coated the azaleas along the front of the building, adding to the charm of the white lights strung around the manicured bushes. It wasn't just the club that glimmered; on our way in I spotted a few women wrapped in fur coats and sparkling with diamond earrings and necklaces.

"I think I should be wearing a tux," Mark said. "And that I should have given my last paycheck to Tiffany's."

"You're the most handsome man here," I replied. That was no appeasing, throwaway line. In his black suit, white dress shirt, and silver silk tie, Mark was super hot. "No need for a tuxedo. And I dazzle on my own."

Inside, the controlled hustle of activity, melody of diners' voices, and muffled beats of disco music from a wedding reception in the banquet room pumped my adrenaline. Zach stood in the entry hall, giving each newcomer a warm welcome. Surprised, I did a quick study of his face for a sign of grief or regret. His expression was unreadable. No one would have criticized him if he had taken the holiday weekend off and hidden at home, with a six-pack or three of beer, a large order of pizza, and an all-sports cable television package. Here he was, though, a new widower, hosting Valentine celebrations. I guessed this was the country club version of "the show must go on."

"I'm glad you're taking advantage of Dad's invitation, Veronica," he said after giving my hand a firm squeeze. "It's a pleasure to have you join us this evening."

"We thank you for the opportunity to see Townsend's in action. The club's beautiful."

After a couple of minutes of small talk, Zach's lips formed a mischievous smile. "Any more meetings with the medium?"

I couldn't tell if the question was a tease or a taunt. "No. I've completed my research."

"Good. I think people who claim to speak with the dead are

dangerous. They give false hope to people at their most vulnerable."

"I agree. It's ironic, though, how Gigi recommended I meet with Agnes. Don't you think?"

"For research only, I'm sure. Gigi didn't believe in that nonsense, either." He gestured to the hostess standing in the west wing's corridor. "Enjoy your evening."

A cool dismissal cloaked in a warm welcome.

We followed the hostess to the dining room at the back of the club. The room was at full occupancy, with young lovers whispering over their place settings, older couples celebrating another year of bliss, and large groups enjoying the mid-winter festivity with glee. A fire kindled in the hearth and the several chandeliers overhead glinted off each table's crystal and china. The soft chords of classical music topped off the elegant atmosphere.

After the attention-absorbing reading of the menu and placement of our orders, Mark and I sat back, enjoyed our table by the window, and toasted ourselves. Mark clinked his glass of Manhattan against my whiskey sour, gazed into my eyes, and said, "For about the fifth time this week, to us." After swallowing his first sip, he added, "I feel I should have memorized a love poem to recite to you, but an English professor I'm not."

"Don't sweat it. I thank you for not reciting the Gettysburg Address."

I took a discreet survey of the room, checking out my fellow diners. I recognized several people who were Saint Augustine's parishioners and a few more who shopped at All Things.

I soon spied Donna and Wayne sitting with a couple at a table in the center of the room. Wayne, noticing me, tipped his head and whispered in Donna's ear. The couple stood, said what I assumed was "excuse us" to their dining companions, and headed toward our table.

"Townsends coming our way," I said from the corner of my mouth.

"Veronica, I'm thrilled you could join us," Donna said before she reached our table.

After she gave me an air kiss, Wayne moved in for a solid peck on the cheek. "Indeed. I'm glad you accepted my invitation."

I introduced Mark and we both expressed our gratitude for the temporary inclusion on the members' list (not in those exact words, of course).

"I hope it will be the first of many nights," Wayne said. "If not as a member, than as a permanent part of the BCT. I want to brag we have an Emmy winner in the family."

I forced a laugh and glanced at Donna, who avoided my look. Was Wayne not on board with her dinner theater dream?

The couple wished us a good evening and returned to their table. Mark's gaze followed them, his brow making a slight ascent when he noted the couple with the Townsends.

"They're dining with Rebecca Wakefield and her husband."

It took me a few seconds to place Rebecca's name with her position. "She's the head of the teachers' union, right?"

"Yes."

"Do you think they're talking about the cost of school books? I've heard book prices are ten times what they were when we last wore school uniforms. Remember those plaid skirts we girls had to wear? With maroon knee-high socks? You guys got off easy with your nice navy blue sweaters and ties."

"I liked those skirts. Particularly when the gals shortened them an inch or two." Mark winked and he took another drink of his Manhattan.

"Yeah, well. Let's have this conversation at the end of the evening. Do you think they're negotiating the next union contract or discussing the weather? Or maybe they're gossiping about all the other county union leaders."

"Maybe all of the above. But let's not talk about them. Happy Valentine's Day, Veronica."

Mark held his glass across the table, soliciting a second "cheers" from me. I obliged and, as far as I was concerned, we were the only two people in the room.

On my way out of the ladies' room after a post-dinner visit, the sound of Frank Sinatra singing "The Way You Look Tonight" drew me down the hall to the wedding reception in the banquet room. I admired the contrasting décor. Tables were swathed in red clothes and topped with all things white: china, roses, and flickering votive candles. The glimmering chandeliers suggested beams of moonlight while a spotlight lit the dance floor in front of the stage, where a DJ had set up his equipment. I couldn't help swaying to one of my favorite Sinatra standards and humming a few additional bars when the song ended.

"Are you crashing this wedding, lady?"

My shoulders twitched; I turned and found Bret standing behind me. His smile indicated he wouldn't call security to escort me from the premises.

"I can never resist a romantic song."

"Me neither."

"It's beautiful." I tipped my head at the room. "You did a wonderful job."

Bret gave a modest shrug. "It was the bride's vision. I just brought it to life."

"Well done." I admired the dance moves of the bride and groom to "Stayin' Alive." "They're good. Very coordinated."

"They took six weeks of lessons," he said, amused.

We observed the party in companionable silence for a minute or two. I spotted Heather across the floor, serving dessert, and returned her smile of recognition.

When the song ended, I asked Bret, "Are you enjoying your job here?"

"I am. I love it. I wasn't looking to leave my job in Niskayuna, but I figured I'd at least hear what Donna had to offer when she called. I'm glad I did."

"What do you mean? You didn't apply for the job?"

Bret gave me a bashful grin. "I didn't. Donna called and asked if I'd be interested in the job."

"Wow. No job application or resume submission? Just an out-of-the-blue call?"

"It wasn't a total surprise. I worked here in high school, a caddie by day and busboy by night. I kept in touch with the family."

"Like they say. It's not what you know, it's who you know."

"It's all about the network." Bret gave me a congenial smile and turned his attention back to the reception.

"I better get back to my table before my hot date eats my dessert."

I walked back down the hall at a slow pace so I could process Bret's tidbit (I knew my hot date wouldn't dare touch my dessert). I recalled Sam Jenkins's gossip about Zach running for the county legislature.

Was Bret the beneficiary of a long-held friendship or did Donna hire him to minimize her son's female temptations? Was she trying to save Zach's nascent political career or his marriage?

I turned the corner and moved toward the entry hall, debating whether Donna's behavior was Machiavellian or maternal. I spotted Donna and Rebecca step into the foyer from the passage leading to the dining room and start up the stairs.

Where were those two going? Did Rebecca have a zipper emergency and Donna was escorting her to the safety pin stash in her office? Were they heading off for some private girl talk? Every move Donna made intrigued me, from her visit with Julia to Bret's hiring; what action would she take with the union lady?

I hurried to the stairs and was up them in a flash, glancing over my shoulder a couple of times to make sure no one observed my stealth moves. I didn't want anyone reporting to management they saw a woman in a red wrap dress charging up the stairs.

I stepped into the upper corridor, which stretched the length of the building. A thick moss green carpet muffled my footsteps. As on the first floor, candle-style sconces hung on the walls, emitting soft light. The paintings were of Adirondack landscapes and not portraits of the estate's original owners. One of the twelve dark hardwood doors along the hall was open, a beam from the office light reaching the corridor. I crept toward it, staying close to the wall, as if it would conceal me if Donna and Rebecca suddenly emerged from the room.

Standing inches from the door, I held my breath and wondered at the silence coming from the room. After a few seconds of continued quiet, I took the bold move of walking by the door. I took three steps, turning my head in a nonchalant move for a glance into the office.

There was no one in the room.

I let out a soft groan and went back to the landing. I stood a few feet from the stairs, deciding my next move. Should I sneak along the other wing with the hope I could overhear Donna and Rebecca's confab through the door?

Wayne's appearance at the top of the stairs ended my short surveillance stint. "Veronica!" To my relief, he appeared delighted to see me.

"My apologies for taking a self-tour. I've always loved this grand old mansion and wanted a peek at the second floor."

Wayne's expression didn't convey disbelief in my lie. "You're most welcome, though all you'll see up here these days is desk furniture and a printer that constantly jams. I'm up here to see what Donna and Rebecca have gotten themselves into. Our coffee and dessert have been served and I don't want theirs to get cold. Did you happen—"

A door at the end of the hall swung open and Donna and Rebecca emerged from the office.

"There you are!" Wayne said, laughing.

"I was showing Rebecca some of our New Year's Eve party photos on my computer." Party photos my rear end, I thought, though I did give Donna credit for the fib's smooth delivery. "Hello, Veronica." Donna put on the phoniest smile I had seen since the last Daytime Emmy Awards ceremony I had attended. Never believe the "It's an honor just to be nominated," nonsense the losers spout after the announcement of the winners.

"I was just checking out the architecture."

Before Donna could add a comment to the odd look she gave me, Wayne waved us down the stairs, trailing behind while maintaining a running commentary about said New Year's party. I kept my lips frozen in a smile so tight my cheek muscles began to ache.

"Enjoy the rest of your evening," Donna said when we neared their table.

I mumbled a reciprocal wish and let my face collapse into one big sag of flesh the moment my back was turned and I was headed for my seat by the window.

"What's wrong?" Mark asked.

"I've been to the Twilight Zone."

Our server swooped in with coffee and dessert. I thanked him, distracted by my escorts' settling at their table. I watched Rebecca slip her purse strap from her shoulder, wrapped it around the black bag, and set it against the back of her chair before sitting.

"The hand that rocks the cradle rules the world. Listen to this." I told Mark about my conversation with Bret and of Donna and Rebecca's visit to the second floor. When I finished, I dug into my slice of red velvet cake and savored its rich flavor.

"Hmm." Mark enjoyed a chunk of vanilla ice cream-soaked apple pie. "I think you're right. Sounds like Donna made a deliberate move to make sure her son didn't have another workplace flirtation. If Zach really enters the race for the legislature, Donna started early clearing his life of anything that might smell of scandal."

My attention returned to the Townsend/Wakefield table. Were the Townsends conducting another chess move in their son's career? Was this Saturday night meal more than a social get-together? With politicians, was there even such a thing?

Donna tilted her head back, laughing, in reaction to something Wayne said. She was proving herself an adept behind-the-scenes player. A terrific political wife transforming into a loving political mom. I would not be surprised if her dinner theater plan included a directing role for herself.

Tracey and I had joked about an *All About Eve* situation between Gigi and Sophie. Did we get the pairing wrong? Was there a power struggle between Gigi and Donna over the theater, with a dash of in-law trouble thrown in to push the duo to a tragic confrontation?

I took one last look at my hosts' table and realized I had caught Wayne in a lie. There were no coffee cups on the table, nor were there cake plates.

So what was Wayne's reason for his trip upstairs? Did he follow me? Or was he going to check on the "New Year's Eve photographs?"

Chapter Thirty-Seven

Mark called Tuesday afternoon with the breaking news. I was in my office, proofreading an ad we were going to place in an Adirondack guide.

"Zach's candidacy is official. He announced it an hour ago."

"Who knew Sam's guys had all the hot gossip first." I turned on my cell phone's speaker, opened Google on my laptop, and typed in the *Chronicle's* web address. Zach's announcement of his run for the county legislature was the headline news on the paper's website.

"Gun control is the centerpiece of his platform," Mark said. "A rather convenient issue for him to advocate, not to be cynical."

"I bet there are many more in the county who'll have the same impression when they hear this announcement."

"A reporter asked him about Gigi's murder. 'Are you a suspect in your wife's death' are the exact words."

"Good!"

"Zach, of course, didn't give a direct answer. All he said was he's passed a polygraph."

I stared at the photograph accompanying the article. Zach stood at a podium in front of the barn's stage, Donna and Wayne at his side. I closed my eyes and considered the symbolism of the setting. Was Zach sending a subliminal message that Gigi approved his political run? Did he want the stage in the background to play on the sympathies of the news audience? Or was the barn simply the most spacious area to accommodate the crowd? The article did state there were club members, employees, and a number of press and local officials in attendance.

"It's interesting Zach's not standing on the stage," I said.

"Humility, real or posed. Zach wants to show he's with the people and for the people by not standing above them."

"You're so smart."

"Notice who's in the group with him?"

I glanced at the faces of the several people surrounding the Townsends and found Rebecca Wakefield among them.

"So did Wayne and Donna secure the teacher's union support at dinner Saturday night? Was the prime rib a bribe, or a thank you in advance?"

Mark chuckled. "Who's the cynic now?"

"You know, I think Rebecca may have had the salmon. Not much of a reward for her powerful union's support. Is she in the Townsends' pocket, or they in hers?"

"I think it's more of an arrangement of mutual benefit."

"An 'I'll give you money and you'll pass legislation that favors my people' type relationship." I looked over the rest of the assembled crowd. A village councilman. The highway commissioner. An assemblywoman. I had seen them all at Gigi's funeral and the lunch at the club. "If Zach wins . . ."

"I'm sure he will, unless he's arrested for Gigi's murder."

I scrolled to the comments section below the article. Several readers had already posted remarks. Zach's announcement scandalized some, evident from the *He killed his wife!* and *Did he kill his wife so he could have a campaign issue?* messages written under anonymous tags. Supporters relied on the usual "innocent until proven guilty" defense.

I scanned through the article again for information I missed in my first read through. "Donna has lined up all her ducks in a row. Supporting Julia's new business. Hiring a man to replace her. And planting the seeds for a new arm of the family business when she assumes the reins." I returned to the top of the page and the group photo. "I wonder if Gigi was a wrench in all these plans."

Mark made a final observation. "You know who's not mentioned in the article, or in the photo? Gigi's family. Neither her parents nor her sister was there. Is it still too painful for them to go to the club, or do they not support Zach? You would think they would be behind him in his stance on gun control."

"I wonder if they will be furious Zach's using Gigi's death as a campaign issue. I'm not surprised the Swansons weren't at the announcement. I don't think they will support Zach until they're certain he didn't kill their daughter."

I read the article again after I got off the phone with Mark and then closed the browser. Would I vote for Zach? With the election eight months off, who knew if he would still be in the race in November. A Townsend victory would install Donna in the club's management seat and mark the end of the BCT.

I said a prayer Zach wouldn't run unopposed.

Chapter Thirty-Eight

I was at my kitchen table eating Cheerios, drinking my first cup of coffee of the day, and reading the *Chronicle* article on Zach's announcement in Wednesday's print edition. An item in the *Police Beat* section on the opposite page caught my attention.

I sucked in my breath at the news of Kenny Pangborn's arrest Monday night in Penny Woods on charges of domestic disturbance and gun possession.

I blurted an expression my father often used. "Holy Moses and Andy!"

Despite Tracey's insistence Kenny had an alibi, I had lingering doubts about him, though I had not pursued my suspicions since our driveway encounter.

I dropped my spoon in the cereal bowl, sending a splash of milk onto the table. I scrambled from the chair and raced into the living room where I had left my cell phone on top of my coat.

Tracey didn't answer her phone, forcing me to blurt a message at rapid speed. "Did you know Kenny Pangborn was arrested Monday? Penny Woods. Domestic disturbance. And gun possession! Call me!"

I went back to my breakfast and the newspaper. What an odd, coincidental juxtaposition of Kenny's and Zach's news. Was one guilty of murdering the other's wife?

I was on my short walk to All Things when Tracey called.

"What'd Kenny do?" I asked without even a good morning to the policewoman.

"Pangborn paid an uninvited, unannounced visit to his estranged wife's home. They'd had a very heated custody hearing Monday morning. Mara Pangborn went really hard against him for his excessive drinking. Pangborn proved her point by downing a bottle of Jack Daniels on the way to her house that night. The neighbors across the street heard him shouting and pounding on the front door and called the police. They found an unloaded gun in Pangborn's car. He doesn't have a permit for it."

"Could it be the gun used to kill Gigi?" I neared the alley and made the daily move of shoving my hand into my coat pocket and wrapping my gloved fingers around my keychain. I'd need it for the stockroom door if I were the first arrival at All Things.

"No. I've told you—"

"Well, if Kenny has one gun, he probably—"

Tracey let out a sigh that shook the heavens. "Veronica, listen to me. And you are not to repeat this *to anyone.*"

I stopped in the alley. I was about to receive confidential police information! I almost shouted at the birds to stop their boisterous chirping. "I'm all ears."

"Pangborn's sister-in-law provided him an alibi for the murder."

"His sister-in-law? She could have lied—"

Tracey laughed. "She has no interest in helping Pangborn. The morning of the murder, Pangborn made another unscheduled call at Mara's house to see his son. It wasn't his weekend for a visit, but Pangborn wanted to take Josh with him to the hardware store to hang out for the day. The sister-in-law was there watching the boy while Mara was at the dentist. She said Pangborn arrived a few minutes after Mara left at ten thirty."

"Which means, if he left the Hearth around ten fifteen—"

"And he arrived in Penny Woods just after ten thirty, he had no time to stop at the barn on his way out of Barton."

"How long was Kenny at the house?"

"He griped to the sister-in-law for ten minutes. Not enough time for him to get back to Barton, kill Gigi, and get out of the way before you and Sophie arrived."

"Well."

"Yes. When Ron interviewed him last month, Pangborn had the good sense to tell him about the visit. I guessed he'd rather face an angry estranged wife and family court judge than be a suspect in a murder."

"So there was no ATM receipt?"

"No. Pangborn's situation with his wife is his personal business. The Barton PD isn't involved in the matter at all, so we kept it quiet. In the same way I promised Nate we would keep quiet about Pangborn's embezzlement."

"A leak-proof department in action."

"If you say anything, Veronica—"

"What's that clanging noise? Oh no, the key to my mouth's Kenny Pangborn compartment just went down the sewer."

Tracey laughed. "Excellent. Have a nice day, Veronica."

I used the key to gain entry into the stockroom. Shoving my cell in the pocket along with the keychain, I exhaled with the relief of finally removing Kenny from the suspect list. I should have given Tracey my complete trust the moment she told me he had an alibi and not cared what it was, but his unscheduled visit to *my* house left me doubting the tale of the ATM receipt.

I flipped the lights on in the shop and walked across the floor to the stairs. "I hope Kenny gets help for his drinking and anger issues."

Those would be my last words on the subject of Kenny Pangborn.

Chapter Thirty-Nine

The sight of Dusanka's determined charge across Carlisle's parking lot on Thursday afternoon snapped me from my three o'clock day dream of Mark and me on a private Turks and Caicos beach, enjoying the fifty-something version of spring break. I had been shelving copies of a new Adirondack hiking trails guide, a task that allowed for entertaining such fantasies.

Dusanka crossed Sycamore, her head jerking left, right, and left before she fixed her attention on All Things' side window, where I stood. I waved when our gazes met. Dusanka mouthed a few words and picked up her pace.

I don't excel at lip reading. She could have said anything from "Let's have coffee" to "I have to sew a wedding dress for a dog."

I moved to meet her at the door. "What's up?"

"She is here! The woman I saw at the theater office!"

So much for the jolt of coffee and amusement of canine nuptials. "At the salon?"

Dusanka wrapped her fingers around my wrist and tugged me outside. "Yes! I believe it is her. She is looking at wedding gowns."

I felt a burst of adrenaline. Could Dotsie's theory about a bridezilla killer on the loose be correct? She'd never stop bragging if one of her conspiracy theories proved true.

I marched in step with Dusanka across Sycamore, through the salon's lot, and into the building's rear entrance.

"I came up to the pantry for a cup of coffee. A *third* cup. I never have three cups of coffee, but today I am tired. I had a lot of sewing yesterday and my eyes are still weary. I passed the showroom and I saw the woman talking with the sales manager. I have not called the police. I'm sure it is her, but not fully. I thought you should see her first. I thought you might know her from your detective work."

I followed Dusanka past the tiny staff pantry and the wall-mounted rack where they hung their coats. My pulse quickened at the first glimpse of an ivory silk corset in the largest of the salon's showrooms.

A woman stood at the far side of the room, her back to us. A brunette, she was taking a thorough look at every dress on the rack.

"That is her," Dusanka whispered in my ear.

"Her" turned around and met my stare.

Julia Rogan.

"Ms. Walsh?"

"Hi, Julia." I walked over to her, Dusanka close on my heels. My next line came out in a matter-of-fact delivery. "You were at the BCT office the morning Gigi was killed."

Julia pressed her lips together, blushed, and moved her glance to the door. Was she going to make a run for it? I slid my foot a few inches across the rug, ready to trip her if she made a sudden dash for the exit.

"I was there to buy tickets." Her voice was soft but insistent.

"Then why lie about it? You said you hadn't been to Barton since leaving your job at the club."

"Should I call the police?" Dusanka asked, nervous.

"No!" Julia's eyes grew wide with fear. "Please. I can explain."

"It's okay, Dusanka." Was it? My head told me I should call Tracey and make Julia explain her actions; my heart said I should hear her out first.

"I was—"

"Julia, what do you think of this dress?" We all spun on our heels to see a woman charge into the room. She wore a ball gown style wedding dress that gave the illusion of swallowing the slim woman whole. Jeweled material clung to her torso while the miles of fabric in the skirt would have kept wedding guests at three-arms' length. Her dark hair draped over her shoulders and down to the gown's sweetheart neckline. "Mom likes it but I think it's too Cinderella-ish. I *do not* want a Disney wedding. I mean, look at the bow in the back." She turned and gestured to the offending ruffle sewn at the waistline. I want something more slinky and sexy."

The woman paused for a breath and a suspicious glance at Julia. "What are you doing? Haven't you picked any dresses for me? Who are these people? You know, I'm paying you for this time. You're here to help *me*."

Dusanka took charge. "I am Dusanka, the salon seamstress. I'm helping Julia find the perfect dress for you." She scampered to the rack, selected two gowns, and held them up for the woman's inspection. "I think this one might fulfill all your dreams." She extended her left arm to show a beaded sheath dress. "Add a glimmering silver sash and you're soon-to-be husband will faint from your beauty."

The woman assessed the dress with a critical eye. "That. Is. Gorgeous." She bestowed on Dusanka a deigning smile. "Thank you, Dusanka." She pronounced the name incorrectly, with a short "a" instead of an elegant, long sound.

"She's not an instant cup of coffee," I said under my breath.

"Julia, carry that dress to the changing room for me."

The monster bride charged out of the room, snapping "Get off" at her mother when the probably long-suffering woman accidentally stepped on the gown's train.

Julia took the two dresses from Dusanka. "You saved my job. Thanks." She looked at me. "I *can* explain. I will. After I finish here."

"All right." I had a mind to visit the dressing room and ask Julia's client to escort her to All Things after the appointment, but the woman scared me.

"You better get a piece of the sale's commission on that dress," I told Dusanka after Julia hustled off with the gowns.

"I think I like it better in my sewing room, helping brides after they pick their dresses."

"I'd hide too if even half your customers are like that woman." I gave my friend a hug and returned to All Things. There would be no more delightful daydreams of skinny-dipping in the Caribbean moonlight. I would be preoccupied with thoughts of the bridezilla's wedding planner.

Chapter Forty

At four thirty, I was arranging a display of Irish-related items for the upcoming Saint Patrick's Day, debating whether I should go back to Carlisle's when Julia, looking timid, walked into All Things.

"I'm sorry I didn't get here sooner. I just finished at Carlisle's."

"Did your client buy the dress Dusanka selected?"

Julia's face beamed. "Yes! She looks spectacular in it. She tried on ten others before deciding, though. And then we had to select a belt, and a veil, and . . . well, you get the idea."

"High maintenance client, to the max."

Julia nodded, her demeanor at ease. "I owe you an explanation. Can I buy you a drink?"

Julia and I placed our beverage orders at the Hearth's bar and claimed a booth. Once she had slipped out of her coat, I asked, "Did you and Zach have an affair? Or should I ask, are you *having* an affair?"

"No." Julia's response was fast and emphatic. "Zach and I did not have an affair."

"A very private lesson on the golf course? Closed-door lunches? It sounds like something happened between the two of you."

My knowledge of her behavior with Zach stunned Julia. "We were discussing Zach's campaign for the legislature."

"Well, I have heard the president discusses policy during his golf games." I put a sarcastic spin on my remark.

I studied her while the bartender set our drinks on the table. Julia's cheeks colored and she avoided making eye contact.

"You didn't have an affair, but something inappropriate went on between the two of you."

Julia took a sip of her vodka and cranberry drink. "Zach and I spent a lot of time together, discussing club business and then his campaign when he decided he was going to run. An attraction developed, but we didn't act on it until one day at their house. Gigi walked in on us making out on the couch. We were brainstorming ideas for his campaign. He wanted me to plan events like fundraising dinners, get-togethers in supporters' homes. We were talking about that over lunch and then we just started kissing."

"Oh yeah, because brainstorming for a political campaign over ham sandwiches really sets a romantic mood."

Maybe I shouldn't have been so snarky. I recalled a scene on *Days and Nights* when my character had a make out session with a hottie twenty years her junior after a five-minute chat about the third-quarter figures. It had been a very profitable third quarter.

However, that was fiction and this was a terrible reality.

"I can imagine Gigi's reaction."

A tear glided down Julia's cheek. "She was furious and humiliated. It is the absolute worst thing I've ever done. I regret it every day. I begged Gigi to forgive me."

She took a gulp of her drink. I noticed her hand trembled.

"Did she?"

"She wouldn't listen. Gigi stopped talking to me. She demanded Donna fire me."

More tears spilled from Julia's eyes. I handed her my cocktail napkin and went to the bar for several more. I watched her for a minute. She was a sorry sight, wiping her cheeks while trying to control her heaving shoulders. I was definitely on Team Gigi, but how I wished she had shown Julia an ounce of mercy. She had obviously forgiven Zach since they were still together at the time of her death.

Don't make assumptions, Veronica, I thought, taking the few

steps back to the booth.

"Thank you." Julia took the handful of napkins and dabbed her nose with one.

That Gigi didn't tell her sister of Zach's infidelity piqued my curiosity. Was her silence with Blair due to a humiliated spirit?

Her eyes dry, Julia fortified herself for the rest of her tale with two mouthfuls from her glass. "When Donna told me Gigi wanted me fired, I threatened to hire a lawyer and sue Townsend's for wrongful termination. Donna backtracked fast when I said I would charge her and Zach with harassment. She offered to help me open my own business."

So the hush money was officially an "investment." "And she made it happen, fast, with an infusion of cash. I saw her walk into your office last month, a couple of minutes after I left. I saw the envelope in her hand."

"Yeah, Donna's an investor. She also gave me a number of names to start building a client list."

I could see Donna's eyes lighting up and almost hear her exhaling with relief at how easy it was escorting Julia from Zach's life.

"Any conditions on her generosity?"

"I had to agree not to bring any clients to the club for a year. And to stay away from Zach and his campaign. I was limited to a small donation to his run."

The ban would expire around the time Zach was, presumably, moving out of his club office and into his new county legislator digs. Interesting.

We were quiet for a minute. I glanced at the bar and saw Whitney sitting at the far end, her arms resting on the bar and her shoulders slumped. The posture of a long, difficult day.

"Why did you go to the theater office the morning of Gigi's death?"

Julia pursed her lips, like a child trying to keep in a secret. "Zach called me the Thursday morning of that week." She let the words linger for a beat. "To say hello and wish me a happy new year."

"That's all?" I didn't conceal my skepticism.

"He said he missed me." To her credit, Julia did nothing to hide her shame. "Zach wanted to get together to talk about events for his campaign."

"What about Donna's ban? Did he know about it?"

"He did. He thought it was stupid. He said he missed me and wanted me to put together a few events for him and told me he'd deal with his mother."

"All right. Did you meet him?"

"I told him I'd meet him for a drink. But we never did."

"Why not?"

"Gigi overheard the conversation. Zach waited until she left the house to call me. But Gigi forgot her cell and went back."

Julia fell silent, drew in a deep breath, and looked toward the bar. I checked on Whitney; she was still sitting by herself, a margarita in front of her. Another troubled soul who needed to confess to an attentive listener? I hoped I had time to fill the role before cutting out for the night's rehearsal (I could always skip the grilled cheese I was going to have at home and have a Hearth burger instead).

"Donna called me the Thursday night. Gigi had told her about the call. She was livid and accused Zach of cheating again. Gigi told Donna she was tired of living with someone she couldn't trust and was going to leave Zach."

Now I knew what Donna and Gigi had talked about before Thursday's rehearsal. At least one of the topics of conversation. Did Gigi summon Donna to the barn to tell her about Zach's contact with Julia, or had Donna gone there to drop her bomb about the dinner theater?

"Donna was furious. She warned me not to call Zach or try to contact him in any way. And if he called me, I was to hang up. I was also to stay away from Gigi."

"But you didn't. You went to see her at the BCT office."

"I wanted to tell Gigi the call meant nothing and assure her nothing would ever happen between Zach and me." Julia's eyes watered. "I considered Gigi a friend. I know *I* ruined our relationship. I apologized to her that morning and promised I'd never talk to Zach again."

"What was Gigi's reaction? Did she offer forgiveness?"

"She was cool, but she did accept my apology." Julia took a hard swallow of her drink. "Gigi said she trusted me more than she trusted Zach. It breaks my heart she died believing that."

"Mine, too."

Laughter from three guys at the bar showed the irony of our conversation during "happy hour." I drank my soda and took a glance at Whitney. She still sat alone, a profile in dejection. She waved at the bartender for another drink.

"Do you have an alibi, Julia?"

"I do. I have phone records and receipts from the ATM, supermarket, and drug store. I met a client at my office at eleven. And the florist two doors down saw me arrive at the office."

"All right."

Julia closed her eyes and let out a sigh a casual observer wouldn't know was an exhalation of relief. "Thank you for listening, Veronica. And for not raking me over the coals."

"You're welcome." I sipped my drink. "What was the real reason for your visit to All Things last month?"

"I really was looking for gift ideas for the Fegans' anniversary party."

"We're still waiting for that order, by the way. It was hard keeping a straight face when you asked how the Townsends were when I knew you had just seen Donna."

"My pathetic attempt to maintain the lie I hadn't talked with any of them since the fall. I worried you suspected me and tried to throw you off the scent. I also hoped you would share what you had learned about the case."

"Like I would tell you. And don't give up your day job. You're no actress. I saw through your act immediately."

Julia allowed a shy smile. "I feel a little better, sharing this with someone. I'm sick about the grief I caused Gigi."

"Do you think Zach killed her?"

"No. Zach would never hurt Gigi." Julia was insistent.

I wasn't so sure. Gigi could have threatened to make his indiscretion with Julia public. Simply leaving him at the beginning of his political career would raise questions and have the press hungry for answers.

"When Donna visited you the day I came to your office, did you tell her I had just been there?"

"I didn't. I knew you weren't really there because of the gala."

"How fast did you figure out I was snooping?"

"Right away. More than your acting reputation precedes you." Julia offered a faint smile. "I didn't dare tell Donna. I didn't want her confronting you, or maybe thinking I had something to do with Gigi's death. She would freak if she knew I was at the office that morning."

"Thanks."

"I told Donna that would be her last payment. I'm done with that family. I thanked her for the support and told her I want to make it on my own from now on. I'm going to start paying her back next month."

"Business is good?"

"Yes. I'm doing well, even without taking clients to Townsend's. I'm permanently banning myself from the club. There are plenty of other venues to patronize."

"Wise choice." I regarded Julia for a moment, bracing for the difficult task I had to assign her. "You need to tell your story to the police."

Julia came close to shedding fresh tears. "I can't! They'll

think I was involved!"

"You said you have receipts and phone records. If you really do, then you have nothing to worry about. You need to tell them about your . . . liaison with Zach. That *might* be helpful to the case."

"They will think I'm accusing Zach of killing Gigi. I don't think he did!"

"If he didn't, there's nothing to fear. You need to go to the police. Right now." I pulled out my cell phone, hoping it would scare the dickens out of Julia. "I'll call Officer Brody and ask her to come here."

Julia reached across the table and grasped my wrist. "Please. Don't call her." She looked at the bar. "Gigi's partner, Whitney Roth, is sitting over there. I don't want her to see me talking with a cop."

I slid across the bench. "Then we'll go to the police station."

Julia spent the next five seconds inhaling a calming breath. "I'll go by myself. I don't want to waste any more of your time."

I took my own five seconds and stared at her, assessing whether I could trust her. I'd let her go on her own, but I'd text Tracey with a heads up Julia was on her way.

Julia departed a few minutes later. I texted Tracey: *Julia Rogan coming to station to talk. Pls confirm arrival.* I almost added *Be ready to issue an APB if she doesn't show.* I finished the last two mouthfuls of my soda and observed Whitney. I considered my options: I could slip by her and avoid an encounter, pony up to the bar and conduct a discreet sleuthing session (in her downcast, possibly tipsy state, Whitney might spill everything except her drink), or sit with her and offer a sympathetic ear of friendship.

I selected the last option. Whitney appeared to have suffered through a bad day and was in need of talking about it. If she mentioned something helpful to the murder investigation, well, I wouldn't ignore it.

Tears pooled in Whitney's eyes when I hoisted myself on the stool beside her. "Veronica! It's so good to see you!" She wrapped an arm around my neck and pulled me against her shoulder. I caught a whiff of tequila.

I extricated myself from the chokehold. "How are you, Whitney?"

"The world is against me, Veronica." Whitney almost submerged her face in her margarita glass.

"I'm so sorry to hear that. Want to talk about it?" I was a sleuth and friend, all rolled into those five words.

"You're a pal." Whitney looped her arm over my shoulder and pulled me close again. "And a client, I dearly hope."

"I'm still looking over my budget."

Whitney whimpered. "If I don't get a client soon, I'm going to be out of business! I won't be able to afford a shingle to hang out!"

"What do you mean? You and Gigi had a long client list."

"Gigi's clients are leaving me in droves. They won't even give me a chance." Whitney thrust her finger in the air, as if jabbing each enemy. "This one decided to hold off on her home renovation. That one doesn't have the money for a redo and her daughter's wedding. So-and-so wants to think about it more before she commits. And Miss Witch of the Northeast outright said she's going to hire another designer!"

I knew I wasn't Miss Witch, and I hoped Whitney didn't think me the "so-and-so."

"I'm sorry." I grabbed a handful of peanuts from a bowl at Whitney's elbow.

"It's not fair." Whitney took an audible slurp from her glass. "They all went with Gigi only because of her in-laws. They all hang together. It's like inbreeding. I'm just as talented as she was."

"Of course you are." I tried putting the reminder of the two ladies who ended up with the same exact living room out of my mind.

"And making matters worse is the insurance woman won't pay out on my cross-purchase policy until the case is closed. As if I killed Gigi!"

Several bar patrons cast curious glances at Whitney. She didn't notice.

"I think that's standard insurance procedure when the death is a homicide."

"That's what the agent said. But I just know she thinks I did it." Whitney didn't speak for a couple of minutes, alternately inhaling her drink and the peanuts. She made a tsk-ing sound. "And Donna won't help me. I asked her to put in a good word for me with her friends and club members and she said this isn't a good time to do that."

"Well, she is grieving—"

"Donna doesn't care. I tried to lock her in for the club decorations for the holidays—"

"Saint Patrick's Day?"

"No. Thanksgiving and Christmas."

"You have to start planning for holidays ten months in advance?" And I thought retail was bad, the way holiday items go on sale weeks before the big day.

"I need a commitment now. Something I can use to attract new clients. Donna said no."

"She probably doesn't want to think about next Christmas right now. And Zach just started his campaign for the legislature."

Whitney waved off my defense. "He won't take my calls. I have to deal with his lawyer. I hope he loses the race." She finished her drink with one gulp. "And I assumed Gigi's clients would stick with me. Out of loyalty. I really thought I'd get some sympathy for losing my business partner."

Her whine left a sour taste in my mouth. "Did you think Gigi's death would translate to more clients for yourself?"

"Of course I didn't!"

I had an urge to tell her she might have garnered more sympathy if she had been a mourner at the post-funeral lunch and not a glad-handing businesswoman scooping up her dead partner's clients. Instead, I needled her for a reaction.

"So the insurance agent thinks you're a suspect. Does that mean you don't have an alibi?" I knew Whitney had told the police she was home the morning Gigi was killed, but I wanted to hear it from her lips.

Whitney's eye-roll gave me the impression she had been asked for an alibi several times. "It was a Saturday morning. I was home, drinking coffee, and brainstorming a client's living room."

Which meant she was flipping through *Architectural Digest* or watching HGTV for the latest in furniture arrangement.

"I don't know why anyone thinks I killed Gigi. I have no motive."

"The business partner is always looked at. Financial trouble is often a reason, or sometimes jealousy."

Whitney didn't respond. She leaned her head against her hand and stared at her empty glass. I prayed she was sober enough to get herself home. I had neither the time nor the desire to be a designated driver.

I remembered Whitney's strong defense of Zach and thought maybe, in light of Donna's abandonment, Whitney's support for the family had crumbled. Gigi hadn't told her sister about catching Zach and Julia in a lip lock, but perhaps Whitney had overheard something in the office. If someone could confirm Gigi was about to leave Zach, the police would have a motive to peg on him.

I said my line, hoping it would cue Whitney. "I heard Gigi and Zach were having problems."

"There was tension between them. I don't know what it was about. Zach called a few times that last week and Gigi snapped at him, saying she was busy or didn't want to talk with him."

"Hmm."

"Gigi had it all. A rich, handsome husband. A great career. The theater, which wasn't such a struggle to keep going thanks to the

Townsends. How she could ever be unhappy . . ."

"Money doesn't buy happiness. A cliché, but true."

"Whatever." Whitney glanced at her cell's screen. "I'm meeting a client in a few minutes. I'm going to the ladies' room to freshen up before she gets here." Whitney slid, somewhat involuntarily, from her stool. "Thanks for listening, Veronica. Give me a call once you've worked out your *budget.*"

I wanted to tell Whitney the clenched-teeth look wasn't attractive. I also thought I should recommend a good tooth brushing (or ten breath mints) be included in her freshening up so she didn't repel yet another client.

"I will, Whitney." I waited for her exit and then asked the bartender, "Can you make sure she drinks a pot of coffee before she leaves?"

"I will, though Whitney usually limits herself to two drinks."

"Usually? Is Whitney a regular?"

"A recent regular. She's been coming in three or four nights a week for the last month."

Drowning her sorrows in tequila or washing away her guilt? I wondered.

"Does she talk your ear off?"

The bartender chuckled. "Whitney's not a quiet one. That's all I'll say."

"I respect the bartender code of silence."

I went into the hall to collect my coat from the rack. A tone from my cell announced a new text.

Arrival confirmed.

I moaned with relief, glad I hadn't screwed up in trusting Julia. I slipped into my coat and charged out of the Hearth, more than ready for a grilled cheese at home and the comfort of becoming Madame Arcati for two hours.

Chapter Forty-One

Sophie was pacing alongside her car when I arrived for rehearsal. She hurried over, opened my car door for me, and practically unbuckled my seatbelt.

"A cop just went into the club!"

"A cop? How do you know that?"

Sophie set us at a slow pace to the barn. "I passed the police station on my way here. A car pulled out in front of mine and I was right behind it until he turned into the club's main parking lot."

"A police cruiser?" Holy smokes. Were they already acting on Julia's "confession" and arresting Zach?

"No. A silver Sonata. I thought it was weird, and interesting, so I followed it into the lot. Guess who got out? It was that tall, dark, handsome cop who responded with Officer Brody when Gigi was found. I don't know his name. And he wasn't in uniform."

"Ron Nicholstone. It's good to see the Barton PD doesn't waste time." I gave her a short summary of Julia's tale.

"I can't believe they made out in Gigi's house! On her couch!"

"Let's keep it to ourselves. I don't want people hearing this gossip from us. It will cause Gigi's family more pain."

"My lips are sealed. Do you think they'll do a perp walk? Will Officer Nicholstone lead Zach out in handcuffs?" Sophie gave my arm a two-handed grip. "Maybe we should go up to the club and see what's going on!"

"Oh, that won't look suspicious at all. We have no reason to go to the club and every reason to get our butts into the barn. We'll know soon enough if Zach's been arrested."

"What if they kick us out in the middle of rehearsal? Just turn the lights off. Say 'Sorry, the club's owner has been arrested for murder. You must leave the premises immediately and never return.'"

"We'll form a human chain so we can find our way to the parking lot. Rehearsal, let's go." I gave her a push to pick up the pace.

When we reached the barn, we both took an instinctive look toward the clubhouse, which stood a couple of hundred yards across a lawn that was emerald green in the summer. Through the trees, I could see light emanating from two windows on the second floor. What drama was going on in the executive suite on the quiet Thursday night?

There might not be a perp walk. Ron might only be asking Zach a few questions, or "inviting" him to the station for a follow up interview. The possibility of Julia confessing to the murder crossed my mind. She could have lied to me but have had the truth coerced from her by Tracey. Heck, Ron might only be there to collect a donation to the Police Benevolent Association.

Entering the barn, I had a final thought on the matter. If the police closed the case that night, it would be with an expected ending, an arrest most in Barton had predicted a month ago. We'd all sleep better knowing Gigi's death was the terrible outcome of a domestic dispute rather than a random violent act in our sleepy village. Yet despite Julia's incriminating evidence against Zach, I had a growing sense we had not reached the story's conclusion.

Uh-oh. Had I finally become Madame Arcati? Method acting, without even trying?

Chapter Forty-Two

Over breakfast at Herman's Diner on Friday, I told Mom everything, from Julia's confession to Whitney's lamentations and Ron Nicholstone's evening visit to the club.

"Do you think you should rethink your conclusion of Zach's innocence?" I asked her.

"Not yet. It would be such a cliché if he did. Man cheats on his wife and kills her."

I shrugged and blurted out the cliché about how a cliché becomes a cliché.

We were counting our money for the meal (we always went Dutch) when Tracey came into the diner. She ordered a coffee and joined us.

Mom dropped her wallet in her purse and slid from the window booth. "You can have my seat, Tracey, and you two can talk *shop*." Her funny twist on the word solicited a snort from Tracey and an eye roll from me.

Tracey sat and sent a puff of air over her coffee cup. "Thank you for whatever part you played in Julia Rogan's confession." She placed her uniform cap on her bench.

"I threatened to call you to the Hearth for an interrogation."

"Interesting tactic."

"Thank Dusanka. She recognized Julia at the salon. Julia was there with a client."

"I will." Tracey took two quick gulps of coffee. "I'm too tired to ask how you connected with Julia to begin with. She mentioned you visited her office in Bolton Landing a few weeks ago."

"You just said you were too tired to as—"

"It was a statement, not a question."

"I was spreading the word about the gala benefit we're holding for Gigi." I elaborated in response to Tracey's raised brow. "And to check her out after I heard something on the club grapevine."

"It's discouraging the vine was more fruitful for you than it was for us."

I waited for the waitress to clear the breakfast dishes and then said, "I understand Ron Nicholstone paid a visit to the club last night. In plain clothes and an unmarked car."

"More grapevine chatter?"

"Sophie saw his entrance. Was he there to question Zach?"

"Ron gave Mr. Townsend a ride to the station for further questioning."

"Are all suspects spared embarrassment by being picked up by a plainclothes officer in an unmarked car?"

"Veronica."

I heeded Tracey's warning tone. "Did you nail Zach with your knowledge of his kissing session with Julia, or drag it out of him?"

"He admitted he had a moment of passion with Julia." Tracey spoke in a low tone. "Like Julia, Zach said it was a one-time event. He also said it had nothing to do with his wife's murder. He swore Gigi wasn't going to leave him, and he wasn't going to leave her."

"Did you take him into custody?"

"No. We still don't have enough to make an arrest. We need to find the gun."

"What are the chances? It was probably tossed in a dumpster or thrown in a lake." I remembered what Heather said about the police swarming over the club's grounds in the hours after the murder. "You searched all over Townsend's. How wide was your search perimeter?"

"We covered every inch of the course, all the surrounding woods, and the bordering streets on every side. We covered a few hundred yards."

"What about the route to Zach and Gigi's house?"

"That too. We also searched their yard and the woods behind their house."

"Sounds like a needle-in-a-haystack search."

"Yep."

We sat quiet for a minute. Tracey drank her coffee and I stared out the window, my mind grasping for new ideas.

"Does Julia really have the alibi proof she claims to have?"

"She does. She was prepared to prove her innocence."

"Do you think there might be another woman? If a man cheats once, the odds are high he'll cheat again."

"If there is another woman, we haven't found her yet." Tracey jerked her head back and finished her cup's last mouthful.

"Gigi's cell phone. Did she make any calls after Dusanka left the office? Maybe she called Zach to tell him about Julia's visit?"

"She made no calls. And she didn't receive any."

"Do you think this case will ever be solved? It's been more than a month now."

"I really don't know." It was an answer imbued with frustration over the dead-end case, not irritation with my persistent inquiries.

I offered encouragement. "You never know when the break will come. Maybe the press will dig up something on Zach while covering his campaign."

"Maybe. If he is the killer." Tracey rubbed her forehead. "I've never been on a case that dragged on so long. I fear it will turn into a cold case and be forgotten."

"Even though Gigi was a member of a prominent family?"

"If we have no evidence, we have no evidence." Tracey grabbed her cap and slid from the booth. "Thanks for the talk, Veronica."

I wouldn't trade my job for Tracey's for anything, even for one minute. "Anytime, my friend. Thank you for keeping Barton safe, Officer Brody."

Tracey tipped her cap and left. I shifted in my seat and watched her cross the sidewalk, get in her patrol car, and pull away from the curb.

What a terrible possibility, I thought, considering Tracey's worry over Gigi's murder remaining unsolved. We would forever wonder the who and the why of the case. The Swansons would never have that bit of closure or witness justice for their loss.

I pulled on my coat and went outside. I turned the corner onto Orchard and began the short trek to All Things.

If the police case was heading to the filing cabinet, I knew my sleuthing days were coming to a close, too. With just one week of rehearsal left until opening night, my access to the club would soon end. When *Blithe Spirit*'s run finished, I'd lose my daily interaction with Sophie, Nate, and the cast. The whole experience would fade to a memory.

Little did I know the case had only hit an intermission. Soon the curtain would go up on the closing act.

Chapter Forty-Three

We were all nervous Friday evening before our Showcase Night performance. The first-time actors had early-onset stage fright— "You can get it out of your systems now," I told them—while vets Jerome, Peter, and Iris had adrenaline rushes that made them excited to go before the crowd and jittery about what might go wrong.

"Erica seems fine," Jerome whispered, "but I'm keeping an eye on Lucy and Kelsey. They look like fainters."

I wasn't concerned about the scene we'd be performing; it was a sideshow to the backstage intrigue. Would Zach be at the club? Did he know Julia had confessed to me? I had a niggling unease about their relationship. I believed Julia wouldn't renew their connection, but guilt might have prompted her to tell Zach she was the one who informed the police of their passionate encounter. I worried she might have called him with an apology for reporting their moment of intimacy to the police. Despite telling me she had kept my sleuthing a secret from Donna, Julia could have told Zach about our conversation, my questions, and my insistence she go to the authorities. In a moment of panic, I prayed I wasn't the swooner Jerome would have to catch.

We waited in the club's sitting room until our performance time in the dining room. Though I had already checked my makeup in the ladies' room, I took a moment to make sure I didn't have lipstick on my teeth. I stood in the doorway, where the brighter light in the hallway would give me a better look at the babe in my compact mirror.

"I'm sorry the dressing room isn't what you're accustomed to."

I spun on my heels and saw Zach walking toward me across the entry foyer.

"Hi, Zach. This is fine. I've had worse accommodations."

"Good."

"Good luck in your run for the legislature. This is the second time you're following in your father's footsteps. First business, now politics."

Zach's response was smooth. "Dad taught me the importance of serving the community. I've done enough hosting of golf tournaments, weddings, and retirement parties. Now it's time to do something to improve the lives of our citizens."

I expected I'd read and hear that talking point for months in his campaign literature and television commercials. "What did Gigi think of your political aspirations?"

Zach's Adam's apple bobbed. "Gigi was very supportive of my decision to run for public office. She understood my desire to serve the community. She was doing the same thing, but in a different way."

"True." I looked over my shoulder into the sitting room. Jerome was in a chair by the door. Our glances locked for a second; his expression indicated he had listened to my conversation with Zach. Jerome shifted his glance, unashamed by his eavesdropping. I didn't care, but I stepped away from the door, not wanting him or anyone else to hear the next part of our conversation. Zach followed me into the foyer.

"And what do you think of your mother's idea to start a dinner theater here at the club? Are you happy she wants to fold the community theater your wife founded into a profit-making endeavor?"

"Mom knows what she's doing. She's always had a killer business instinct, so I know the dinner theater will be a big success."

Zach seemed unaware his killer instinct remark was an unfortunate slip of the tongue.

Sophie appeared at my side. "Hey, Zach. Have you heard from Julia lately? I miss her."

Zach seemed taken aback, but recovered in a flash. "I haven't. We're both too busy with work to have the time to catch up. I hear she's doing very well in her business, which makes me happy. Julia deserves her success. And I get to claim some credit. I taught her everything she knows." He gave us a wink and hurried down the center hall.

"He has some nerve," Sophie muttered.

"So do you. It was very bold of you to ask him about Julia. You caught him off-guard."

"Yeah, but I don't think I shook him hard enough."

"I don't know about that. He did flee the scene. You only said a few words and he almost cracked."

"I'll be more loquacious next time. But now you have to snap out of sleuth mode. It's almost time for the performance."

The cast mingled with our audience after the performance. The enthusiasm warmed us veterans and eased the nerves of the first-time actors. Sophie and I stood at the edge of the group filling the dining room; we enjoyed watching our friends soak up the glory.

"I'm proud of you, Sophie. You've done an award-worthy job pulling this group together and getting the best out of us."

Sophie gave a Mona Lisa smile. "Let's hope the full dress rehearsal goes as well as the one scene we did tonight."

I laughed. "Typical director. Never completely happy."

"I take that as a compliment."

"Please do."

An attractive blonde in her mid-forties emerged from the crowd and headed our way. She wore black wool slacks and a pale-green cashmere twin set. Best of all, she held a checkbook.

After introducing herself, Claudia Sheldon declared how excited she was to meet me. "I grew up watching *Days and Nights*. You were always my favorite."

We talked for a few minutes about the soap and then Claudia held up her checkbook. "May I buy two tickets for opening night?"

"You absolutely can," Sophie said. She led us to a table by the door, where a BCT volunteer was selling tickets and accepting donations. Sophie selected two tickets while Claudia began writing the check.

"I make this out to the BCT, correct?"

"No. Please make it to the Barton Community Theater."

"Oh." Claudia scribbled the date on the check. "My husband wrote a thousand dollar check to you in November made out to the BCT."

"Thank you very much. We appreciate your generosity. I guess the bank didn't care that he put the theater's initials on the check, so long as it went into the right account."

"I suppose. It *was* cashed right away." Claudia filled in the amount she owed for the two tickets. "Will you be sending out thank-you letters soon for last year's contributions? For tax returns? I suppose you have another week, until the end of February, to mail them." Claudia seemed embarrassed by her question.

"I'll get a letter in the mail to you first thing in the morning. I'm sorry for the delay."

Donna, a martini in her grasp, came up behind Claudia. With a clenched smile, she watched Claudia make the final flourishes on the check and exchange it for the tickets.

"How are you, Claudia dear?" Donna brushed her cheek against Claudia's. "Come talk to Bret about that reception Kurt wants to have. Veronica, mingle! Everyone wants to meet our resident Emmy winner!"

Donna linked her arm through Claudia's and guided her away from the table.

"Strange," Sophie said in a soft voice.

I noted her blank stare. "What's up?"

"It's odd Claudia hasn't already received a thank-you letter for her contribution."

I followed her gaze to where Donna, Claudia, and Bret sat at a table along the wall.

"It is?"

Sophie faced me. "Gigi was very good about sending letters right away after we received a donation. She'd usually mail the letter out the same day, or the next day at the latest."

"Maybe she didn't handle the check."

"No, she saw them all."

"Perhaps she meant to write the letter and then something came up and she forgot. Or maybe the letter was lost in the mail. Or Mr. Sheldon could have opened the mail the day the letter arrived and never told his wife."

"Maybe." Sophie was still doubting and distracted.

"It's not a big deal. Claudia didn't seem to mind the delay. Put the letter in the mail tomorrow and it will be done."

"Gigi would be mortified a donor had to wait four months for a thank you."

"You can omit that detail the next time you and Agnes talk with her."

Sophie smirked and returned her attention to Claudia. Her preoccupation with the Sheldons' check puzzled me. The matter fell under Nate's purview, so why not hand it off to him?

I'd soon be reminded to always listen to my director.

Chapter Forty-Four

My Saturday morning bakery order included a chocolate-glazed chocolate doughnut for Sophie. It was still warm when I arrived at the BCT office, where I would spend an hour or so helping her with a mailing of ticket orders.

"Yummy." The huge piece she had in her mouth muffled Sophie's praise of the doughnut. "Thank you."

"You can start eating healthy when you turn thirty." I hung my coat and sat in the visitor's chair.

She took one more bite of the doughnut and set it on the desk. "Listen to this. I checked the donor database this morning for the Sheldons' donation before writing a thank-you letter. Guess what? The Sheldons aren't in the database."

"Administrative oversight? That would explain why the Sheldons didn't receive a letter."

Sophie's look was skeptical. "Gigi was good at entering contributions and sending out the letters. And if it wasn't in the database but was on the monthly bank statement, Nate would have caught the error and corrected it."

I chased from my mind the vague suspicion Tracey had of Nate and his possible mismanagement of BCT funds. "Are you thinking Claudia is wrong about the donation?"

"I don't know. I Googled BCT, to see if there are any businesses in the area that go by that name, in case her husband did business with the company and Claudia thought the entry in their checkbook referred to us. There aren't any. This is really bothering me. I think someone stole the check."

My mind jumped to Kenny Pangborn. Did his embezzlement include the Sheldons' check? No, I decided, remembering he was gone from the BCT before November, when the Sheldons made the donation.

"All right. Let's not jump to conclusions. We'll call Claudia and get more information. Maybe she can send us a copy of the cancelled check. If we're lucky, there will be a signature on it."

"I don't have the Sheldons' phone number."

"We'll call Bret. The Sheldons are club members, so their phone number must be in the club's records. If Bret won't give us the number, maybe he'll contact Claudia and ask her to call your cell."

Sophie picked up her phone and tapped her finger on the screen. Putting the phone to her ear, she stared at me, her countenance tense. "Hi, Bret." Sophie moved her glance to the window and gave a smooth explanation about needing the Sheldons' number to confirm a contribution. "I want to make sure we give them proper credit."

I gave Sophie a thumbs-up signal when she looked back at me.

"Oh . . . okay . . . Thanks." Sophie tossed the cell phone on the desk. "Bret says Claudia is at the club right now, having breakfast. He's going to ask her to stop by here when she leaves the club." Her frown told me her worry hadn't eased. "I hope Claudia doesn't think we mishandled her donation. That would look really bad."

"We'll tell her the contribution wasn't entered in the database and you're not allowed to add it if you haven't seen the check. That's at least half-true. You can blame a *volunteer* for the error. And write the letter now and print it out so you can give it to Claudia."

Sophie's shoulders relaxed and her expression brightened. "That makes sense!"

"Feel free to call me O' Wise One."

Claudia swept through the door fifteen minutes later, glowing from the winter weather and delicious food from the Townsend's kitchen. "Good morning!"

I returned the exuberant greeting, wondering if she had a Bloody Mary or mimosa (or both) with breakfast.

"Bret said you have a question about our donation?" Claudia pulled off her sunglasses and gloves and tucked them in her purse.

"Yes. Here's our thank-you letter. Please accept my apology for the delay." Sophie stood and walked over to Claudia. Following my script almost word-for-word, she punctuated her request for a copy of the cancelled check with a polite smile.

"Oh, sure." Claudia swept and tapped her index finger across her cell phone. "Gigi had questions, too, but she didn't ask to see the check."

"*Gigi*?" Sophie cocked her head and gave Claudia a puzzled look. "She knew about your contribution?"

Claudia glanced up from the phone and nodded. "I called Gigi the day before she was . . . before the poor woman was killed. I asked when we'd receive a thank-you letter because I was getting our receipts together for our tax return. I got the impression Gigi wasn't aware of our donation. She asked if I had mailed it or hand-delivered it."

I realized I was holding my breath, waiting for the conclusion of Claudia's tale.

"What did you do?" Sophie asked.

"My husband wrote the check and asked me to give it to Donna Townsend at a lunch for the botanical society I was attending at the club."

"I see." Sophie's tone was neutral; her expression gave no indication of relief or concern.

Claudia showed Sophie a shot of the cancelled check and then agreed to send it to the BCT's email address.

"Last night, I didn't say anything to you about talking with Gigi about the check, because I thought it would sound as if I was blaming her for not sending us an acknowledgment letter." Claudia slid the letter into her purse.

"Not at all," Sophie said. "I'm glad we finally got this all straightened out. I apologize again for the long delay."

Claudia expressed her anticipation of our opening night, bid us a good day, and left.

"Was that helpful?"

Sophie didn't respond; instead, she pecked at her laptop keyboard, the screen's brightness reflecting off her scowl.

"What's wrong?" I stood behind her, looking over her shoulder at the laptop.

Sophie had logged into the BCT's email and opened the attachment containing the JPEG file of the Sheldons' cancelled check.

"Look here." She held her finger to the screen, indicating a bank stamp on the back of the check. "The check was deposited at the Bank of the Adirondacks." She swiveled in the chair and looked me in the eyes. "We don't have an account at that bank. Donna stole the check."

Chapter Forty-Five

"Are you sure the BCT doesn't have an account there?" I asked after thirty seconds of processing Sophie's declaration and accusation.

"Yes, I'm sure. Our account is at Chase."

"Are you certain the BCT doesn't have two accounts?"

"We're not breaking the bank with one account. There's certainly no need for two."

I ignored her snappy tone. "That's not the only reason to have two accounts." I sat down, leaning my forehead against my hand. Did Donna really steal the Sheldons' check? I didn't understand why she would. A thousand dollars was pocket change to her.

"Are you thinking this is why Gigi was killed? Is this the smoking gun?" Sophie uttered the words in a whisper colored with fear.

"We need more proof than one cancelled check. We need information on this Bank of the Adirondacks account."

Sophie leaned back, dropped her hands in her lap. "How are we going to do that? We don't know anyone who works there."

"Yes, we do." I reached for my purse. "She might not be able to talk with the dead, but she can certainly tell us how much money they had."

My reference to Agnes lit a spark in Sophie. "She can ask Gigi about it!"

I placed the call to Agnes. "I think she'll be of more help giving us copies of the account's recent statements."

Agnes answered on the second ring. After exchanging pleasantries, she asked, "Would you like to contact Gigi again?"

Again? I didn't consider initials and emotions a conversation with the dead, but I wasn't going to get into a debate with Agnes. I couldn't show my skepticism of her *gift* when I needed her to break bank rules.

"Not today, thanks. Sophie and I are doing some filing here at the BCT office and she noticed a few statements from the theater's account with your bank are missing. Could you get us copies from the last six months?"

It was Sophie's turn to give the thumbs-up. She then folded her hands and struck a prayerful pose.

"You can access the statements on our website. It will take just a minute to download statements from the last year."

Darn twenty-first century technology and its gift of instant self-service.

I stammered. "Um, I don't think Sophie has the password."

"Why don't you ask your treasurer? Nate Kelton, correct? He should know the login name and password."

I rested my head against the back of my hand. I should have called Bret for the Sheldons' phone number and made Sophie deal with Agnes, her hero. If I truly was the Wise One, I would have chosen the easier task.

A few seconds of silence passed. "Does this have something to do with Gigi's murder?" Agnes certainly had a talent for reading the minds of the living.

"Yes." I drew in a breath and decided to bring Agnes into my confidence. "A few months ago, a couple who are club members gave a one thousand dollar donation to the theater. The check was made out to the BCT, which is not the theater's official name. And we just learned the check was deposited at your bank, where we don't have an account. We have a copy of the cancelled check, if that will help."

Agnes's response was a drawn out hum. "I see." Her pause lasted only a few seconds but felt like ten minutes. "Do you have the check in front of you?"

I jerked the laptop to see the screen. "Yes."

"Read me the numbers on the last line of the bank stamp. It should be a ten-digit string."

Containing a yelp of delight, I read the numbers.

Agnes hummed some more and murmured, "Yes. I see. Hmm . . ."

I had the same feeling I have when I'm in the doctor's office, trying to determine the state of my health with a clumsy interpretation of her humming and facial movements.

"I'll bring the statements to your house this afternoon."

My heart thumped against my chest. "We can pick them up, if that would be easier. I don't want you to go out of your way."

"Not at all. You're on my way home. It would be better for me to drop them off."

I appreciated Agnes's discretion and caution. "I'm not going to get you in trouble, am I?"

"Not at all. If necessary, I'll say I made an honest assumption and was wrong."

"Thank you, Agnes. Can you also find out who the signers are on the account?"

"I can do that."

Sophie gave me a high-five when I ended the call. "Agnes will be at my house at one thirty."

"This might be the break we've been waiting for! And all because Claudia Sheldon wanted to pay for her tickets with a check. Imagine if she had asked Nate for the thank-you letter, or decided to forget about it? We should call Nate and tell him about this."

Sophie's suggestion gave me pause. Was I jumping to the wrong conclusion by assuming Donna was involved in the mystery? What if she gave the check to Nate for deposit in the theater's legitimate account and he stole it?

"Let's keep this to ourselves for the time being." I stared at the check image on the laptop's screen. "Print out the email from

Claudia, and the check. Then forward the email to your personal account, and delete the email from the BCT inbox. And delete the message you send yourself."

The situation might end up nothing more than an innocent mistake, but if it wasn't, I didn't want anyone at the BCT to know what Sophie and I had discovered.

Chapter Forty-Six

Sophie and I picked up sandwiches at the deli and went to my house. Over lunch at the kitchen table, we went over the details provided by Claudia and tried to guess Donna's role in the great check mystery.

"It doesn't make sense that Donna would steal the check. Maybe she accidentally deposited the check in her account, or the club's account." Sophie chomped on a pickle. "Agnes didn't give you the name on the account, did she?"

"No. But I would think if it was a Townsend account, or Donna's personal account, she wouldn't be printing statements for us. And I would think Donna would correct the error as soon as it was discovered."

At one fifteen, Sophie began pacing a route from the front hall to the dining room, into the living room (with a pause to look out the window), and back to the front hall. I sat on the couch and read the *Chronicle*, which made no mention of the murder investigation or Zach's political campaign.

"Agnes is here!" Sophie, on her tenth round, dashed from the window into the hall. I joined her at a slower pace. "I'm suddenly really nervous about what we find out." She pursed her lips and wrung her hands.

I opened the front door for Agnes, my curiosity rising when I saw the white clasp envelope in her hand. Did the envelope contain a break in the murder case, or symbolize a wasted Saturday?

We gathered at the dining room table, a cup of tea and turkey sandwich in front of Agnes. I couldn't ask her to disregard bank rules and not at least offer her lunch.

I opened the envelope and withdrew its contents: a stack of about forty pages, with the most recent statement on top. *BCT* was the account's name, a P.O. Box its address.

"Donna Townsend opened the account three years ago. She is the sole signatory."

"Donna was our treasurer that year," Sophie said. "But Gigi should have been a co-signer, and Donna's name should have been replaced by Nate's when he became treasurer."

Flipping through the pages, I acknowledged Agnes's and Sophie's remarks with a nod. On my quick glance over the statements, I noticed there were a few deposits every month, in amounts from a few hundred dollars up to five thousand dollars, with two or three checks drawn and a few cash withdrawals.

"I also looked at recent activity," Agnes said. "Several withdrawals of a few hundred dollars each have been made. And last Saturday morning there was a withdrawal of fifteen hundred dollars."

"Uh-huh." I passed half the stack to Sophie and went to the last page of the most recent statement. There were two check images on the page, both written to Townsend's and signed by Donna. On the memo line of one check, drawn for one thousand dollars, was *Office Rent*. The second check, in the amount of five thousand dollars, was marked *Barn Rent*. The dates on both checks were from the week of Gigi's death.

I thumbed to the December statement and found another one thousand dollar check for the office rent. For November, October, and September, there were rent checks for the office and barn, plus a five thousand dollar check marked *Barn—Opening Night*.

"I thought the BCT didn't pay—"

"We were charged for the opening-night reception! And Showcase Night!" Sophie, indignant, thumped her fist against the table. She answered my unfinished question. "No, we don't pay rent or pay for use of the barn. At least I thought we didn't!" Pique colored her face. She picked up a page and fluttered it. "I wonder if Gigi knew about this. Was there some secret deal between her and Donna?"

She looked across the table at Agnes, who had listened without comment while chowing down on the sandwich.

"You can ask Gigi! Contact her! It's urgent!"

Agnes showed no offense at Sophie treating her like a telephone operator. "Gigi can't give you advice on this, dear." Agnes, calm, dabbed her lips with a paper napkin. "Thank you for the sandwich, Veronica. It was delicious." She rose from her chair. "Please call me if you need more assistance."

I walked with her to the front door. "We appreciate your help, Agnes. It looks like we've uncovered a case of embezzlement at the theater."

"Be very careful with this, Veronica." Agnes glanced over my shoulder at Sophie. "And you, too, dear."

The hint of foreboding in Agnes's voice chilled me. I almost believed she was conveying a message from Gigi.

Sophie and I went back to the dining room and spent the next fifteen minutes going over each statement, line by line.

"Unbelievable. Donna stole our checks and funneled the money back to herself through the club. What a crook!" Sophie's face was red from her rage. "Can we call Nate now? I think we need to tell him."

"I need to tell you something, first. And then we need to call Tracey Brody."

"I can't believe Donna wants to replace us with a dinner theater!" Sophie's outrage grew until it became palpable during the relating of my conversation with Donna at the Hearth. "Doesn't she have enough?"

"My guess is she wants to make her own mark on Townsend's

when she takes it over after Zach wins his election." I gestured at the statements. "And now it looks like she stole money from the theater to support her argument that the BCT doesn't raise enough money to survive on its own."

I had a flashback to my conversation with Blair. Donna, she had told me, was the one who had gathered and packed Gigi's clothes and a few of her possessions in the home she and Zach shared. It was Donna who had encouraged Zach to clear out Gigi's things. Did Donna use that as an opportunity to go through Gigi's drawers, looking for evidence that might alert police to the bank account? A diary. A note scribbled on a scrap of paper. A thank-you letter to the Sheldons, not mailed until Gigi talked with Donna?

Heather had told Sophie and me Donna'd had breakfast with a friend at the club the morning of Gigi's murder. Maybe, though, Donna had time for a traipse across the grounds to the barn.

"I'm going to call Tracey."

I first made copies of the statements and filed them in a folder in my desk drawer. I wanted the copies for future reference (the near future). Mark would get a look at them that night. I put them out of sight so Tracey wouldn't confiscate the folder.

"I have some information that will be of interest to you," I told my policewoman pal a couple of minutes later.

"No quips. This must be serious."

"It's no joke you might soon need an arrest warrant for the most powerful woman in the county."

"I'm on my way."

My pulse soared a minute later when I heard a siren in the distance. I trusted it was a coincidence, an ambulance or one of Tracey's colleagues out on an emergency response. Our stack of statements needed careful handling, not a blaring announcement.

Chapter Forty-Seven

Tracey alternated her glance between Sophie and me and the bank statements, giving each serious attention.

Sophie and I took turns giving a narrative of our discovery. Sophie began with our introduction to Claudia at Showcase Night and then gave a minute-by-minute account of her database search and accompanying thoughts. I picked up with Claudia's office visit and my drinks date with Donna. I didn't explain how we obtained the statements, hoping Tracey wouldn't notice the gap in the chronology.

"If this isn't the theater's account, how did you get these statements?"

Drats.

"From a friend."

Sophie's cool response elicited a few seconds stare from Tracey before she moved her glance to me. "Have you checked with Nate Kelton?"

"We haven't talked with anyone about this yet," I responded.

"Except your *friend*." An amused grin twitched on Tracey's lips.

"We thought it best to share it with you, first."

"Thank you."

"This gives Donna a motive for Gigi's murder. If Gigi went public with this embezzlement—"

"*If* it is embezzlement."

I acknowledged Tracey's interjection with a one-shoulder shrug. "If Gigi pressed charges against Donna, the case would have serious repercussions on Wayne's career and Zach's campaign."

"The BCT wouldn't even have to press charges," Sophie said. "Simply dismissing her from the board, and the gossip that would follow, would damage the Townsend name."

"Let's say Donna did have a motive to kill Gigi. Your theory is sound, but Donna didn't have the opportunity to murder her daughter-in-law. She was with Rebecca Wakefield from nine until ten forty-five that morning. They played two sets of tennis and then had breakfast at the club."

"Are you sure Rebecca was with Donna the entire time? I mean, they probably showered after the match. Or maybe Donna went up to her office to make a phone call, or do some business, or something."

I appreciated Sophie's grasp for straws and looked to Tracey for a sliver of possibility.

Tracey shook her head. "There was no time for Donna to go to the barn and shoot Gigi."

"So much for the simplest explanation being the correct one." Sophie expressed her disappointment with a click of her tongue.

I agreed. We finally had a solid lead, but the evidence pointed at the one person who had an irrefutable alibi.

Tracey slid the statements into the envelope and stood. "I assume you have copies, Veronica." She held up the envelope and gave me a wry look.

"But of course."

"For the time being, let's keep this to ourselves. We don't need any distractions from the murder investigation."

"We should do something before Donna steals any more money from the theater," Sophie said.

"You should have enough to think about with your opening night next weekend. How are your final rehearsals going?"

"Everyone's doing great. We'll see how it all comes together at Monday night's dress rehearsal."

Sophie stayed on the couch while I accompanied Tracey to the front door. When I returned to the living room, she was standing at the window, watching the light snowfall that had started during Tracey's visit. I sank onto the couch, feeling a sudden fatigue.

"I don't know if I'm disappointed we didn't solve the murder, relieved Donna didn't kill Gigi, or angry that Gigi didn't tell someone about the Sheldon check the second she hung up with Claudia. Why didn't she tell Nate right away?" Sophie said.

Or did she? I wondered. Was this another instance of Nate not speaking up about financial problems at the BCT? Was he shielding Donna to keep his computer contract with the club? Could he have known about this bank account all along and looked the other way to protect his business interests?

Sophie crossed the living room and sat in the chair opposite me. "What if she *did* tell Nate? You don't think . . .? Is that why Tracey told us not to tell anyone?" Aghast, Sophie clapped her hand over her mouth. "Could he have—"

I stopped her before she voiced my fear. "Tracey doesn't want us talking because gossip spreads like wildfire. And she doesn't want us pointing fingers at anyone, especially since we were wrong about Donna being a killer."

"But I think we're right about her being an embezzler." Sophie groaned and closed her eyes. "What a mess."

We lapsed into a silence that let me consider the day's information overload. I regretted wasting Tracey's time, summoning her to an urgent meeting only for it to end on an anticlimactic note.

Yet . . . Tracey took the bank statements with her. Those pages were evidence against Donna, but for possible embezzlement, not murder. Tracey wasn't investigating a financial misdeed, so why did she need the statements?

I remembered Agnes's remark about recent withdrawals. It hadn't registered before because I was intent on studying the statements.

Agnes mentioned a withdrawal of fifteen hundred dollars the

previous Saturday. Mark and I had gone to the club that night for a Valentine's celebration. The Townsends dined with Rebecca Wakefield and her husband, and Donna and Rebecca had slipped away for a closed-door session of "looking at New Year's Eve party photos."

Zach's political career commenced three days later.

I retrieved my copies of the bank statements and checked the January statement. There was a withdrawal of fifteen hundred dollars made the day before Donna and Rebecca met at the club for tennis and breakfast. The day Gigi died.

Rebecca Wakefield, a powerful union boss, was Donna's alibi, a Townsend friend, and a political colleague. Did the Townsends purchase her support of Zach's candidacy with a stack of hundred dollar bills? A down payment the morning Gigi was killed and the remainder over dinner at Townsend's?

I had a flash of inspiration about the deposits in Donna's phony account.

"What do you know about the Sheldons?" I asked Sophie.

"Besides that they're very generous? Nothing."

I got up, hurried to the family room, and returned with my laptop. "What's Claudia's husband's name? Did Donna say last night it's Kurt?"

"Yeah."

I typed *Kurt Sheldon* in Google's search box and received several dozen hits for his name. I first checked his public LinkedIn page and learned he owned an IT company headquartered in Barton neighbor Bear Lake. The county was included in the list of the company's top clients.

"This is the guy who beat out Nate's company for the county computer contract!" Sophie's outrage on Nate's behalf was sweet and ironic because a minute before she was about to accuse him of murder.

I closed LinkedIn and scrolled down the Google results page. I spotted a link to a *Chronicle* article. I opened it and read the paper's article on the county's awarding its technology business to Sheldon's company thirteen months earlier.

I connected Donna's meetings with Rebecca Wakefield, the two fifteen hundred dollar withdrawals, and why Kurt Sheldon asked his wife to give their donation check to Donna and not to Gigi or Nate. The pieces formed a plausible theory. I grabbed my cell phone.

"I have an idea and we need Agnes's help to prove it."

Chapter Forty-Eight

The rest of the weekend passed without further developments. My theory preoccupied my thoughts through Saturday night's canasta game (I didn't utter a word about the day's discoveries to my fellow card players), Sunday morning Mass, and the afternoon rehearsal. Except for a few shared knowing glances, Sophie and I kept our interaction to all things *Blithe Spirit*. Nate's cheerful presence did nothing to dispel my nagging worry over his possible knowledge of the scandalous bank account.

I kept my cell phone clutched in my hand Monday morning to the point where my fingers stiffened and became numb. I was anxious for a call from Agnes, for her signal we had found the final puzzle piece.

Sophie called every thirty minutes. "Did Agnes call yet?" "Have you heard from Agnes?" "Do you think she got caught?" "Maybe Gigi told her not to help us!"

At eleven thirty, I answered her call with, "A watched pot never boils. Go have lunch and do some visualization exercise about dress rehearsal. I'll call you after I've heard from Agnes."

"Promise?"

"We are in this together, my friend."

Agnes called five minutes later. "Can you get away for lunch, Veronica?"

I invited her to dine at my home, offering to pick up sandwiches at the deli. I hung up and exhaled away the morning's agonizing hours of anticipation. I sought the closest chair—the rocker in All Things' Christmas corner (a quiet location after weeks of being the busiest spot in the shop).

I wondered if I should include Sophie. Though I had promised I would call when I heard from Agnes, I had no news to report. Sophie needed time to envision the scene in Charles Condomine's living room and not take part in the potential drama in mine.

Agnes showed up on my doorstep holding another white clasp envelope and a box of Pepperidge Farm cookies. "Dessert."

We had a working lunch at the dining room table. In between bites from our sandwiches, Agnes read aloud the names on every check deposited in Donna's BCT account since she opened it. I wrote the names on a legal pad. Rebecca Wakefield, Kurt Sheldon, and a host of other familiar names had given money to the shadow "theater" Donna operated.

Political theater. I shook my head in disgust at the extent of the corruption.

"Have you ever seen a case like this in your job?" I asked Agnes.

"Not with such deep implications. I shouldn't say that. A small loss for a nonprofit with a cheating employee is devastating. A wife whose husband cleared out their account suffers tremendously. Cases that don't make the front page can cut as wide a swath of pain as the very public cases."

I imagined the story on the *Chronicle's* front page. Color photographs, bold headlines, above-the-fold coverage. I'd get no satisfaction knowing I was the anonymous source who cracked the case.

After Agnes left, I spent a half hour filling out my list of names with details about each individual and company. Using Google, I found their titles, business associations, and connections to Wayne Townsend and the county government. A few, like Kurt Sheldon, had won lucrative contracts with county agencies. Others had lobbied for, and won passage of, important bills before the legislature.

I had always considered my cozy, charming village a sanctuary from the crazy world. I liked to think the people we elected to local office were more honest, more diligent in their leadership than those in state and national positions.

I was wrong.

I called Sophie and confirmed our suspicion of a political cesspool, then called the plumber who would take part in the draining of it.

Chapter Forty-Nine

"Does Wayne Townsend have an alibi for the morning Gigi was murdered? He didn't play tennis with Donna and Rebecca, by chance? A two-against-one match? Or maybe he had a three-hour breakfast in full sight of the entire club staff? Or a dental appointment for a triple root canal?"

"None of the above." Tracey crossed the threshold into the front hall. She removed her cap, but left her jacket zipped. "What's going on?"

"I think Wayne killed Gigi. Does he have an alibi?"

"No." With a resigned look, Tracey removed her jacket and walked into the living room. "He had an eleven o'clock meeting in Lake George with the county HR commissioner."

"That's it? What time did he leave Barton? Can he account for himself before he arrived at the meeting?"

"He wasn't asked. What do you have?"

I picked up the envelope from the coffee table and handed it to her. "Scans of every check deposited in Donna's BCT account. Every single check is from someone with business before the county, or someone who had an interest in Wayne Townsend winning his race for county executive."

Tracey sat on the couch and opened the envelope. A copy of my list was the cover page for the statements.

"That's a summary of the *contributors*. More like a cheat sheet, emphasis on cheat. I made copies, just in case your set blows away, or you accidentally drop it down a sewer or shredder."

Tracey's response was a droll, "You're quite an

organized woman, Veronica."

"What did you do with the statements we gave you Saturday?"

"I showed them to Chief."

"And?"

"Police business, Veronica."

"Did he ask where you got the statements?" Would Tracey get in trouble for not getting a warrant? I worried. Would Agnes lose her job?

"Yes. I told him a friend of the theater gave me the statements. He knew immediately you were my source."

"Those exceptional deductive skills are the reason he's the chief."

"I'll pass along the compliment." She looked over the check scans without further comment. Tracey hunched over the papers, her jaw tight and her brow furrowed, her eyes moving from top to bottom of every page in a slow absorption of the facts. After five minutes, she shoved the papers into the envelope. "Do not discuss this with anyone." She slipped on her jacket and cap.

"I won't." Though I trusted her, I'd call Sophie back and remind her to keep quiet. To Agnes, my anonymous source, I'd send a message via Gigi.

If Gigi only knew how prescient she was putting me in contact with Agnes.

Or maybe she did know.

Chapter Fifty

I took a chug of antacid before leaving for dress rehearsal. I didn't need it to combat stage fright, but to calm rumblings caused by a cast of emotions that had invaded my stomach.

I felt excitement over the rehearsal, where we would finally see the results of everyone's hard work. I was jittery about it, too, worried something would go wrong, such as a part of the set falling or an actor suddenly stricken with laryngitis or the flu (that vaccination Gigi told us to get didn't cover every strain of the virus), or someone showing up with an epic case of memory loss. A wardrobe malfunction was also at the back of my mind. I tried to clear my mind of all those thoughts so I didn't find myself in a self-fulfilled prophecy in an hour's time.

In addition to the typical actor's nerves, those bank statements had created a deep well of anxiety in me. The prospect of facing Wayne and Donna at the dress rehearsal scared me, but not quite stiff. Not only would I have to play Madame Arcati on the stage, I'd also have to act the part of a know-nothing behind the scenes. I prayed I could pull off the dual role.

I saw Sophie for the first time that day when I scooted from the makeup room into the hall. I pulled Madame Arcati's red wool cape around my shoulders and fastened the top button.

"Don't forget to undo that before you make your entrance," Sophie said. She wore a bulky black turtleneck, faded jeans, a weathered pair of sneakers, and a look of apprehension. "So you can just whip it off and hand it to Kelsey."

I smiled; Sophie had wardrobe malfunction concerns, too. "I will."

Our lighting guy passed through the hall. "Break a leg, ladies."

"Thanks." Sophie grabbed my arm and pulled me down the hall to the back door. "Have you heard anything from Tracey?" Her whispered question was loaded with worry.

"No. Have you seen the Townsends?"

"Donna's out front, talking with Nate." Sophie's expression darkened. "I'm really freaked out by all of this, on top of being a wreck about dress rehearsal." She covered her eyes with her hands. "I can't breathe."

Good grief. "Take a deep breath and hold it to a count of three."

Sophie did the exercise several times. "Better. A million questions have been running through my mind all day since you called."

I cut her off before she could reel off every single one of those questions. "Put it all out of your mind. We have to forget about it and trust the police are untangling the web. We have a show to do. Tonight, we're an actress and director, not two sleuths trying to solve a murder."

I stood in the wings, awaiting my cue. I checked that my cape's button was unfastened—it was—and fussed at the velvet gloves I wore.

Kelsey walked off the stage and stood beside me. A shot of adrenaline pulsed through me when Jerome said, " *'You go and meet her, darling.'* "

I took a step forward and, projecting my voice, uttered my first line. " '*I've leant my bike against that little bush, it will be* perfectly *all right if no one touches it.*' "

Kelsey and Erica spoke their lines and then I walked onto the stage. All my preoccupations with Donna and Wayne and secret bank accounts vanished. I was no longer on a stage in a barn in the cold Adirondacks, but in an English country home on a summer's evening.

A few minutes later we finished the scene, moving to the back of the stage as if we were heading to Charles Condomine's dining room. When the stage lights dimmed, I glanced over my shoulder, sneaking a peek at our audience.

The lighting in the room, though dim, was bright enough for me to make out the people seated at the two tables set up ten feet in front of the stage. Sophie sat at one table, intent on the show and the notes she was taking about everything from the performances to the lighting to the layout of the set. Wayne, Donna, Zach, and Bret sat at the other table. Donna's expression was one of wonder, while Wayne appeared amused by our show. Bret, like Donna, seemed enchanted and with us in Kent, England. Zach had his head lowered, his attention fixed on his cell phone. There's one in every crowd.

I exhaled and with a "one scene down, six to go" count in my head. Or so I thought.

Chapter Fifty-One

We breezed through the first two acts without a hitch, taking short breaks between the acts. Lucy, Jerome, and I were midway through the first scene of Act Three when the offstage drama began.

I was standing in the wings, awaiting my cue to reenter the scene when a cell phone rang in the audience. While Lucy and Jerome continued undistracted, I peered into the dim room to see Wayne lifting his phone to his ear. Sophie, sitting at the table next to Wayne, shifted her attention from the actors to the county executive.

Thirty seconds later, Wayne stood up and walked toward the entrance to the backstage hall. I think I was the only one who noticed Sophie follow him moments later.

" *'Call her in—she's got to get me out of this.'* " Lucy, crying, took two heavy steps toward Jerome.

Jerome, speaking his line, moved to the set's dining room door, through which I would enter. " *'Madame Arcati—would you please come in now?'* "

I hurried to center stage, turning left and right, my eyes wide with excitement. " *'Is the darling still here?'* "

I continued glancing around the stage, spinning and looking for Elvira, whom Madame Arcati could not see.

When Jerome directed me to the piano (on loan from the club), I turned and not only saw Lucy sitting on the piano bench, but also Sophie standing in the wings off right, waving both arms and mouthing my name with a frantic spark in her eyes.

I ignored her, walked to the piano, and spoke my line.

"Veronica! Veronica! Come here!" Sophie's sharp, urgent

whisper didn't distract Lucy from delivering her line. I wondered if she thought Sophie's display was intentional to test her concentration.

Sophie kept flailing and beckoning through Jerome's dialogue.

I said my next line, " '*Home*,' " with a turn to the audience. It was fortunate I had but one word to say, for what I saw stunned me speechless.

Chief Price, in his police uniform, and the district attorney (still wearing a dark suit and tie at nine p.m.) strode into the barn. Tracey and another police officer stood by the front door. I went slack-jawed, giving a blank look to Lucy and Jerome. They knew the expression was off-script.

" '*Madame Arcati*?' " Jerome asked.

I gave him a fleeting glance, noted Chief Price's stealth walk across the room, and caught Sophie's creeping move onto the stage.

"What are you doing?" mouthed Nate, his hands raised in a questioning stance, from the opposite wing.

"I hear the spirit of Ruth beckoning!" I improvised before hustling off the stage. Sophie latched onto my arm and dragged me down the couple of steps from the platform and into the hall. "Where's Wayne?"

"That's what I've been trying to tell you! He went out the back door. Why would he go out in twenty degree temps to talk on the phone?" Sophie's words came out fast in a rising note of panic. She pulled me to the rear exit. I glanced over my shoulder at the closed door at the other end of the hall and wondered what was going on in the main room behind it.

Clutching my wrist, Sophie pushed her shoulder against the door. The two of us stumbled into the frigid, starless night. A light snowfall had begun during our rehearsal.

Wayne stood near the corner of the barn, under a halogen lamp attached to the building. The fixture, several feet above him, cast Wayne in a sort of spotlight.

He was still on his phone. "How do they know? What proof do they have? *Did someone turn on me?*" Wayne, furious, snapped out a lineup of expletives.

I pulled Sophie close to the building so our presence was less obvious to Wayne. "Stay still," I whispered in her ear.

Wayne ended the call a few seconds later and looked around— deciding which way to make a break for freedom? His pensive glance fell on us.

"Shouldn't you ladies be inside?" I admired Wayne's deft switch from irate, dirty politician to cool-headed gentleman.

"Is everything all right, Mr. Townsend?" Sophie asked with equal calm.

"Fine. Fine."

I imbued my voice with cheer, my hardest bit of acting of the evening. "Why don't you come back in with us? The show's almost over." In more ways than one.

Wayne didn't budge from his position. "I'll be there in a moment." He put his hands in his pockets and appeared to clutch something. Car keys? "Go on in. I'm right behind you."

I turned to the door, ready to charge inside and alert the police in a volume that would project my voice clear to Orchard Street.

Sophie started toward Wayne. "Soph," I said through clenched teeth.

Ignoring me, Sophie's stride picked up its pace and became a determined march. "You should come now. We don't want you to miss a moment, Mr. Townsend." Sophie moved into the circle of light and was ready to take Wayne's arm when he reached into his suit jacket.

"No!" I screamed when I saw the gun he withdrew.

Wayne grabbed Sophie's arm and yanked her to his side.

"You killed Gigi!" I prayed someone, inside or outside, heard Sophie's screech.

"You don't know anything!" Wayne groped at Sophie's jeans.

"Give me your car keys!"

Sophie struggled against Wayne, almost succeeding in shoving him to the ground.

He steadied himself and pinned Sophie against his body, holding the gun to her side. "The keys."

His command sent a shiver through me. "Sophie, give him the keys."

Sophie, seething and panting for breath, dug into her pocket and produced a keychain. When she moved to throw the keys out of reach, Wayne gripped her wrist and wrenched the keychain from her fist.

"This is your doing!" Wayne tightened his hold on Sophie and gave me a murderous look. Figurative, at the moment, and I prayed it stayed that way.

"No, Wayne, it's your doing." I took a few steps toward the pair. "Gigi found out you and Donna are laundering your bribery and kickback money through a phony BCT account. Someone asked for a thank-you letter for her husband's *donation*. You killed Gigi so she wouldn't bust up your sweet moneymaking deals." I drew closer with another two steps, stopping at the light's edge. I wasn't moving in for a gun grab; I hoped my proximity would calm Wayne and move him to a peaceful surrender, or at lease prompt him to release Sophie and run for a getaway car.

"No one got hurt and Gigi knew that. She looked away once, she should have looked away a second time."

"What do you mean? Gigi knew you were taking advantage of the BCT? Did she know about the secret bank account?" Sophie, more enraged than frightened, made a wriggling attempt at escape.

Wayne tightened his hold on Sophie. "When I ran for county executive, Gigi found out I took donations under the BCT name and against my public pledge to entirely self-fund my campaign."

"Scumbag."

Wayne ignored Sophie's insulting epithet. A politician, he had probably heard worse. "She found out the same way, when someone's wife asked her for a letter for her tax return. Said her husband gave me the check. I said my mea culpas, swore I only took a few checks for my campaign, and reminded Gigi of the many benefits she was enjoying through her business and marital association with the Townsend family."

"Slime bucket." I didn't voice my agreement with Sophie's observation, but I held the same opinion. Wayne was the stereotypical politico: all public talk of community service while standing first in the self-service line in private.

"But last month Gigi found out you didn't take just a few checks," I said. "And she wouldn't look away twice."

"I tried to talk sense into her. I offered her some of the money—"

"Gigi couldn't be bought," Sophie said.

"I told her she would ruin Zach's political career. She didn't care. She was going to leave my son. She wanted to take the whole family down."

I heard the creak of the back door opening, but didn't dare turn to see who was joining us.

"You were already a success, Wayne, and I hate to say this in light of your despicable behavior, but you've done good things for the county." I doubted a contemptuous glare would shame Wayne, but I gave him one anyway. "You threw it all away for the sake of greed. You just had to have more. You've destroyed the Swanson family, your wife, and your son. I guess Zach was going to continue the *proud* family tradition of *quid pro quo*." I drew in a cleansing breath and got a whiff of the beach.

"Zach was *not* involved in any of this." Donna stopped at my side and held out her hand. "Wayne, give me the gun."

Wayne's only move was to lower the gun an inch.

"Zach didn't know you bought the teacher's union endorsement for him?" I asked, incredulous. "He didn't know you were using a phony BCT account to launder money?"

Donna's head jerked in surprise. "No, he didn't. It was Rebecca who demanded money for her support."

"She wanted to be a taker instead of a giver," Wayne said, his tone more bitter than a cup of black coffee.

"That would have been the last bribe, if I had anything to do with it. And I would." Her voice faltered. "Did you really kill Gigi, Wayne?"

He answered, "Claudia Sheldon called Gigi looking for a *thank-you* letter for the thousand Kurt gave me. Gigi was going to go to the DA."

"Oh, Wayne." Donna ran her hand across her eyes and let out a cry of grief. "You should have told me she knew. I would have talked to her, convinced her to stay quiet."

"I tried that, Donna." Wayne addressed his wife in a sharp tone. "I tried to convince her keeping quiet was the best for all of us. She just wouldn't listen. I didn't want to hurt her, but I couldn't let her destroy us all."

"I was going to put a stop to all of this when Zach won his election. That was the point of the dinner theater. Once the BCT became a for-profit theater, we could no longer accept those *donation* checks."

"Your dirty dog husband would have found another way to do his filthy laundry." I'd have to suggest Sophie pursue a playwriting career. She had quite an ear for dialogue.

"It would have been harder. And maybe Wayne would have decided he had enough. I was so naïve." The last part Donna whispered, as if speaking to herself.

"Did Nate know about your phony account?" I asked. I didn't like asking the question, but I needed to know the whole truth.

"Nate?" Donna appeared astonished by my query. "Of course not. Only Wayne and I knew about it."

I heard footsteps approaching from behind at the same moment

Tracey and two of her colleagues appeared from around the building's corner, holding their guns at their sides. Wayne uttered an oath commonly used to describe a hopeless journey up a creek.

"Put the gun down, Mr. Townsend." The male voice came from behind me.

Wayne released Sophie. She hurried to me; I put my arm around her shoulder and guided her away from Wayne, Donna, and the officers.

"Lay down your gun." Tracey, her order delivered in a neutral tone, took several steps toward Wayne.

Wayne lifted the gun to his head. He was once again alone in the spotlight.

"No!" Sophie screamed.

Donna addressed her husband in a soft voice. "Wayne, please. Put down the gun. Don't do this."

With my breath and heart crowding my throat, I watched Wayne consider his wife's plea. His hand holding the gun gave a slight tremble and his defiant gaze remained fixed on Donna. A muscle flexed in his cheek in three quick bursts. Finally, he lowered the gun.

"Put the gun on the ground," Tracey repeated.

Wayne bent his knees and made a slow descent to the snow-dusted ground. He placed the gun at his feet and straightened, both hands in the air. Stripped of his authority and swagger, Wayne transformed into a forlorn man.

With Tracey reciting Wayne's rights, one of the officers placed Wayne in handcuffs, another standing close in case Wayne made a final, desperate move.

Donna watched, weeping. I lay my hand on her shoulder for a small measure of comfort, until Tracey gestured me away.

I looped my arm through Sophie's and walked her to the back door. "We don't need to see anymore. Are you okay?"

"Yeah." Her exhalation lasted a good ten seconds. "That was intense."

Nate stood inside the door, holding it open a crack. Over his shoulder I saw the cast and crew crowding the hallway, confusion the collected look.

"What happened?" Nate asked.

I put my arms around him and gave him a tight hug. It was an expression of my relief for the murder case's resolution and joy over his innocence in the sordid deal. It was also a wordless apology for harboring suspicions of him.

"I just might have to host opening night at my house," I answered. "The barn just became unavailable."

Chapter Fifty-Two

Fifteen minutes later, I stood in the backstage storage room with Tracey. She related the timeline of events since I gave her the deposits information that afternoon (which felt like a month ago after the night's action).

"I brought the deposit statements to Chief Price and connected all the dots for him, as you did for me. Chief called the district attorney. He asked us to email copies of the statements ASAP. Once the ball got rolling, it gathered speed fast."

"When Sophie and I went outside, we overheard a minute of Wayne's phone conversation. I think someone tipped him off to his impending arrest."

Tracey's eyebrows shot up. "I'll let the DA and Chief know."

"This is a sad story, from beginning to end."

"It makes the BCT all the more important to the community. We all need an escape once in a while."

The BCT was a piece of the sad story; it had just landed between a rock and a hard place.

Tracey read my thoughts from my sudden frown. "I'll do whatever I can to help the BCT find a new home." She offered her hand. "Thank you for your help on the case, Veronica."

"Does this mean I get a police pension?"

"You're not vested in it, and you never will be."

"Well, I thought I'd give it a try. It doesn't hurt to ask."

Her grip on my hand tightened. "And shred your copies of the statements. You're officially fired from your role of amateur sleuth." She released my hand and pointed at my attire. I was still in my

Madame Arcati clothes. "Now focus on your part in the play. I'm one of your biggest fans and I expect a stellar performance."

"If I'm fired, I don't have to take orders from you anymore. But I'll grant you that final command."

"I appreciate it."

I walked out, allowing myself a moment to entertain the fantasy of Dusanka and Tracey forming a Barton chapter of the Veronica Walsh Fan Club.

"Get over yourself," I mumbled.

I continued down the hall, feeling unburdened for the first time in the new year. Yeah, my spirit was rather blithe.

The cast, also still in costume, had assembled on the stage, filling the set's sofa and chairs. Nate sat on the stage floor, his elbows on his bent knees and his chin resting on his folded hands. A few members of the crew also sat on the floor, while others rested on chairs they had pulled from backstage and from the tables where our jailbird audience had earlier perched. Bret was a part of the group, sitting at the side of the stage in a wingback chair.

Sophie held everyone's attention with a recounting of every moment of our investigating adventure. She sat on the sofa; Iris beside her with her arm around Sophie's shoulder.

"Veronica figured it all out," Sophie said when I climbed the stairs to the stage.

"I couldn't have done it without you," I said when the group's applause ceased. I gave Sophie's knee a pat and plopped into the sofa space between Iris and Erica. "You were very brave to go after Wayne. Foolish, too, pal."

Sophie disregarded my gentle admonition. "I wasn't going to let him get away. And I sure wasn't going to let him steal my car!"

"He might have taken you with him," Kelsey said.

"If he had made me his getaway driver, I would have crashed the car."

Jerome, being his practical self, spoke. "Obviously, we won't have opening night here. Nate, do you know if the high school is available?"

"I'll make the phone call first thing in the morning."

"Let me know if you need a space," Bret said. "I might be able to get you into another hall."

"Thanks," said Nate.

We were all quiet for a minute, feeling the weight of the evening's drama and the worry for the show's future.

"We didn't finish the show. Are we going to have another dress rehearsal?" Lucy gave Nate and Sophie a concerned look.

"I'll ask about the gym's availability this week when I call the high school. Between basketball games and their drama club's rehearsal, the gym's usually booked."

"There's always the grammar school," said Sophie.

"And Saint Augustine's school." I offered up my elementary alma mater.

"We could use some divine help. We almost lost our director and Madame Arcati for good." Erica rested her head on my shoulder and gave my hand an affectionate tap.

"It certainly wasn't our best dress rehearsal ever," Iris observed.

"Remember the old theater adage. Bad dress, good show." Jerome chuckled, his eyes glistening.

Meaning if your dress rehearsal is a disaster, your opening night will be a huge success.

"In that case," Sophie cracked, "we're sweeping the Tony Awards."

Chapter Fifty-Three

Sophie and I hovered over a plate of cookies in the hallway of Saint Augustine Elementary School. Framed photographs of the Catholic school's graduating classes, my own included, hung on the walls, causing a flashback to the days when I walked the halls (no running allowed!) in my plaid uniform, black Mary Jane shoes, and knee-high socks.

The show's opening night was a sold-out success. There were no flubbed lines (though Erica panicked five minutes before the curtain rose, crying "My mind is a blank slate!" and swearing she had forgotten all of her lines—she didn't), prop mishaps, or sound or lighting difficulties. The audience gave us a well-deserved two-minute standing ovation at the curtain's closing; we gave each other hugs and high-fives backstage.

In light of the murder case's resolution, the production indeed needed a new venue. After checking the availability of Barton High's auditorium (and learning it was booked), Nate secured use of my parish's school gym. The backstage space being the size of a box for a child's shoes, the cast prepared for the show and did wardrobe changes in the kitchen. Though I hated the reason for our need of Saint Augustine's stage, I appreciated my full-circle moment and calmed the nerves of my castmates by sharing stories of my first acting performance, playing the Virgin Mary in my second grade Christmas show on that same stage.

We also needed a new source of after-show refreshments. A number of suppliers readily stepped forward to help us celebrate. A caterer friend put together trays of delicious finger foods. A beverage dealer tossed in a few cases of soft drinks. Rizzuto's delivered cellophane-wrapped plates of cookies and a sheet cake an hour before show time. Dusanka kicked in a platter of apple strudel and the Swanson family, who attended the show, arrived bearing two trays of Gigi's favorite brownie recipe.

"I don't think we'll be performing *The Mousetrap* or any other murder mystery anytime soon," Sophie said, munching on a pink Italian leaf cookie.

"I take that to mean the Barton Community Theater will continue to act another day." I grabbed a lace cookie and bit into it, savoring the crunch and the chocolatey goodness.

"Yes. We're not going to let a corrupt murderer end our fun."

"You'll always have my support."

"You're the best, Veronica." Sophie pushed the rest of her cookie into her mouth and gave me a hug I returned with great affection. "Any time you want to direct a show, or act in one, let me know. I know! You can do a one-woman show!"

"Maybe . . . someday. But I like being part of a cast. I'm a team player."

"Remember, it's a standing invitation."

"Veronica, nice picture!"

Nate's voice pulled my attention down the hall, where he stood in front of one of the framed portraits. I couldn't believe there was still space on the walls for photographs from the 1970s classes.

"You haven't changed a bit," he added, a grin lighting his face.

"Don't you dare say I still have the same hairstyle!"

Ignoring several amused glances, I swiped another cookie and nibbled on it, searching the crowd for my personal cast of characters. There was my mother, beaming with pride, talking with Anita and Nick Rizzuto. Carol was chatting with Jerome and Iris. My canasta pals surrounded Dotsie, who was probably expounding on another conspiracy theory. Plus the All Things team, Tracey, Dusanka, and Agnes. Yeah, I'm friends with a medium.

My gaze settled on Mark, who was standing near the trophy case with Carol's husband. Mark, my all-in-one leading man, favorite person, and crime-solving partner. We exchanged winks.

"Thanks for the invitation," I said to Sophie, "but I'm going back into retirement."

I had more scenes to play in my real life.

About the Author

Jeanne Quigley grew up reading mysteries, watching soap operas, and vacationing in the Adirondacks, never imagining these pleasures would be the inspiration for her Veronica Walsh cozy mysteries. Unlike the fictional Veronica, Jeanne has never been a soap opera star, but she has worked in the music industry and for an education publisher. She lives in Rockland County, New York and is a member of the Sisters in Crime.

jeannequigley.wordpress.com
facebook.com/jeannemquigley